Clan Ravensmith

Book 1

The Beginning

JAMES WILLIAM PEERCY

Three-Sided Coin Publishing

Clan Ravensmith Series

Book 1: The Beginning
Book 2: The City of Taika

Books in the Xun Ove Series

Book 1: The Wall Outside
Book 2: Partition Majik
Book 3: Twisted Fates
Book 4: Tainted Soul
Book 5: The Vulkodlak Curse
Book 6: The Unicorn Twist

Clan Ravensmith – The Beginning, Book 1

Published by arrangement with the author.

For information write:

Three-Sided Coin Publishing, P.O. Box 2695, Sherman, Texas, 75091

www.ThreeSidedCoin.com

Manufactured in the United States of America

ISBN-13: 978-1-937491-04-8
Library of Congress Control Number: 2019918605

DEDICATION

The character, Ord, the six-foot dwarf, was inspired by my friend, Bill Wiedemer, who I met as a blacksmith at the Texas Renaissance Festival. What is true or untrue in this manuscript, only he can tell you . . . and perhaps Bob the pixie as he zips through the mystical forest.

ACKNOWLEDGMENTS

I wish to express sincere appreciation to family and friends. In particular: Claudette Peercy for all the hard work she put into prepping this book; Clifford and Dianne Peercy who never set limitations on what I could become; and the readers who like a great story based upon the truths of life with just a little pixie dust thrown in. A special thank you also goes to ChandaElaine Spurlock and Gina Champange for their guidance in helping to keep me on track.

To all of you, highest commendations.

PROLOGUE

Words always tell a story, whether they comprise full sentences or are a single name. When the whimsical and mischievous Bob, the pixie, found this manuscript, the first of several scrolls, in the library of Väinämö, a great mage, little did the pixie know what it contained.

Yet, he recognized a single name, Ord, and remembered how Jonna had first met the six foot dwarf when repairing the Partitions of Majik during Twisted Fates. Had this scroll led up to that meeting? Bob certainly did not know.

In Bob's own words, "I, Bob, being of sound mind and pixie in body, recovered a lost history in the stacks of scrolls that comprised Väinämö's library. And, I, Bob, being of a trickster mind and tiny in body, sneaked it from the shelves."

With a sprinkle of his pixie dust, you stand beside him.

"Here," he shoves the first of the manuscripts at you, "read it quick before Väinämö comes back. I'll let you know my thoughts at the end."

CHAPTER 1

Clang.

As the hairs on his arms stood up, Ord, the six-foot dwarf, gripped his massive, dwarven, two-sided hammer.

Where are they? he thought, towering above his kinsmen. *I know those blue-skinned goblin pond scum are here some place.*

Beads of sweat ran down his head where his helmet pressed snugly against his temples and soaked his beard with its two braided sides. His mustache was wet against his upper lip. The stench of heated body odor rose around him, only to be whisked away by the beating of dragons' wings above his head. While the dragons fought aerial combat against each other, dwarves, blue goblins, and dark elves faced one another on the ground.

He remembered Dimur's words, his platoon leader, *Beware the earth.*

A sword plunged toward his plate-mail chest armor as he turned to the left. He dodged but not enough.

Gasp.

It screeched, metal on metal in the golden sunlight, and jolted him backward until it angled off.

He exhaled after the sharp blow. At the same time, he swung his center-balanced war hammer at an upward angle.

Snap.

The sword his hammer met shattered, breaking into metal shards the size of small, spinning, assassin blades. Some pieces bounced off his fellow armor-clad dwarves. Other pieces found their marks, followed by gulps of pain, with nicks and cuts among the blue-skinned goblin enemies and maybe a dark elf or two.

Clang. Crash.

Ord slammed one side of his hammer against a dark elf's plate-mail armor. He reversed direction, and let the other flat side of his hammer strike a blue goblin, crushing the blue goblin's arm.

The elf, wearing the plate-mail, flew backward and toppled two other dark elf warriors.

A dark elf archer leaned out from behind his shield-bearing partner.

Twang.

Two arrows leaped from the archer's bow aimed at Ord's platoon.

Thud.

Findor, his friend, a dwarf two-thirds the size of Ord, bellowed. One of the arrows pierced between the joints of Findor's banned armor, passing through the dwarf's shoulder. It struck the inside of the round shield attached to his back. The arrowhead shattered upon contact with the metal shield but left the feathered end of the wooden shaft sticking out of Findor's body.

Findor roared, his voice heard despite the noise of the battle around them, and surged forward into the fray, cutting a path to the dark elf archer. Beneath Findor's two hand axes, both, the dark elf shield bearer and the dark elf archer, fell.

Ord stayed with Findor protecting his friend's flank.

Twang. Clatter.

As the archer's bow hit the ground, the bowstring snapped. Both ends sprang out and tripped a dark elf warrior who had rushed up to help.

Ord struck downward with his great hammer as the dark elf warrior stumbled.

Slam.

The dark elf, which had tripped on the bow, did not rise again.

Ting.

An arrow ricocheted off Ord's shield kept in place on his back.

Whoosh.

From behind Ord, a crossbow bolt zipped by the right side of his helmet. At the same time, he heard a goblin's battle cry behind him. He swung the great hammer low as he turned to face his attacker.

His war hammer parried the goblin's mace, stopping the goblin from trying to strike the back of his legs. The goblin bashed his shield into Ord, attempting to drive Ord back as he raised the mace for a downward blow.

Findor rammed his armored, unhurt, shoulder into the goblin, knocking the goblin sideways. Ord looped his war hammer up over his head and brought it down on the goblin's collar bone.

Crunch.

Without waiting for the goblin to hit the ground, both Ord and Findor battled their way back to their platoon.

Through gaps in the throngs of warriors, Ord spied a trio of blue goblins forcing their way to Ord's position. Swords clanged, even against the dark elves that refused to shift out of their way. Wearing leather sleeves and black iron chest armor, the lead blue goblin shoved through to Ord's position, eyeing Ord with a gleam in his eye.

No, you don't, Ord thought.

Goblin leg bones snapped under the weight of Ord's great hammer. The blue-skinned warriors screamed. They fell backward into their comrades, crumpled to the ground, and were trodden by the warriors who pushed to take their place.

A roar came from the blue sky above. Whether it was from friend or foe, Ord could not tell. The ambient heat around Ord and his comrades intensified, as orange and red dragon flames licked down.

The goblins and dark elves pulled back, giving a wide berth to Ord and his comrades.

"Platoon Fimi, defenses up," Captain Dimur shouted above the turmoil.

The dwarves around Ord closed ranks, snatched their gold trimmed shields from off their backs, and held them over their heads, weapons at the ready. The overlapping shields formed a bright, shiny, metallic barrier against the death soon coming from above.

Ord dropped to one knee to bring himself closer to his comrades' height. He raised his shield, the hammer-inlaid tribal design of his family crest catching the yellow sunlight. In the shield's shadow, he spied a red dragon. It turned around for a second pass and zeroed in on his platoon.

"Left side sinister. Right side hold," ordered Dimur. "Dwarven archers ready your bows."

The dwarven platoon divided, and Ord found himself at the inside front edge of the split group.

A second burst of flame from a black dragon shot down from Ord's left. It was followed by dragon drool which fell from the sky and oozed down a dwarf's round shield.

In orange and red, the fire burned downward from the red dragon at their defensive shields. It licked around the edges and scorched the ground outside their perimeter. The dragon drool, still rolling off a shield, hit the ground like liquid fire consuming what little plant life had not been trampled by the battle.

The black dragon bellowed as a group of small green dragons charged it in the air.

A green dragon used its claws and ripped across the black dragon's left wing. The wind forced open the wound as the black dragon turned to engage the green, tearing it more.

The black dragon desperately flapped to gain more height but plunged toward the ground. It used its good wing to slow its momentum before heavily landing on the outskirts of the battlefield.

The ground shook. Rocks bounced. A dust cloud rose to choke the warriors near it.

The red dragon twisted to snap at another green dragon, cutting short the red dragon's intended second pass at the dwarven platoon. It flew in a curved flight path and drove the smaller green into the jaws of another waiting black. The red dragon swooped around for a third pass at the dwarves.

Ord watched as the creature winged from updraft to updraft, lifting higher and faster than a third green could match. Then, it turned. Holding its wings straight out, it soared down at its maximum speed.

Twenty dragons circled: black, red, green, and gold. The dragons flew across the sky roaring challenges to each other and defending the side they supported on the ground.

With a black dragon chasing them, three green dragons swooped upon the blue goblins and dark elves. They sprayed fire and grabbed warriors with their razor-sharp claws glinting in the yellow sun. A single green dragon cut from the group, turned, and engaged the black dragon.

A gold dragon and a black dragon slammed together in midair. With jaws snapping and dagger-like claws ripping across their reflective scales, both tumbled toward the ground. The gold caught the neck of the black in its strong muscular maw.

Snap.

The black dragon's wings stopped. Its head fell to the side. Its claws released from gripping the gold dragon.

The gold dragon launched upward, straining to maintain flight with both their masses. Its great wings angled its path toward the northern side of the battlefield and released its hold on the black dragon.

The black dragon plummeted toward the ground over the reserve troops of the blue goblins. Those that saw it falling ran. The dragon's body crashed onto the field of battle.

The earth shook. Goblins screamed and were crushed beneath its weight. Dark elves retreated as rocks shot up to pelt down from the sky. Dust billowed into the heavens. As the dragon's blood fed the dirt, earth golems rose bursting from its surface. Dimur's words, *Beware the earth*, had even more meaning to Ord now.

Despite the turmoil in the sky and on the battlefield, Ord kept coming back to the red dragon as it careened toward them. The hinge of its wings to maintain its dive, how the bones adjusted in flight to accommodate the wind, and the downward thrust it could generate for last minute changes all factored into his thoughts.

It was a marvel of engineering, a mountain of death to those it did not favor. One miscalculation by the red dragon, and it could crush the dwarven platoon like the black dragon did to the blue goblins.

Is this the best place for us to stand our ground? he thought.

While their dwarven shields could hold off the flames, this did not solve the problem of the dragon's attack. He glanced at the earth beneath his feet, leery of seeing the earth golems rise from it even if they managed to take the red dragon down.

The rugged surface was made of hard dirt and porous rock. The platoon was wide open, protected only by the metallic shields above their heads. And while the shields would hold off Hades' fire, something the dragon spewed from its mouth, they certainly could not stop a dragon crashing down upon them.

There must be a better way.

As if in answer to his thoughts, a breeze flowed through the platoon of dwarves. The dust beneath him swirled. The dirt cleared by the swirl gave way to a glint of light that caught his eye.

Maneuvering his foot, he scraped the ground around the glint until an amulet in the shape of a small hammer with a double twist in the handle sparkled in the light. He set his great war hammer down on its head and reached toward the amulet with his free hand.

Clang.

"Ord," the dwarf on Ord's left side shoved Ord with one hand, "watch what you're doing with that shield. Keep it up."

The push was enough. Ord snagged the edge of the amulet's chain with his gauntleted fingertips and brought it up to eye level.

At its touch, images formed in his mind. Pictures of events appeared in snatches: a tall grand forest spreading across the hill country, an ocean withdrawing from a sandy shore leaving desert, and a flood filling a valley. Flashes of creatures appeared: a wolf that walked on its hind legs, a multi-tentacled water monster, a woman with a fish tail, and the appearance of a great golden dragon larger than he had ever seen.

Ord allowed his shield hand to waver to the right. The shield tapped Findor's armor.

Clang.

"For the love of the dwarven kingdom, pay attention," his friend bellowed.

In Ord's mind's eye, the golden dragon mouthed his name. "Ord."

Ord looked up at the dark red dragon as it zoomed closer. The tips of its wings vibrated in the wind as it drew in air to fuel its fire.

Inside his skull, the words of the golden dragon came to life. His eyes grew wide.

"Ord," the golden dragon in Ord's mind's eye mouthed, "throw the amulet."

How is this possible? he wondered in awe.

"Ord," the golden dragon said in his mind, "you must throw it."

Ord lowered his shield until the bottom hit the ground.

Thunk.

"What are you doing?" Findor said and then elbowed him hard. "Ord."

"You wanted another way. Here is your chance," the golden dragon assured Ord.

Ord dropped his shield entirely. It clattered to the ground.

The dwarves around Ord murmured in confusion.

"What in the dwarven kingdom is going on?" Dimur, the platoon leader, hollered from the other side of the platoon. "Shields at ready!"

Hefting the amulet in his hand, Ord eyed the dragon.

How can my throw possibly reach it?

"Ord," the golden dragon pushed, "throw it, now."

Ord stood up from his kneel, wound back, and hurled it into the air.

The amulet rose higher than any other dwarf could have thrown it, but the distance was not enough. It reached its peak only a quarter of the way to the diving red dragon.

Before the amulet could descend, an arrow, black against the blue sky, rose from behind Ord. The tip of the arrow snagged the center of a link on the amulet's chain, whizzing the small hammer three-quarters of the way to the dragon. And yet, it, too, could not go high enough.

A raven soared in from the left flank of the dragon, snatched the amulet off the arrow before it fell, and rose still higher with the beat of its wings.

The dragon roared at the bird then hissed hot air from its nostrils. However, the dragon's gaze stayed focused on the dwarves below. The bird banked away from the steam and then, with a tight change in direction, beat its wings to get above the dragon's body.

With a jerk of the dragon's great head, the reptile snapped its glistening teeth at the raven and flapped its wings once. This altered the dragon's flight path from a horizontal dive to an angled twist.

The thrust of the dragon's wings shoved the raven outward to soar beyond the smoke from the sides of the dragon's mouth. The bird guided its descent toward the dragon's angled body, allowing the wind to carry it faster.

It descended above the dragon's neck, opened its claws, and let the air flow catch the amulet. The amulet dropped to the dragon's back catching on one of the boney ridges that tracked the dragon's vertebrae.

A burst of light grew brighter than the sun. Ord threw his arm over his eyes, turning his head away. As the glare faded, the blue sky was clear. Only a wisp of sulfur filtered down on the wind.

From the front right of the platoon, a hoard of arrows launched toward the dwarves' defensive stance. Ord snatched up his shield and dropped to the level of his comrades-in-arms.

"Hold position," Dimur shouted.

Ting. Thunk. Ping.

The arrows slammed into the superior dwarven shields as they glistened yellow in the sun. The barrage of projectiles bounced and thudded with only a few appearing to stick and then fell off.

The war hoots of the blue goblins and the thunder of the dark elves grew louder. They pressed toward the opening the platoon had provided when defending against the dragons.

"Close quarters," Dimur bellowed above the battle roar.

Closing the gap between them, the two dwarven groups attacked their enemies from both sides. Weapons clashed against shields. Armor bent at the blows. Blood was drawn, feeding the earth beneath their feet. And the war cry of enraged earth golems rose from the ground.

The goblins, dark elves, and dwarves turned from each other to battle the golems for the golems were on no one's side.

Arrows stuck. Some passed through. All left holes in the golems though the weapons did not slow them down. The more effective hammers crushed them into dirt. Axes chopped the golems into pieces as dwarves swarmed over them before they could reach full height. As soon as the golems were destroyed in one section, the three enemies turned on each other, again.

In Ord's head, the battle cries from both sides, enemies and allies alike, merged into one as his hammer rose and fell. It was a rhythm of death and destruction, the twisting of metal and those who wore it. The breaking of bones and the shatter of weapons aided the undesirable song.

During those endless strikes, parries, and clangs, Ord realized the noise of battle had stopped, and he stood alone on an empty battlefield: no bodies, no comrades, and no enemies.

Before him sat a great golden dragon with its tail curled about its body. It was the same dragon who had told him what to do with the amulet, the tiny hammer with the double twist in the handle, the amulet he had found on the ground.

He held perfectly still, dumbfounded, confused as to how this great beast had arrived and where his kin had gone.

"Ord," the voice of the female dragon boomed, "you must find the Branwen to know the path home. Seek the true Guardian of the Mundgurun. All is not lost."

"What are you talking about?" Ord shook his head. "I already know the path home, and every dwarf knows the Mundgurun was destroyed ages ago. The Guardians are dead."

The dragon snorted. Leaning forward, she eyed him closely. "Not all."

The vision of the dragon vanished. His hammer appeared in his hands still in mid-swing. The opponent in front of him leaped back. Battle cries hit him like a wave. However, the clang of metal as it struck metal, the weapons that hit shields, were all washed away as horns blared from every side of the battlefield. The abrupt clamor knocked him to his knees.

Ord struggled to his feet. His mind reeled. He raised his war hammer to strike again.

"Hold up, lad." His friend, Findor, clapped a strong hand against his arm, unable to reach his shoulder. "Didn't you hear the call?"

Ord's wounded friend, the arrow still in one shoulder, pointed across the battleground with his good arm. More dragons, elves, goblins, and dwarves, had fallen. The golems, which had risen from their shed blood, were now piles of dirt upon the earth.

Dark elves rode on horseback, carrying away their dead on makeshift stretchers. As supplies for all sides were taken somewhere else, wagon wheels bounced over the rocky landscape.

When Ord glanced up at the sky above them, it was empty of the battling dragons. Over the farthest mountains, the last dragons soared into the sunset.

He looked back at his friend, eyes wide with disbelief. "The battle is over?"

"A truce." Findor nodded at the flags of recall fluttering in the wind on both sides. "Perhaps uneasy," they could see the darting glances of those enemy warriors who did not wish to stop the bloodbath, "but a respite nonetheless." Findor glanced at his shoulder where the dark elf's arrow had pierced between a small gap in the armor. "At least I go home with a souvenir for the wall." He grinned.

Dimur scowled and stepped toward the center of the platoon after conferring with a runner. He wiped the scowl away as he realized all eyes were on him. "We fought well and are privileged to return to our families. Pull back and tend to the wounded. We break camp in the morning."

"Captain, what happened?" Ord hefted his hammer, feeling every achy muscle as the adrenaline of battle drained away. He set the bottom edge of his shield on the ground and gripped it by the top.

In a murmur, the same question rippled through the other dwarves, growing by the second.

"Do you not see the flags? Did you not hear the horn?" Dimur, his face turning red, grunted. "There is a truce." He pointed at Ord. "And after the stunt you pulled today, you better be glad it is. You have your orders." He turned sharply and led the way back to their camp.

The murmurs lessened as the dwarves ambled behind Dimur, stepping over the bodies of their fallen enemies. Crews of dwarves, not involved in the battle, were approaching from the camp to retrieve their own dead.

Ord helped his friend, Findor, retrieve his weapons and shield. He peered across the battlefield as he secured his own shield and war hammer to his back. He noted the dark elves had finished recovering their dead.

Did that mean the dark elves were responsible for the truce? he thought.

The blue goblins still worked to remove their own one by one. The black dragon, which had fallen, lay where it was near the enemies' encampment among the piles of destroyed earth golems.

Beyond the black dragon, other dragons had died. Although no gold dragons showed across the field, smaller green and a red lay unmoving, a testimony to the horrors of a race fighting its own kin.

What could have happened to make the three armies call a truce? Ord shook his head, trying to make sense of the situation. *Not that I am complaining, but without a good reason, it would simply start all over again.*

Ord and Findor headed toward the dwarven camp with Findor in the lead.

"It doesn't make sense." Findor threw a backward glance as the opposing sides continued to withdraw from the field of battle. "We had no clear winner."

"No," Ord wrinkled his brow, "it doesn't." Catching up to walk beside his friend, Ord looked over at Findor's shoulder. "Hurt much?"

"Tickles like a feather," said Findor, pointing at the end of the arrow. "Want to try it?" He chuckled, reached up and punched Ord on his plate-mailed upper arm.

Clang.

Findor cringed and lowered his arm. "Guess the war adrenaline is wearing off, my friend. Thanks for reminding me."

Ord chuckled. "What are friends for?" He looked closer where the arrow penetrated Findor's shoulder. "It does need to be checked. It is hard to tell what it hit inside the armor."

Trudging up the hill, both dwarves made the crest and gazed upon the circle of large boulders marking the location of their camp. The boulders were used as part of the camp's defensive boundary. Where there were gaps between the boulders, stone barrages had been stacked. Guards walked their posts.

A long line of dwarves had formed leading to the entrance. They were greeted by a sentry who strode their line but refused to let them pass.

A dwarven lieutenant walked in front of the sentry and handed out small, triangular, metal trinkets of bronze, gold, and silver. Without hesitation, the lieutenant handed a gold one to Findor. He eyed Ord, looking up at the much taller dwarf. With some hesitation, he passed Ord the same color trinket and said, "Someone likes you today. Pretend you hit your head."

The sentry watching Ord snickered.

"Why?" Ord held his trinket up in the light. The gold color reflected in the last throws of the setting sun. "This is for officers and those whose wounds could be sever. I am neither."

The lieutenant shrugged. "Orders are orders." He continued down the line toward another platoon.

Faint grumbles came from those ahead of Ord in the line. The phrase 'human half-breed' caught Ord's attention. He took a deep breath, his muscles taut.

"Come on." Findor warned Ord with a glance and started into the camp. "Let them dream of the mugs of ale a golden trinket will give them." He reached his good hand over and gripped his shoulder where the dark elf's arrow had plunged through, applying what pressure he could. The wood shaft and feathers shifted slightly as he walked. "I need to get this checked."

Disgruntled looks continued to be cast their way as the two walked on. They turned right inside the encampment, passed down an alley between tents, and stopped where those with the gold trinkets could rest.

Bonfires burned scattered with enough distance between them to give some privacy for conversation. Dwarven seats had been set up around the bonfires along with small folding tables used to hold the dwarven mugs and meals.

Findor picked a vacant, outer-edge, bonfire. He dropped his shield beside a chair. Using his good arm, he undid the strap that held his helmet on his head and set the helmet on top of his shield. He sniffed the air. "I need to get the filth of the dark elves off this armor." He glanced at the arrow still in his shoulder.

Ord removed his own shield and added, "And the blue goblins putrid smell."

"Aye," Findor agreed.

The firelight reflected from Ord's shield crest, a war hammer with a long straight handle held by a gauntleted fist. He leaned the shield against one of the tables and then pulled his great war hammer from the holder on his back.

It had remained true in battle. It had served his family name well. It, too, he placed beside the table along with his helmet.

A field doctor in old armor rattled up to them. The doctor carried a leather bag over his shoulder and a wooden bucket filled with hot, smoking water in his left hand. He glared at them both. "Well, what are you waiting for? There's more to see than the two of you." Putting the bag on the ground, he pulled a small bowl from it and placed the bowl on the table.

Findor pushed his shield away with his left foot to give the doctor more room to work. He took a seat, handed the doctor his gold trinket, and sat up straight, allowing the doctor to see both his front and his back.

The doctor eyed Findor's back, placing his left hand on dwarf's shoulder. "Clean through. That's a good sign." Without warning, he snapped off the broken arrowhead sticking out of the dwarf's back.

Findor flinched and drew three sharp breaths. "Come on doc," he blurted out, "where's the ale first?"

The doctor raised an eyebrow at him and handed him a short piece of wood. "Ready?"

Findor shoved the wood between his teeth. He mumbled with the wood in his mouth, "Why all the . . ."

Placing his right hand on Findor's shoulder, the doctor jerked the rest of the arrow out of Findor's front.

Findor gasped, cutting through the wood with his teeth. When his breath come back he finished, ". . . torture?"

The doctor started to toss the arrow pieces into the bonfire, but Findor caught his wrist.

Findor spit out the broken wood. "No warning? Really?" He nodded toward the arrow pieces. "Give those to me. I'm taking them home."

The doctor showed a wisp of a smile. "Souvenirs?" He shrugged. "Suit yourself."

Ord helped the doctor undo the buckles holding Findor's shoulder armor in place. The banded plate-mail remained firm to Findor's arm.

The doctor grinned at Findor. "Ready for some more fun?"

In the middle of Findor's single nod, the doctor ripped that off too. Dried, dark, blood stains filled the interior.

Findor swore in a language Ord had never heard before. When he finally finished, he more politely said, "Son of a goblin lover, where in hades did you get your bedside manner?"

The doctor only nodded. "Go ahead, son. Get it all out." Then, he shook his head as he studied the wound. "That will have to be cleaned." He dipped the small bowl into the bucket of water and pulled out a cloth from a pouch on his belt. Placing the bowl back on the table, he soaked the cloth in the bowl and reached toward Findor's shoulder.

Findor flinched.

The doctor smirked. "What are you afraid of? You faced a horde today, lad." He pressed down firmly on the shoulder, allowing the hot water to dissolve the dried blood and began to clean the wound.

With a grimace, Findor growled, "You clean wounds like sandpaper on metal."

The doctor smiled. "You have your profession. I have mine."

Fresh blood oozed from the wound as dried blood dissolved with the water. Once all the dried blood was gone, the doctor applied a paste to Findor's shoulder both on the back and the front and then wrapped it with a shimmering gold material. The scent of turmeric drifted up from the patch.

"There. It's the best we can do until we get you home." The doctor rinsed the bowl clean and stepped back from Findor.

Findor raised the arm up with a grimace. "The best, eh?"

The doctor glanced at Ord and snorted. "Where were you hurt?"

Ord raised an eyebrow. "Hurt?"

The doctor pointed to the gold trinket in Ord's hand. "Someone's idea of a practical joke? I'll get to the bottom of this." He headed away from the fire, leaving the bucket and bowl.

Red and orange flames danced against the blackness as darkness fell. Findor started to spout off again as the doctor stepped from the firelight, but Ord laid a hand on his friend's good shoulder. "Let it go. We'll be home soon enough."

He picked up Findor's banded plate-mail shoulder piece and studied how the arrow had successfully slipped through the bands. There was a tiny space, smaller than the end of his pinky, where the joints of the bands merged. It had taken a very good archer to make that target.

A lad came by and handed out mugs of ale.

Findor continued to fume. "Never could figure out why they let the quacks come to the battlefield while the real doctors stay at home." His expression brightened as he observed the ale in his hand. "Oh, well. At least the golden trinket buys the best ale."

Ord sat back in his dwarven seat. It creaked as he shifted.

Picking up Findor's armor, he used the bowl to dip more water and washed the blood stain out of Findor's shoulder piece. His thoughts drifted back to the battle. "Wasn't it odd how the red dragon disappeared?"

Ord's friend raised his mug of ale. Admiring it, he placed it to his lips and drank deeply. After licking his lips, he wiped the rest of the foam off with the sleeve of his good arm. "Red dragon?" He sighed, satisfied.

"You know . . ." Ord glanced up at the stars. A few clouds had started to form but nothing to worry about. ". . . the one who vanished." He placed Findor's cleaned armor on the ground to dry.

Findor extended his wooden mug toward Ord. "My friend, I think you need this more than I."

Ord continued, not paying attention to Findor's response. "And it doesn't bother you I stopped in the middle of the battle to throw a hammer amulet?" He squinted as he picked up his own mug. "Come to think about it, Dimur didn't seem amazed either." He tasted the ale, and his eyes opened wide. "Stout."

"All I saw," Findor waved it away, "was your shield drop out of position before the black dragon took a second pass. Had it not been distracted by the green, you would have been one cooked dwarf."

Ord shook his head, watching the bonfire. "That's not how it happened."

"Tell it to Dimur in the morning." Findor yawned as the ale's strength bit him. "Had we not been in the midst of battle, he would have pulled you from the ranks." Ord's friend struggled to keep his eyes open. "Better to spend your time fixing your armor than to worry about things we can do nothing about."

Ord's voice became cold. "You think I'm making this up?"

"No," Findor's voice dropped lower as he closed his eyes. "It's just," he yawned again, "something you're not going to figure out tonight."

Ord glanced at his armor. It required only superficial repair and functioned just fine. As all dwarves in the community, each family had their own special design. His family used a type of woven flax seed to line the inside of the metal so the overlaps did not rub together. This kept down the metallic clatter as he moved during battle.

Thud.

From the corner of his eye, Ord spotted something strike the soggy ground beside him in the exact spot he had cleaned Findor's armor.

Findor jumped and swatted at the air, not quite awake. "Perfumed elf-kissing mosquito. I hate mosquitos."

Ord raised his eyebrows and glanced over at his friend. Findor was dreaming, but whatever had hit had been real. Looking down, he eyed an arrow sticking into the ground beside his seat. It was an excellent shot in a gap about an inch wide between Findor's armor and his chair. Even in the flicker of the firelight, he recognized the design.

A dark elf's arrow?

He tensed his muscles and then forced them to relax. Whoever had shot the arrow was behind him among the tents. With an aim that good, and he without his helmet on, if the archer had wanted to kill him, he would already be dead.

He reached over and pulled the arrow from the dirt. Attached to its wooden shaft was a small piece of parchment. Drawing his family knife from his boot, he cut the fine string holding the parchment in place and slipped the paper off.

A note written in the Dwarven language had the printed words, "Be ready." Warning bells went off in Ord's brain.

Why in Hades would a dark elf warn me of anything?

He rose to his feet and staggered. His head swam. Grabbing hold of the seat to stabilize himself, he gazed across the camp.

Dwarves fell on every side. The sentries were down. Using dubhruya, the ability most dwarves had to see in complete darkness as if it was only dim light, he spotted to his left a long, dark, billowing, horizontal fog approaching the camp entrance. It loomed closer, growing larger by the moment, slithering around objects until it appeared to swallow them whole. The hairs on Ord's arm stood up.

Dark elves materialized from the fog, outside the dwarven camp, as its wispy bulk pushed its way over the stone walls and boulders. Bows and quivers adorned their backs. With swords sheathed, they strode into the campsite on steps so light, had Ord not seen them, he would have never heard their approach.

"Findor, we have been drugged," he whispered. He grabbed hold of Findor's good arm and shook it.

His friend's head fell to the side, mouth open, as he began to snore.

With Ord's vision swirling, he staggered away from his seat. He had to hide. He had to slip away.

The flickers of the campfire faded behind him. He passed dwarven tables with half-eaten meals. The tents he approached appeared distorted reminding him of creatures from a child's nightmare. He swayed, struggling to stay upright, drawing upon every bit of strength as he placed one foot in front of the other.

His right leg folded first followed by his left. As he dropped toward the ground, Ord reached out to snag a wooden post. He held it just long enough to keep from smashing his knees against the hard-packed earth. Then he collapsed, dropping sideways. His lungs heaved as he fought against whatever concoction had been put into the ale.

Who has done this?

He fought to open his eyes and to listen to the sounds in the encampment.

Approaching footsteps, he struggled to think.

The noise was distorted and deafening. Every tone throbbed inside his skull. He watched dark elves lift up dwarven heads around the bonfires, look at their faces, and turn away.

They are hunting for someone, but who could it be?

Distant dark elven words floated on the wind to Ord's ears in the quiet of the darkness. He struggled to understand them through the distortion caused by the drug.

The shadow of a dwarf was cast by the firelight of a large bonfire. Yet, this dwarf walked upright in full control of his faculties. The dwarf said in a gruff voice, "He was here, I tell you. I saw them give him the gold trinket."

The dwarf's voice seemed familiar to Ord, but the distortion of the sound made it difficult to recognize who it was.

"Your intelligence is somewhat lacking," a dark elf coldly said.

"If you want to find the key," the dwarf growled, "you will have to do it my way."

Ord sought to rise but his limbs would not obey him. The sound of light footsteps came from within the tent to his right.

The wind caught the edge of the tent flap. As it flicked out, a slim elven boot worn by a thin dark elf stepped toward him.

He tilted his head enough to see a large dark cloak in the elf's hand, but he could not see the face.

"Shh," a female voice warned. "Be silent or you will die."

With a swish, she dropped the cloak toward Ord. It descended in slow motion, completely covering him. Everything went black, his eyes closed, and he fell into a dreamless sleep.

CHAPTER 2

Thud. Bump. Thud. Bump. Thud. Bump.

Ord thought it was the beating of his heart.

Am I dreaming?

A bonfire glowed in front of him, but he felt no heat. Findor's head fell to the side. Billowing clouds rose from the darkness filling the dwarf encampment. The shadow of a dwarf, at first small, grew huge in front of Ord as the dwarf walked closer to the light of a bonfire. The dwarf casting the shadow was the same dwarf that had been unaffected by the drugged ale. And, a female dark elf stepped out of a tent near Ord to drop a black cloak on top of Ord's body. The thick black cloak still lay over him.

Am I awake or asleep?

Though no light penetrated the cloak, the dubhruya, the dwarven ability of his race to see in the dark, kicked in. He picked out in shades of gray the edges of the cloak lying against a grained wooden floor. Of course, *that* meant he was lying on wood, not the ground. *This* meant he could be somewhere else other than the encampment.

He slowly moved his stiff fingers, which had been abused on the field of battle, and noted he was still wearing his gauntlets.

Thud. Bump. Thud. Bump. Thud. Bump.

As his mind cleared, he realized part of the sound came from his helmet. It sat on its side, not more than a foot in front of him, rocking under the motion of whatever he found himself in.

A boat, a wagon, or something else? he wondered.

Although he could not imagine what *something else* might entail, he knew enough not to immediately rule it out. His studies in the library to be a sage had opened his eyes to many ideas.

Waves rocking a boat, in general, were gentler on items than the motion he saw his helmet make. In addition, the battle where they had fought had been landlocked, so unless he had been out for a very long time, a boat was less likely to fit his situation.

The *something else*, at the moment, was an indefinable mystery. Only when all other options had been ruled out would he go in that direction.

The hits were sharp on the thud and light on the bump.

Wheels?

Based upon the circumstances, there was one type of transport that would cause his helmet to rock that way even under a heavy cloak: a wagon as the wooden wheels rolled over some bumpy path.

Where am I?

He adjusted one arm and felt the hinge of metal at the joints. A glance toward his feet showed the plate-mail armor still in place. The metal joints of one of his gauntleted hands quietly complained as he flexed his fingers. He had not oiled his armor the night before.

He stretched his back muscles trying to keep his movement to a minimum in case he was being watched. As if being in battle wasn't enough, sleeping in his armor made it worse.

Back muscles ached. His shoulders felt tight. Moving his hands and finding himself not bound, he decided to take a chance and slowly sat up.

The black cloak slipped off his face and piled in folds at his waist. The wind went by at a steady breeze. Taller than the two-foot wagon walls, he stared at a forest of green conifers while he steadily rode by in the bed of a wagon.

The needle-like leaves of the trees decorated the forest floor in browns, yellows, and greens. They also told him he was still in the higher elevations of the mountain range not far from where he had fought in the battle. Although, he was not sure of his direction.

The wagon continued its bouncy ride, as if unperturbed by the fact that he was no longer asleep. Full burlap sacks had been piled around, sufficient to hide his previously still form from watching eyes.

A large wooden box was secured against the left front side of the wagon walls. It rocked each time the wagon rose and fell but did not slip away from the corner.

Probably attached with bolts through the boards of the wagon, he thought.

A lock, hanging three inches from the top of the box, held the lid of the box shut. The shank of the lock looped through a metal ring built into the box side.

He took his first good look at the driver, or rather, two drivers. Due to Ord's height, he could easily see the backs of both over the top of the wagon walls. He could also see the road ahead where two horses pulled them down the path. Within a few minutes, the driver on the left offered the reins to the driver on the right. Both wore exterior dark cloaks, keeping the details of who they were a mystery. By the swaying of their bodies, they were both fatigued.

If I am not a prisoner, what am I?

He reached for the dagger in his boot but found it gone. Also, his family's war hammer was nowhere to be seen. The last he remembered, he had left his large, two-handed, great hammer by the bonfire at the dwarven campsite.

No weapons, he puzzled, *but no bonds.*

He pushed the rest of the cloak off his legs and quietly scooted closer to the drivers.

From the dark cloaked driver on the left, a male voice tolled in the common tongue, "You are permitted to rise, dwarf, but come no closer. I will not have the smell of you upon me twice in three days."

"Aidan," a female scolded from the right, "he is our guest." She thrust the reins toward the male driver, who grunted in acceptance. Raising her right hand, she pulled the hood of her cloak back. As the hood slid off her head, it revealed long, pitch-black hair, dark skin, and elven ears as she turned around to smile at Ord.

"I am Jada." She motioned to the male beside her. "This is Aidan."

The male beside her grunted and said, "That's not my name."

"It is for the purpose of this mission," she sweetly reminded him. Her eyes dropped back to Ord. "It was we who saved you from the hunt."

"Saved me? Why?" Ord watched Jada's steadfast eyes, noting her palms were down and her gaze never flinched. There was a mystery behind those eyes, but the sparkle in them seemed to indicate she spoke the truth.

He sighed and thought, *Whatever is going on, she certainly believes she did it altruistically.*

And though it appeared they had saved him, he sensed something more to the story.

What are they not saying?

"We are enemies," he said, focusing a leery eye on Jada. "The dwarves and the dark elves are at war."

She lifted her chin as if schooling a child. "The kingdom is at war. We do not share their beliefs. To prove our intentions, there is a gift attached to your belt."

The number of trees thickened around them as the slope of the trail declined.

Ord looked down. He hadn't noticed it before, but a small, flat bag hung from his belt on his left side. He raised a single eyebrow in Jada's direction. "You gave me a leather bag to prove you are who you say you are?"

Jada chuckled. "Open the bag."

Is this a trick? he thought.

Ord undid the buckle, which held the bag to his belt, and then lifted the bag to chest level. Using both hands, he loosened the drawstrings. With two fingers, he pulled the top open. Unlike leather, the mouth of the bag stretched though it should not have. However, other than that one fact, he saw nothing to indicate the bag was of exceptional quality.

"Now," Jada continued in a whimsical tone, "reach inside."

Ord tentatively poked two of his gauntleted fingers into the top. The mouth of the bag expanded. He slipped in a third and watched it stretch again. Soon, he reached his whole hand inside but felt nothing. The bag, itself, never bulged though it should have. "What am I looking for?"

"It's a bag for collecting eggs. We call it an echor. No matter how many eggs you put inside, they will not hit each other and will be kept at exactly the right temperature."

A wisp of mountain air brushed by them, stronger than the breeze they generated by the moving wagon.

Pulling his hand out, he closed the bag. "Okay." His forehead wrinkled. "But I have to ask, 'Why only eggs?'"

Continuing to smile, Jada stared at his facial features as if looking at something he did not know existed. "That is its function."

The dwarf grunted and glanced away. "Yeah, this definitely convinces me of your intentions." He rolled his eyes as he laid the bag on the wagon floor beside him. It scooted back and forth as the wagon moved down the trail.

"Why don't we talk about why I'm here?" Ord peered into her face as his own became without emotion. "A truce had been called. You invaded our camp and broke the peace."

She did not blink. Though her smile sobered, it remained on her face. "The truce was called by those who commanded a single battle." She shook her head. "They had no intention of honoring that peace. We fight a greater war, you, I, and Aidan."

Ord leaned back against a pile of the burlap sacks and folded his arms. "I fight for my people by my own choice. You cannot force me to fight a war for you."

"Nor would we try," she assured with a single shake of her head, leaning toward him in sincerity. "We have a common enemy and only by working together can this enemy be subdued. The battle you fought with our kind was a symptom. It can only be cured by winning the greater war."

He listened to the urgency in her words. He gazed upon the uncompromising determination in her eyes.

"You believe what you're saying," he agreed, "but how can I know it's the truth? Taken in the night? Given an echor? A bag? And my weapons are gone?" Ord waved his hand at Aidan and Jada. "And I have two dark elves to guide me to a fate of which I have no clue." He huffed. "Perhaps you did not understand. I fight for the kingdom of the dwarves, for the protection of my family, and the honor to stand along my comrades-in-arms."

"And you will again," she said, her face beaming. "We ensured that you would by saving your life two nights past."

"And the other dwarves?" He watched her closely.

"It was not their lives that needed to be saved."

He kept his arms folded. "You talk in riddles."

"It is because you hear only that which you want to know." She tapped her ear. "A condition from which many suffer."

Her answer vexed him. He considered a sharp reply but her words, which included *two nights past,* clung to his thoughts. "Wait, I've been out almost three days?" Ord wrinkled his brow as he tightened the fold of his arms. "Perhaps you should start from the beginning."

Aidan choked on his own laughter. In the dark elven language, he said, "I told you, these dwarves mine too many stones to be smart. It is all the vapors from the deep."

Ord raised a single eyebrow and answered in the dark elven language, "Perhaps you overestimate your intelligence."

Jada smirked, fought to hold it in, and finally chuckled. "It seems our dwarven friend knows our tongue."

Aidan scowled as guided the horses more to the center of the trail. "He is a fool," he resumed in the common tongue. "I would have kept that knowledge a secret until I could have used it to my advantage."

"No," Jada gazed into Ord's eyes. "He is a friend to trust. Anryulong was right."

The wagon jarred as it hit a deep hole in the dirt trail. The dwarf unfolded his arms to steady himself, using his right hand to grip the wagon wall. Words slowly came to his mind as he thought over what had been said. "And Anryulong is?"

"A golden dragon." Jada's brown eyes were so comforting, so open, Ord was forced to look away.

The vision Ord had on the battlefield flashed through his thoughts. He whispered, "Find the Branwen." He looked up at Jada, searching her face. "I don't understand."

"The name is from an ancient dark elf legend. The Branwen is your guide home," her eyes sparkled, "if you wish."

Aidan pointed up ahead. With his other hand holding the reins he pulled back, slowing the horses. "We're coming to the fork in the trail. Be ready."

Jada turned to the front and replaced her hood. The redwood tree trunks were thicker here with a few trees reaching thrice the height of the average conifers. The smell of smoke wafted through the forest. After a short curve in the path, a chimney, made of white and red stone, came into view between the branches. It appeared to be a part of a lodge made of logs.

Aidan said in muffled dwarven words, "Do not speak. Do not say who you are. If asked a question, simply point in my or Jada's direction. If we are not around, play dumb. Do you understand?"

A smirk crossed Ord's face, but he said nothing. Without any reply, he shifted around until his back was to the front of the wagon.

After a short pause, Aidan continued. "Good. You are in enemy territory. If they feel you are anything other than our slave, you will be killed. If you speak, they will cut out your tongue. Now, remain facing the back of the wagon, eyes down, with all humility."

Ord adjusted where he sat, but the thoughts rolling through his mind were anything but humble.

Enemy territory? Why didn't they say that before? But I'll be babysitter to a babbling goblin child before I'll be a dark elf's slave.

He picked up his helmet and placed it on his head.

I'll not be going to face goblins without a way to defend myself.

The heavy burlap sacks would be fine for a quick knock-me-down, should he need them against the goblins, but they wouldn't do any real damage. His shield was nowhere to be seen. His gauntleted fists could be like hammers, but he preferred the swing of a weapon, his family weapon, the great war hammer.

The wagon sharply dropped, one wheel hitting in a hole.

Something bounced in the box to his right giving a metallic ring. He could have sworn he saw the shine of metal through one of the cracks in the rectangular box.

Weapons? Did they have his weapons?

Using his fingers, he reached over and traced the edge of the top of the box all the way to the lock. With the right tool or a heavy hammer, it would be easy enough to break open.

Ord mulled over Aidan's words and scowled.

The toe-sucking dark elf is right. I'll pretend to be a slave for as long as I can hold my temper.

He certainly never imagined himself as boastful as Findor, his friend since childhood. However, playing a slave to dark elves set his teeth on edge.

Surely slaves didn't wear plate-mail? Wouldn't that be a dead giveaway even without a weapon?

He whispered, "This will never work."

Aidan glanced back at him. "Shh."

The horses slowed. To Ord's left, the curve of the trail brought them around the north east end of the large wooden lodge, giving a full view of the chimney composed of red and white stones. A hitching rail ran the length of the longer north wall beginning just west of the chimney.

As the wagon started to parallel the northern side, heading west, the front door on the east wall opened under a small porch. From it, a blue goblin stepped out and stared at the wagon.

Aidan gave the reins to Jada, who turned the wagon toward the mid-center of the north wall, cutting off Ord's side view of the goblin. The wagon had no sooner pulled up to the hitching rail than it dipped and bounced in the front.

Ord looked to the right front and spotted Aidan lightly landing on the ground. The elf silently pointed a finger at Ord before the dark elf headed around the corner toward the east front door.

Startled birds squawked and took flight from farther away in the forest, rising into Ord's view of the sky. A raven soared above him. Goblin voices came from the northwest beyond the end of the lodge. Toward the back of the inn, near the voices, Ord spotted a stable for the horses through the trees.

Without the noise of the wagon's movement to mask so many other sounds, he heard the front door screech open. The bongs and bangs of goblin music came from within the lodge until the door closed.

Ord squinted at patches of goblin blue skin that flickered between the trees. The hairs on his arms stood up and he realized, *I am being actively watched.*

Dark elves were bad enough, but he could not stand blue goblins. They were never considered very smart by dwarf standards. They rarely did anything but pillage and destroy. He had never heard of them using buildings like this one, only huts scattered throughout their villages.

Fighting to keep his composure, he let his gaze drift to the locked box and then to the ground behind the wagon. Large stones had been cleared from the parking area. The stones had been used to create a makeshift border for the path that led to the barn.

There, that is what I need: a single large stone. With it, I can break the lock on the wagon box.

He still sensed he was being watched, yet subtle glances showed no one was about.

Jada is too quiet. Could she sense the goblins too?

He placed his hands on the floor of the wagon and flexed his arms testing how quickly he could push himself up, should the action be required. Despite his strength, plate-mail armor was heavy and certain startup movements could be slow.

Goblin, spoken between at least two, came from the forest around the horse barn. He peered through the trees but could not see the blue goblins that spoke.

Aidan's words rolled back through his mind, *Eyes down with humility*. His face flushed in defiance.

I would rather face them openly in battle.

A goblin swore toward the back of the house. Ord glanced to the left side of the wagon.

Leaning against the wall of the lodge, a blue goblin glared at him. It tilted its head as if summing the dwarf up then sniffed the air. "Caught in the war, were we?" Its tongue flicked out as if tasting Ord's scent. "And freshly, too. No time to bathe? Perhaps we should relieve you of that wonderful armor?"

The word *we* made Ord doubt this blue goblin's intelligence, even more than what he had been taught, until he heard footsteps to his right side. Using his peripheral vision, he spotted the second blue goblin approach. Watching both sides of the wagon as best he could, he turned his head to stare at the back, pretending to ignore both.

Ord repeated to himself, *Don't speak. Don't speak . . .*

He fought to keep his tongue, but he couldn't decide whether it was because of Aidan's warning or his conversation with Jada.

"Well trained, this one," the goblin on the left side mocked as it walked toward Ord. "Perhaps he already had his tongue removed." The goblin casually reached into the wagon and smacked Ord on the side of the helmet.

Bong.

Ord gritted his teeth and fought to keep from clenching his fist.

You'd be kissing my great hammer if I had it, he thought.

The goblin switched to pat Ord on the top of his helmet.

Bong. Bong. Bong.

Every pat stabbed at Ord's control. Although his muscles tensed, he continued to play by Aidan's rules.

Where is that stupid dark elf? And why isn't Jada saying something?

"Daarkob," the second goblin said from the right side of Ord.

Ord fought to keep from reacting as the second goblin leaned closer, his voice grating on Ord's nerves. "We'll get no sport from this one today."

The hairs on Ord's arms stiffened, and he knew, *There are more than two.*

The reek of skunk odor, a form of cologne among goblin men, wafted toward him on the wind. Ord fought not to cough.

As if the insults aren't already enough, now they are trying to gag me to death.

Two more goblins stepped from the forest, approaching the back of the wagon. The first of the two newcomers said, "Daarkob, Steepberd and I want in on the fun."

Now Ord was caught on three sides.

Why, by all the beardless women, isn't Jada saying something? Surely she sees what is going on?

"Sure, Clob," Daarkob said on Ord's left. "Vigar and I don't mind sharing. There's plenty of fun for all."

The skunk odor grew worse. Ord wrinkled his nose more.

"Hey, dwarf," Daarkob said. "How did you grow so big? Did they tie up your feet and stretch you taller?"

Ord felt his face grow hot.

When the war broke out, Ord's greater than standard height had made him an asset in combat. He was twice the size of the other dwarves and taller than most humans. It also made him the center of attention when his platoon took to the field.

Despite the commotion his height caused among his fellow dwarves, there was never a question of not going to war. It was a duty he felt deep within. Picking up his family war hammer and sheathing his father's boot knife, he had marched off to help defend the kingdom.

The warrior training had been brutal. With the call to arms and little time for practical experience, the instructors had been merciless.

But it did not matter. Intelligence lit his eyes. Determinism set his jaw. He would defend the dwarven kingdom to the end.

"What are you, a dwarf or a human in dwarf armor?" pushed Daarkob.

The other goblins chuckled.

Ord's muscles knotted until they were rock hard. Had it not been for the armor, the goblins would have seen his chest rapidly rise and fall.

Keeping his eyes steady on the back of the wagon, he pinpointed the location of each blue goblin, studying their stance and looking for what weapons he could see.

Bang.

Daarkob popped him on the back of his helmet, jerking Ord from his thoughts.

Ord's neck whipped forward before he caught himself.

"Did I tell you to look away?" Daarkob sneered.

Vigar, the goblin on the right side of the wagon, egged his friend on. "That's it, Daarkob. I think you've finally got the attention of the beard-loving hanky-toting oath breaker."

Ord glanced toward Vigar.

The goblin spat. The saliva hit the front of Ord's armor and ran down the plate-mail. "That's right, dwarf. When we are through with you, we'll ship your body back in pieces so your battle commander can plead in mercy before we take his short stubby head."

Ord roared. He grabbed Daarkob by the head and heaved him up into the air.

Click.

The neck snapped as the goblin soared over the wagon bed to crash down on his friend, Vigar.

Clob lowered the back of the wagon and threw out burlap sacks, trying to clear a path to Ord. Steepberd leaped into the wagon bed and fought to stay balanced, landing on a sack that Clob was trying to pull. Clob swore, the end of the sack he had grabbed ripping off due to Steepberd's excess weight.

Goblin voices rose from the back of the lodge.

Steepberd, facing Ord, slipped a knife from the sheath at his waist and jumped at the dwarf. The goblin stabbed multiple times, trying to get the knife to penetrate the shoulder joint in Ord's armor.

The weight of Steepberd knocked Ord sideways and pressed him against the wooden wagon bed. Ord spotted the front seat of the wagon as he fell back, but Jada was not there. He grabbed Steepberd's knife hand with his left hand and struck the goblin's chin with his right metal gauntlet so hard even Findor would have lost focus.

Crunch.

As the goblin's jaw smashed, Steepberd dropped his knife.

Ord thrust the blue goblin backward. The goblin slammed into Clob who had leaped up into a bag-cleared path. Both goblins tumbled off the end of the wagon and thudded against the ground.

Ord snatched up the goblin knife before it finished clattering on the bed of the wagon. With a quick turn, he jammed the blade between the shackle and the crossbar of the lock and then twisted the handle of the knife with a jerk.

Snap.

The shackle and crossbar separated.

He huffed.

Good quality blade. Bad quality lock. The lock certainly wasn't made by dwarves.

He tossed the broken lock off the back of the wagon and heard a satisfying *thunk* as it collided with the top of a goblin's head.

Throwing back the wood lid, he caught sight of the contents. His eyes brightened. Both his great hammer and boot knife were there along with other things: square folded linen, knapsacks, and waterskins. He tossed the goblin knife into the crate, drew his father's knife from it, and placed it into the sheath inside his boot. Gripping the great war hammer with his right hand, Ord turned, bounded over the filled burlap bags, and jumped from the back of the wagon.

Thud.

His feet struck the ground barely missing the two goblins who had been knocked out the back. One lay unconscious. The other groaned. The dust clouds of his landing blew away in a gentle breeze.

He waited, but no one came from the forest or sides of the lodge, despite the goblins lying in plain sight at his feet.

The ground rumbled. Shouts from goblins rose from behind the lodge to the west. The horses attached to the wagon stirred, stamping their feet and pulling against the tether that held them there. With dwarven fury awakened, he bellowed, "Bring it on, you witless blue goblin scum!"

Howls and hoots from screaming goblins came from the rear of the building. The rumble became a tremor. The lodge swayed as the building shook. Still filled with rage, he stomped toward the back corner of the building, ready to pick a fight.

To the south west, barely seen above the trees, the mountain above them quivered as boulders, rocks, and dirt rolled down its incline. Trees overturned, broadening the destruction in the wake of the landslide.

Goblins rushed from the forest to fill the clearing around the back of the building from farther up the mountain. Their hands thrashed as they screamed in terror, a horde of blue-skinned madness rushing in an uncontrolled mob.

Ord jumped back against the side of the building, holding himself as flat as possible while the stampede of blue bodies swept past. The horde's path curved around the corner, somehow avoided the wagon, and raced beyond it toward the trail.

Dust filled the air from the running feet. The goblins that fell were trampled. Colonies of birds took to the air, darkening the sky as if thundering clouds floated overhead. A single raven circled through them watching what took place from above.

The horde thinned but remained steady as seconds went by while the shake of the ground grew worse. The lodge rocked. The logs groaned.

The stones outlining the path to the stable jumped. Leaves on the trees shook loose and fell. The branches of the trees waved to the creak of snaps and breaks.

Ord turned to run. He spotted Jada sitting in the wagon front seat, as if she had never left, holding the reins to steady the horses. The tether had been removed from the hitching post. Her features showed no concern about the descending landslide.

Coming from around the front of the building, Aidan leaped onto the left front seat beside Jada and caught Ord's eye. "What are you waiting for? Get in and secure the backboard." He took the reins from Jada.

The dwarf bounded over to the wagon even as Aidan fought to walk the horses backward. The right rear wagon wheel bumped against the bodies of the two blue goblins. The horses panicked, surging back and forth.

Aidan swore in dark eleven as Jada took the reins. He jumped from the wagon and dragged one of the goblin bodies from behind them as Ord grabbed the other.

The wall of the groaning lodge leaned. Clay tiles slide from the roof and crashed to the ground beside the horses' hooves.

Ord leaped for the wagon bed as Jada turned the horses. While the dwarf was still in the air, Aidan climbed into the seat beside Jada.

Jada flicked the crop above the back of one of the horses. The wagon jumped forward as the horses leaped into a gallop.

Ord landed in the wagon bed, slamming down on the unlevel bags.

Gasp.

The jolt knocked the wind from him. He slide backward and snagged a stack of heavy burlap sacks to stop him from sliding out the tail of the wagon.

"Secure the backboard," Aidan hollered again, taking the reins from Jada.

The wagon raced forward, cutting through the horde of goblins that sprinted down the trail. Blue goblins dodged out of the way as the wagon gained speed.

The road curved. The right side of the wagon rose as it balanced on its two left wheels. Bags slid toward the left side, bringing the wagon close to tipping.

Ord slid with them but snagged hold of the right wagon wall before moving too far. Slipping on the wooden wagon bed, he planted his feet against the inside of the left wagon wall. This stabilized him and the burlap bags.

Aidan leaned right, keeping the reins in his left hand while his right grabbed onto the wooden bench. Jada stretched to the right, grasping the end of the bench with both hands.

With the weight stabilized, the wagon slammed down on all four wheels. Jada fought to sit back up. Aidan released his hold on the wooden seat and grabbed the back of Jada's black cloak to help her.

The burlap bags rose into the air about half a foot as the wagon jarred against the ground. They collided into Ord as Aidan drove the wagon faster.

The bags pounded Ord toward the backboard. He shoved them toward the center of the wagon bed and rotated his body until only his head extended out the back of the wagon.

Dust billowed up behind them. With his left hand, he held onto the nearest wagon wall and secured the great war hammer in his back sheath. The backboard bounced with every bump in the road, bashing at his fingers when he reached to secure it.

He snagged it with his fingertips and then slowly raised it up. Inching his left hand close enough to hold the backboard in place, Ord slid an iron hook through the first iron loop to secure it.

A goblin, seeing the wagon moving faster than he could run, lurched out to catch the backend. It missed and tumbled down into the dust. Another blue-skinned goblin darted in from the right, but its hands slipped off as the wagon jostled by.

The avalanche reached the back of the lodge. Logs splintered and snapped. The chimney cracked and the red and white stones tumbled. Blue goblins were swept away as the clouds of dirt and rolling rocks swallowed the lodge whole.

The edge of the cataclysm surged by with the loving touch of the landslide nipping at the wagon wheels. Trees crashed behind them. The wood of the wagon strained as branches slapped against it.

Ord dropped the last iron hook into the last iron loop, grabbed hold of the wagon's left side panel, and worked his way up the bed of the wagon until he was behind Jada and Aidan.

"What happened?" he said, unable to pull his eyes from the calamity that ripped down the mountainside.

The lid to the open wood crate rattled against the side of the wagon. With one hand, Ord closed it, surprised that nothing had fallen out.

"You spoke," Aidan snapped. The dust billowing behind them rose higher into the sky.

Jada remained quiet while the sky darkened above. As the dirt continued to rise, she reached back and removed a linen cloth from the wooden crate, handing it to Ord. "Use this until we get inside to breathe through." She slipped a black cloth, tied around her neck, up over her own mouth and nose. Adian placed the reins in one hand and did the same.

Ord accepted the gray cloth. He removed his helmet, wrapped it around the lower half of his face to cover his nose and mouth, and placed the helmet back on his head. "My actions couldn't have done that." He waved back toward the debris, the roar of the landslide and the cloth forcing him to raise his voice.

The avalanche swept over the trail they had come by and dumped into a shallow valley. The debris accelerated, hit the bottom, and then slammed into the far side of another rising peak. Dust and dirt shot into the air as the blowing wind shifted it back in their direction.

Jada's voice remained low, but somehow it could be distinctly heard. "We will not be able to come back this way for a while. Some of the goblins have survived, enough to be witnesses that we traveled this direction."

Aidan nodded. "There are other paths." With a quick turn of his head, he scowled over his shoulder at Ord. "I pray we will not need to lose another."

"You can't blame this on me," Ord shot back. "I didn't cause the avalanche."

"But you did make it necessary," Jada said quietly.

He bristled. "How? The goblins were attacking me. What choice did I have?" He stopped. His eyes went wide as he stared at Jada. "You did this?"

Ping. Ping. Pong.

Pebbles struck Ord's helmet. Dirt and rocks rained. The air became a murky brown. Aidan fought to keep the horses on the path and at the same time use the trees for cover.

"We need shelter, at least until the cloud finishes its descent." Jada pointed toward a barn whose outer attachments had fallen, though the main structure seemed intact. Weathered oak planks, darkened by the years, covered its outer walls.

Two large doors met in the middle on the east side that faced them. Against the north side of the barn, rubble from the avalanche lay strewn. And, although he could not see it, Ord suspected the western side was the same.

Aidan urged the horses toward the damaged structure. The wagon wheels crunched over broken branches as they drove around the trees. The rain of debris lightened, but they could see darkness in the sky heading their way.

Farther down the slope, in front of the barn but more north, the remnants of a logged house stood. The foundation logs used to secure the upper structure to the ground remained, but the house proper had been taken by the landslide.

Aidan stopped the wagon ten feet from the double doors and handed the reins to Jada before dropping to the ground.

Creak.

The two doors covering the entrance of the barn groaned open as Aidan pulled back the left door first and then the right. He stepped inside, peering into the shadows. Only the wind blowing between cracks could be heard from within the barn. At a wave of his hand, Jada directed the wagon in.

Ping. Pong. Ping. Ping.

The pebbles rained down faster, bouncing off Ord's armor. He glanced back at the murky air descending toward them and then at the inside of the barn.

It would be so easy to escape at this moment. A rush to the road and down into the valley is all I need to do.

He sighed.

But they don't act like I'm a prisoner. They claim to have saved my life. Yet, they do not tell me where we are going.

He remembered the red dragon diving through the air at his comrades-in-arms. He recollected the black, dark elf, arrow that had shot upward to help lift the amulet as Ord's throw had fallen short. And last, he recalled the raven, who had dropped the amulet on the dragon, in a final swoop.

The facts were incomplete. The golden dragon had known what was about to happen, he was sure of it. Somehow, he, himself, was connected to the fates of these two dark elves.

Realizing Jada did not have any protection from the falling sticks and stones, he stood up behind her and held his arms over her head. She coached the horses into the barn.

Ting. Clang. Bang.

As if an intelligence knew they trying to hide from the storm, larger stones bashed against Ord's armor as Aidan, Jada, and Ord passed into the depths of the barn. The roof vibrated as thousands of rocks beat upon it, filling the barn with a roar.

Aidan slipped outside, stayed close to the wall under the roof overhang, and pulled the right barn door closed. The falling debris slammed against the wood, bouncing off the door planks to settle both inside and out of the barn. When both doors were pulled closed, Aidan dropped a long wooden bar into place to hold the doors tight.

Ord wrinkled his brow and raised his voice to be heard over the roar. "Are we expecting someone?"

Aidan gave a curt nod and then moved to the front of the wagon. He hunted under the wooden seat and retrieved his bow.

"Quickly," Jada stepped to the ground and held out a small bag for Ord to take. Her voice, despite the roar of the rocks on the roof of the barn, remained crisp and clear. "You almost lost this."

The dwarf gawked, accepting the echor. He grasped the side of the wagon, leaped over it, and land with a heavy thud even with the straw on the ground. "You saved the egg collector?"

"It is a precious gift." With a stern look, her eyes caught his. "You should treat it as such."

He reached out to take it, but she did not immediately release it.

Jada looked him in the eye. "Remember the Branwen."

He blinked. "Perhaps you should tell me the story of the Branwen."

She turned away to face the barn floor, slipping the black cloth down off her nose and mouth and wearing it like a scarf.

Ord studied the bag.

How are the two, the echor and the Branwen, related? he thought. *What do all these things have to do with the golden dragon?*

Yet, there were no answers. He buckled the echor to his belt, removed the cloth from his nose and mouth, and put his helmet back on. Turning, he watched what Jada did next.

Assuming a squatting position, she brushed the straw away next to the wagon. "We need to make a circle of protection." With her left hand, she reached under the wagon and used her other hand, the right hand, to draw symbols in the air, gradually working her way completely around their ride.

The horses snorted but kept their feet still while she moved beside them. The roar of the rocks filled the barn.

As she reached where she began, the straw leaped away from inside of the circle, landing outside the border. She started around the wagon a second time.

"What are we being protected from?" Ord said, following her and noting each symbol she drew in the air. His dwarven eyes adjusted to the dim light though what he saw still remained in color.

"From that which follows behind and now knows we are here," Jada said, focusing on her last symbols, as she drew them with an air of expediency.

With the straw gone, she stood up and watched Aidan place his quiver upon his back. He then reached to remove the driving harness from the horses, but she caught his eye in warning. "We will need them ready. It is essential you be on the left side of the wagon." She looked to Ord. "Please take the right."

The horses flicked their ears and shifted their heads as she left their side.

Aidan threw her a questioning glance as he moved to the left side. He stayed within the cleared circle she had created but placed three feet between him and the wagon.

Reaching into his quiver, he pulled an arrow with a large hollow head. Inside the head was a thick black substance. For a brief moment, he stared at it as if he did not recognize why it was there, shrugged, and dropped it back into the quiver. The second arrow he pulled had a smaller, more normal, arrowhead.

Jada answered Aidan's glance at her with a whisper, "It is his test."

Ord positioned himself to the right side of the wagon, his hammer at ready on his shoulder. He studied the depths of the barn, noting the glances of the horses toward the darkness.

Stairs ascended to the loft on the south wall. The loft had been built in an L-shape, creating a second floor that extended halfway toward him along the right rear wall.

Beneath the loft, storage bins had been set. On the wall above the bins, tools for farming hung. He had never known goblins to farm anything, let alone create wooden structures of such size as this.

Taken as a whole, this barn could not have been created by blue goblins. They would never have taken the time. It was more like . . . "Humans lived here?" He glanced back at Jada and spotted Aidan watching him.

Jada nodded. "Before the blue goblins, this was once a human village."

She absently tapped her lips as she turned around to face the wagon. "I will need a few things to complete the circle." Climbing into the bed of the wagon, she sat upon the burlap bags nearest to the box where Ord had found his weapons. Neither of the dark elves had commented on his way of *unlocking* the box nor had they mentioned anything about him taking his weapons out.

From a bag hidden inside her black cloak, she pulled out a white stubby candle almost used up, a dual-edged ornate knife whose obsidian handle had been carved into the shape of a raven, and a golden apple whose surface appeared unblemished. These she placed on the lid of the closed wagon box.

Eyeing the surface of the apple, she placed the dual-edged knife blade preciously parallel to the apple's core and cut the apple in half.

Ord's stomach grumbled.

Then, she reached a second time into the bag beneath her black cloak and withdrew a small cloth tied at the ends by a leather string. Untying one end, she let it drop open to form a spout. From the small cloth she sprinkled yellow powder onto the fruit, closed the apple pieces together, and set it by the candle. She carefully put the knife and small cloth away.

Ord smelled floral pine needles as the breeze, which slipped between the cracks in the barn planks, wafted the scent in his direction. "Lavender and rosemary?"

"For one from the depths of the dwarven mines, you have an unusually good nose, dwarf." Aidan snickered. "That must be a fluke."

Ord raised an eyebrow toward Aidan. "For one so sour, you have a sense of humor, elf."

The horse on the right had stopped moving its head and stared into the darkness of the barn. The one on the left whined and stomped its feet.

Jada cupped her palms around the candle's wick. As she mouthed words, Ord watched a flame ignite. The light reflected from a ring on her right hand, middle finger, a ring Ord had never noticed before.

She looked at Ord, meeting his gaze as if she noticed him spotting the ring. "Be diligent."

As the flame grew brighter, the horses settled in quiet bliss. However, the hairs on Ord's arm stood up.

He turned away from watching Jada to view the barn's interior details. "Diligent for what?"

The barn filled with the noise generated by the stones beating against the roof. All the way to the edge of the inner circle, the light from the candle shone out brighter than should be possible. Yet somehow, the glow appeared muted beyond the circle's barrier. It took on an ugly, orange, radiance as if discolored by something else in the room.

About a foot above the floor, humanoid images formed. Some were tall, others short. An aura of energy traced their outlines.

Ord stared. He held up a hand and watched one of the shorter images mimic his movements. In that instant, he sensed the outline had once been a young boy, no more than a child. The other images paid Ord no attention.

He lowered his free hand. The young boy's image did the same.

Ord said, "What magic is this?"

Though he knew Jada was behind him, her voice seemed to come from all around the barn. "These are those who walk in the shadow, taken by those of the dark. They call for our help, beings trapped in limbo and lost between two worlds."

The dwarf squinted at the figures. "And they've been here all along?"

"They are drawn during eruptions of violence like the landslide we have just incurred. Raw power holds them here, attached to this world, but unable to enter or flee. They are not the ones to fear. Those who follow are."

A scream cut the air outside the barn. The air around those from the wagon grew cold. Ord's breath came out in icy puffs as a shiver rippled up his dwarven spine.

CHAPTER 3

The barn doors shook. Through the interior the sound echoed despite the pelting of rocks against the roof. The wind howled, gaining strength outside the building and beating against the wooden planks. Between the boards of the walls, the gusts whistled through the cracks. The light outside dimmed as if twilight had fallen. The images of the beings faded until they could no longer be seen.

"But who are they?" Ord looked toward Jada when she did not answer.

Her eyes were closed as she mumbled in a language not entirely elven.

He looked to Aidan. "What is she doing?"

Aidan stared into the blackness on his side of the wagon. Though his voice was emotionless, the tightening of his jaw was obvious. "She is hiding us. Pray she can succeed."

The wind batted against the barn doors. The doors bounced, rattling the hinges. The wooden bar, which held the two barn doors closed, curved inward. The barn timbers creaked.

The combination of the rock strikes against the roof and the creaking timbers did not sound good to Ord. While he had seen the strange beings with his own eyes, there was something about their presence that did not fit the story Jada told. And though the blowing wind and pelting debris were working together to rip the building apart, he wondered about what Jada had not said.

Boards groaned on every side. The hair on his arms stood as something shifted closer from the darker recesses of a corner. A skunk odor, carried to him on one of the gusts of wind, reached his nose. The hay floor near the barn wall lifted. He spotted a flash of blue goblin skin. Other areas on the floor stirred within stalls and in corners. The wind caught the straw and whipped it into the air.

"Aidan, Jada, we've got other troubles."

Aidan loosed his cloak. It slipped off his shoulders to the ground.

A blue goblin leapt from the loft above them toward the wagon. Why Ord had not detected them before made no sense.

Aidan's dark elven arrow struck the goblin through the heart. The goblin's body fell to the ground landing just short of the circle. The horses, partially breaking from the calm that Jada had settled over them, uneasily shifted.

A second goblin rushed toward the horses. Ord swung his hammer. The great war hammer passed beyond the circle with a bone crunching strike. The goblin tumbled backward before it could reach the circle perimeter. Gusts of wind slammed against the outside of the barn.

"Why are they revealing themselves now?" Ord blurted out. "Shouldn't they be hiding from the storm?"

A third goblin sprang into the air from the loose hay next to a storage bin. It dropped dead before its feet reached the ground with a dark elf arrow through the goblin's neck.

"They are controlled by the beings outside the barn," Aidan said. He eyed every corner on his side, keeping his bow at ready.

"All beings have free will," Ord countered as he shifted his gaze toward any moving shadow. Beyond the cracks in the stall walls, blue flashes of goblin skin continued to appear, although none of the goblins seemed anxious to show themselves. With what little light shown between the cracks in the outside barn walls, Ord could see others beyond the barn fighting the wind and coming in their direction.

Rocks struck them, knocking them to their knees. Others were thrown to the side, swept away by the wind. A few were slammed against the outside of the barn, only to collapse against it. Those that remained conscious fought, crawling toward the building as if caught in a trance.

Aidan shook his head, replying to Ord's statement. "Not if you give it up. The beings outside are trying to make us show ourselves by using the goblins to break Jada's spell. We were briefly seen because of the avalanche. And now, due to Jada's circle of protection, are not seen anymore. It takes focused power to track us."

"Why don't *those beings outside* come in themselves instead of using the goblins?" Ord growled. "I don't like races who can't handle their own battles."

Aidan scrutinized the hay bales beyond the circle of protection to the west side of the barn. Cutting off the natural light from that section, the hay had been used to set up low walls three feet high.

He aimed at a bale, which slid a half inch forward, and said to Ord, "It is easier to let the goblins fish us out."

In a stall to Ord's right, hay rose into the air. It fell off the head and shoulders of two blue goblins who scrambled to their feet. For an instant, Ord caught sight of two tunnels, both a shoulder-width wide, leading down into the ground before the hay covered them up.

The goblins rushed Ord. His hammer smashed into one but missed the other. He braced for impact but instead of feeling the collision, watched as the creature slammed into a transparent domed barrier. Ripples of orange shot out in all directions as the goblin violently shook, falling back unconscious.

Jada groaned. Her words, not understandable by Ord, rose and fell.

The light of the candle flickered in a wind Ord could not feel. The brighter light, within the circle of protection, momentarily dimmed.

"What was that?" The dwarf gawked at the edge of the circle and darted a quick glance toward Aidan.

Aidan snapped, "Protect her."

Another entranced goblin stepped within range. Ord's hammer found its mark. "What do you think I'm doing?"

Wood cracked above them. A stone shot through the hole in the roof and struck the top of Jada's mystical shield. Orange ripples radiated out as the rock bounced down until it dropped into the hay.

Jada gulped air as her lungs labored. Though the volume of the words dropped, they did not stop.

Aidan spun to the left and let loose an arrow. A blue shadow dropped by the far wall.

"What's wrong with her?" Ord slipped closer to the front of the wagon and eyed a blue mass as it rose from beneath the hay near the farthest side of the barn. Multiple dirty hands and arms could be seen as if the group of goblins had clawed their way up from under the ground.

Aidan retorted, "They are draining her. Every strike against the circle of protection shortens the time she can hold it."

Ord hesitated as he watched the blue mass separate into individual goblins. Three emotions tore up his insides: fear of this force that could take control of the blue goblins, an uncanny concern for this female dark elf, and the knowing that she and Aidan were keeping out details he should know.

He had seen the caring in Jada's eyes: a caring more than for herself, more than for her people. She fought for the beings of this world in a battle Ord could not even fathom. And yet, there was more. Something inside him knew there was.

How could these mystical beings outside the barn have tracked them?

A sense of understanding passed through him like the hunter knowing where the hunted hides.

It isn't me they can track. If so, I would have encountered them long before now. It is Jada and Aidan. Somehow, these two dark elves are tied to these mystical beings and had revealed themselves to them through their actions.

Remembering the orange ripples, he was also sure, if he could keep the attackers further away, there would be less chance they could exert a strain upon her circle of protection.

He zoomed in on where the huddled, blue mass had been, but it was almost gone. In its place, a horde of blue goblins stumbled about as if without instructions. The hair on his arms stood straighter.

They are about do something. I can feel it.

Whatever it was, their numbers would devastate the circle of protection, and he could not let that happen.

If the end of my hammer can pass through unscathed, why can't I?

"Then perhaps I can help her," Ord replied to Aidan's retort and stepped beyond the barrier.

"Ord," Aidan shouted, "no."

A goblin war cry came as the remains of the disorganized mass divided. They all charged the circle.

Ord planted himself for battle. "You will not touch her."

With his hammer, Ord jabbed the first running goblin to reach him in the midsection. The goblin's vertebrae cracked. The second goblin dropped as his leg bones shattered from the weight of the great war hammer's touch. Ord looped back to put the goblin out of its misery with a slam to the head.

The third blue goblin gasped as Ord bashed into its side with the war hammer. The goblin flew across the room and went silent as it bounced off a barn wall.

The bodies of two enemy goblins slammed backward as Ord struck the first with his hammer, knocking the first into a second.

Thud.

Their two heads cracked together.

Another goblin stabbed at Ord with a pitchfork, only to have the metal end crumple at the touch of his swinging hammer. The shaft snapped as Ord altered his hammer's glide to curve back and collide with the goblin's weapon. Before the goblin could jab with the splintered end of the shaft, Ord struck the goblin directly in the chest. The goblin spun off to the right to land face down on the barn floor.

The next goblin swung a scythe, but the wooden handle was no match for the blunt force of the war hammer. The scythe split, the metal end flying off to stick into a wooden stall. The goblin stabbed with the remaining pointed handle toward Ord's face. But before it could reach him, Ord brought the hammer down on the goblin's head.

Heart heaving and muscles bulging, Ord searched for another opponent. They were down, all of them, some by his own hand and others by Aidan's arrows. He scanned the right side of the barn from corner to corner.

A slight flutter in the hay, almost imperceptible, had he not been looking straight at it, stirred from the far back corner. His heart beat faster as he rushed in with the hammer ready . . . before screeching to a halt. His feet slipped on the straw. He grabbed the nearest post to keep from falling.

Lying in a small curved alcove was a baby goblin. It stared up at him with its light green eyes.

There was no fear. There was no taunting. It didn't have any of the prejudice that the world in which they lived might breed. As it gazed up at him, it cooed.

Ord slowly lowered his hammer. He set the weapon down on the ground beside him and pondered the baby, while the roar of the debris striking the roof lessened. The wind, which tore at the outside of the barn, abated by degrees. His own heart steadied as the adrenaline of battle drained away, and yet, at the same time, something inside him stirred, just out of reach. He watched the goblin child smile up at him, the fright from the battle washing from her features.

The crunch of dry hay sounded behind him. He spun around to face Aidan and Jada as they approached.

Aidan scowled and swore in dark elven before continuing in the common tongue. "You abandoned the circle."

Jada placed a hand on Aidan's arm. "Ord is discovering more of who he is."

Ord blinked at both, feeling his insides twist. "I don't know what you're talking about." He hurried away from the baby and headed for the wagon. When he made it to the horses, he purposely kept his back to the elves and the goblin child, while he checked the animals for damage even though he knew nothing had made it through the circle of protection.

He grunted abnormally loud and said, "Aidan, I applaud you. You kept the horses from harm *almost* as well as a dwarf."

There was no response behind him.

Ord glanced toward the dark elves and caught sight of the baby who continued to gaze in his direction as Jada picked the baby up. He nervously avoided the baby's eyes.

He felt his heartbeat quicken and thought, *What is wrong with this child? Why is it looking at me?*

When he glanced back at it, the child's smile brightened.

He turned away and spotted the light as it filtered between the planks in the barn door. Through the cracks between the outer wood, he caught glimpses of the outside.

Pebbles and stones littered the ground. He knew a landslide could cause this phenomenon. However, the presence of so much debris concentrated at this one location and petering out about fifty feet beyond, felt unnatural.

It seems to confirm Jada's story that we were under attack, he thought, *so why wasn't there more damage?*

The stones varied in diameter from pea-size to rocks as large as his fist.

With that type of falling barrage, it should have caved in the roof of the barn.

He walked toward the back of the wagon, closer to the doors.

Could Jada's circle of protection have helped with that too?

Ord cleared his throat. "I take it the circle of protection is no longer needed?"

"They are gone," Jada assured. "Your distraction was enough. You correctly deduced what had to be done."

He felt a flicker of anger. "You were waiting for me to do that? You knew I would do that?" He turned back and looked at Jada, Aidan, and the goblin baby. "Couldn't you have just told me what needed to be done?"

Jada looked down at the tiny goblin baby. She whispered, "And what will we do with this little one?"

Ord spotted the baby still staring in his direction and glanced away, focusing on Aidan who seemed highly amused. Ord fought to ignore the strange stirrings he felt when he looked at the child, although he did turn back to view Jada with the baby.

"Leave him," Ord said. "I'm sure the mother will be back after the storm."

Remembering the debris outside, his own words hit him hard as he thought, *No one could have survived outside, and if the mother wasn't here already . . .*

He glanced at the fallen goblin bodies.

Surely, she had not been one of the attacking goblins?

He swallowed as the horror of what he may have done hit him. With a tight throat, one by one he checked the fallen goblins but found only male warriors. Their bodies lay where they had dropped. He traced the paths they had made coming from the stalls and the dark corners. They had emerged from the ground through holes in the earth, many of which had been covered by hay and boards to hide the entrance.

He peered down into one of the holes. While he might be able to fit down in one, it would be a tight squeeze.

Aidan walked up behind him. "Thinking of going down for a look?" The dark elf smirked.

"Should we?" He glanced over at Jada and the goblin baby. "Maybe its mother is somewhere down there."

"Maybe," Aidan shrugged, "but if she was, it probably wouldn't matter now. I would think if the tunnels didn't collapse due to the avalanche, they would not be safe to enter after." He rolled his eyes. "But be my guest. From what I'm told dwarves like dank, dark, holes in the earth." He touched his chin. "Much like rabbits."

"I think you've mistaken dwarves for dark elves," Ord shot back.

"Think so?" Aidan grinned and nodded toward Ord's hammer. "We will test that theory someday."

Aidan drifted his gaze to a goblin body within three steps from them. He leaned near the dead goblin, placed a foot on its chest, and pulled his arrow out. The gaping wound bled, feeding the dry hay on the barn floor.

"In any case," he continued, wiping the arrow clean in the hay beside the goblin, "we need to gather the dead into one pile." Kicking a broken pitchfork away from another goblin's body, Aidan moved to a third. "And while I don't care what you do, whether you follow the tunnels or not, Jada may have different ideas."

Ord pointedly said, "Why does it bother you that she wants me on this quest?"

Aidan removed another arrow from another goblin body and then shoved the body next to another. "I didn't want you on this journey to begin with." He pointed at Jada. "It was her choice."

"Ord," Jada said in a low voice, "what shall we do with the baby now?"

Jada's words grated on him. He looked down at the hole and thought of the goblins who had just been killed. Dragging a goblin body closer to the others, Ord picked up a goblin dagger and wrinkled his brow, thinking, *What type of mother would leave her baby here?*

But he knew the answer. He gripped the wrist of another fallen goblin warrior and dragged it to the growing pile Aidan had created, tossing the goblin's short sword near the north wall of the barn.

Clang.

It hit another sword Aidan had already dropped there.

Ord continued his thoughts, *A desperate one . . . or one that had been killed.*

He drew a deep breath using it to steady his determination and said to Jada, "If what you have told me is true, this is no journey for a baby." He hesitated, unsure of his own spoke words as he said, "We have no choice but to leave it." All the things he had ever been taught about blue goblins surged into his mind.

Blue goblins are the enemies of the dwarves, no matter how small . . . but can I believe that staring into the baby's eyes?

His insides ached at the thought of walking away. The child could not care for itself.

To leave a baby defenseless, he continued the debate in his mind, *lying in a barn to an unknown fate was . . . Could he even say the word?*

Levity rose in Jada's voice. "It's a she, Ord." In her arms, the female dark elf rocked the blue goblin. "Six months. Newly weaned." Jada looked away from the baby as if seeing something written above it in the air. "Force weaned. The mother is gone and will not return." Her heart filled with compassion. "And she is hungry." Jada turned to Aidan. "Get me the rations. And Ord--"

Ord's eyebrows rose. He involuntarily stepped back, part of him dreading her next words but he did not know why.

"Please, find me some milk."

The dwarf's eyes became round. "Milk? Now? After a landslide?"

The elf nodded once. "Quickly. Timing is crucial."

Ord thought back to what Jada had said about him stepping outside the circle of protection to fight the goblins and wondered at her words.

Could she see the future?

He studied her and the baby. "Surely you brought some if you knew this was going to happen?"

Jada shook her head. "If I did, it would be in the wagon."

She turned toward him while still smiling down at the baby, and then shifted her pleasant gaze to look him in the eye.

"Ord," she continued, "the ability to know things, things most others don't, is called The Sight. It is a gift we can have but never make entire use of. It becomes more difficult when we are emotionally involved because our emotions distort it to what we want it to say instead of what is. As a dark elf mage, I have this ability. However, being a mage is not a requirement to have the gift."

She stared into his eyes. "So, you see, I know that if the drink for the baby is here, you will be the catalyst for finding it, whatever may take place for this to occur, whatever decisions you choose to make during the discovery. Do you understand?"

"No." Ord stepped back, eyeing the baby.

She sighed. "A truthful answer is the beginning of knowledge. Rest assured, do as I ask, and all will be explained."

He continued to walk backward, as if to escape from something he knew was happening but could not think of a way to stop it. He bumped into the wagon. The wagon rocked. One of the horses turned to look in his direction.

Ord hurried around the horses to the other side. After the twilight of the thunder of the falling rocks, each footstep he made seemed louder than it should. The hinges of the wagon crate groaned eerily in the quiet.

He rummaged through the wagon crate, noting the cut rectangular cloths of before but found no milk. "You have nothing here except waterskins."

"You'll have to find it outside," Jada continued as if seeing more only now, as if feeding him additional information only after he had chosen what to do of his own accord. "There may be some in the cellar near the house."

"You know there's a cellar?" he asked.

Jada looked at the baby and allowed it to play with her finger. "Don't worry, little one. Ord is going to find you something to eat."

Frowning, Ord skirted around the wagon and eyed the long timber bar that had successfully kept the two doors shut. Stress cracks had formed along its length. The pressure against the outside doors had warped the already old wood.

He gripped one end of the timber and used the hole through it to pull. It slid an inch and jammed tight, held in place by the way the wood no longer remained straight. With his left gauntleted hand, he traced the bar, identifying the largest stress cracks and noting where they met. Hefting his hammer in his right hand, he calculated the distance in proportion to his swing, and struck it with the great war hammer.

The wood splintered at the point of impact. Pieces flew. The sound of the wood breaking echoed off the barn walls.

With every strike he felt relief, relief to choose his own actions, relief to choose his own life. Jada's talk of The Sight had him both curious and nervous as he thought, *How could anyone know anything that the five senses did not show them?*

Of course, there were those recorded in dwarven history who had done this but the ability to do it had never been given a name. The Guardians were one of these groups, ancient warriors who had protected the dwarven people from the beginning of time. And yet, for all their great abilities, there were no Guardians today.

A final strike splintered the remaining section of the bar. Using the great war hammer as a wooden mallet, he knocked the two pieces of the bar free from holding the barn doors closed. Placing his shoulder against one of the doors, he shoved outward. It pushed out enough for him to scrape through but then stopped.

There are too many stones on the outside, he noted to himself.

The wood scratched against his armor as he pressed through from the inside of the barn to the outside and stared at an entirely different world.

Trees were barren of leaves. Branches littered the forest floor. A layer of dirt covered everything, hiding the path that led to the barn door. The pebbles and rocks close to the barn piled up as if some hand had poured out a holocaust at their location.

The brownish hazy air smelled dusty with visibility at no more than a hundred feet in any direction. A gentle wind whistled through the branches, gradually blowing the dust toward the east.

No goblins were in sight, but he did not relax his hold on the hammer. He reached down with his left hand and tossed rocks away from the door until he could swing it fully open. Standing up straight again, he looked toward the house of which only the foundation remained.

Could milk really be there?

It made sense, and yet, it did not. If the goblins had claimed the housing of the humans, maybe something had survived that the goblins had not already ransacked.

But milk? For that to happen, the takeover would have to have been done in the last day or so, and unless it was kept cool, the milk would already be sour.

With his ears tuned to the slightest sound, he worked his way through the rubble toward the foundation of the house. The round pebbles and large stones shifted beneath his feet making each step treacherous, despite his caution.

The log house, which should have been above the foundation, had been entirely ripped away, leaving only a wooden floor. The main outline of what was left could be identified by a southwestern pile of rocks along the slightly raised rectangular shape of the foundation.

He knocked away some of the rocks still gathered on top of the wooden floor. Gaps existed between the wooden planks. The wind whipped the dust that had settled, and the dust poured down through the gaps in the wood, piling in even lines upon the ground next to the foundation footings. Two coins beneath the floor caught the brownish, dim light and managed to flash in brief intervals as more of the airborne dust continued its journey to the east.

He used his gauntleted left hand to sweep away parts of the debris, while keeping his war hammer held in his right, in the hope of finding a horizontal pantry door. Though the barrage of rocks had ceased and the attacking goblins had stopped, he was wary of any power that could force another to do its will.

Ord walked every square foot of the remaining wooden floor, clearing rocks, tossing branches, and brushing away dirt. No opening for a cellar appeared, hinged or otherwise.

He grumbled to himself and said, "This is getting me nowhere."

With his war hammer, he smashed some of the cracked floorboards. Then, dropping to his knees and with his left hand, he checked the ground beneath the floor foundation. It was solid packed earth. If there was a cellar beneath the house, this was not the way to access it.

Ord stepped off the wooden floor in the direction of the barn, noting the accumulated branches were thicker at this location. He tossed the branches to the side and used his foot to shift the dirt and rocks. As the area cleared, it revealed a border of stones implanted into the ground. This extended out from the wooden foundation about five feet. With the head of his hammer gripped in both hands, he used the handle end to tap within the border of stones.

Thump. Thump. Thump.

An odd, hollow, wooden sound came from the ground beneath. It was small and only over part of the area. He dug with his left hand and found the edge of a stone step.

The more he dug, the deeper the steps went. About three feet down, he spotted the end of a buried broken plank sticking up where it should not be. The horizontal wooden cover beneath the dirt appeared to have been struck by a huge weight, busting up the cover and allowing dirt to freely flow in.

He brushed away the rest of the filth exposing the broken cover. With his fingertips, he hooked the edge of the cover and pulled out pieces of the wood. Dust whirled into the air blown away by the gentle wind as he laid the pieces to the side.

A branch snapped.

Eyeing the area around him, he listened. The snap did not repeat. Only the wind's slight whistle could be heard as it blew through the now leafless trees.

He set the hammer down beside him but kept glancing up at the forest. Cautiously dropping to his knees, he used both hands to shovel out the soil from the hole he had found. As the pile grew higher, the tops of gourd-shaped clay bottles emerged.

The smell of dirt mixed with a slightly sweet, slightly pungent odor rose into the air. It grew stronger as he dug deeper, the soil changing from dry to damp.

The sudden onset of the landslide must have crushed the bottles, he thought.

Some of the busted boards appeared to be shelving. He pulled out a broken clay bottle and had almost decided this was a waste of time, when he lifted another that had not been damaged. Turning it slowly in front of him, he checked for cracks in the fired clay.

No cracks.

He uncorked one of the bottles and sniffed. The sweet and pungent odor was strong. If not sour milk, it had to be yogurt.

Yogurt makes sense, he thought. *It can last so much longer than milk.*

In a way, the landslide had helped to preserve the lower bottles in the small cellar from the falling debris.

Though he heard no one approach, he looked around at the land. The brownish air had lightened. He could see twice the distance of when he had first emerged from the barn. There were some trees that had not entirely been de-leafed.

Ord placed his war hammer in the leather sheath that hung on his back, hefted out three of the undamaged clay bottles, and started toward the barn.

He walked slowly over the dubious surface of stones and dirt carrying the three bottles. The trees, barren of leaves, gave him an unearthly shiver for they were found mainly around the barn as if the rain of stones had been directed only at them. It confirmed what Jada had said about their attackers and made him wonder who these beings were that could control both the goblins and nature.

Behind him to the north, goblin cries came from the destroyed goblin lodge. Even now, the lifeless eyes and still bodies of those who had fought to make it to the barn lay buried in the stones and dirt.

With glances toward the lodge, he kept watch on the area around the barn and thought, *It is only a matter of time before the survivors come scavenging through the ruins.*

Behind him at the lodge, through the brown dirty air, now turning tan, smoke swirled up. He had no doubt hot embers slowly ate at the wood left by the avalanche.

How many goblins had been killed? he wondered to himself. *Had the goblin baby's mother been one of them?*

He found himself frowning but forced it away.

Death is a natural process of life, he continued, *and I have done the same in war. So why in the dwarven kingdom does this goblin baby affect me?*

There had been a dwarven girl he liked in his hometown, before his growth spurt had hit. He had always thought they would one day have a family, but it could never have been. Once it was known he was growing so much taller than those around him, her parents would no longer let them associate together.

Could the goblin baby be causing a paternal instinct? he wondered. *Surely not. I don't even know what that means.*

His logical mind said there was no room on this quest for a child, if it was a quest, if the dark elves were telling the truth. Yet he could not shake the connection between the golden dragon and Jada's words. All the events that had transpired, the golden dragon amid the battle, the dark elf's arrow that had aided his throw, and the raven that had helped to vanquish the red dragon, combined with the conviction he had seen in Jada's actions.

His instinct said there was more to this story. His curiosity wanted to see it through. And yet, for the second time, he realized he had the perfect opportunity to leave.

Ord stopped. The barn stood in front of him. He swung around to stare north.

Just past the lodge, hidden by the hazy air, was the trail that would take him home. On foot or not, it would take him home.

He held still as if suspended in time, listening to the wind. Findor was back at the camp, and even if the dwarven army had already packed up, his friend would be looking him. His parents would expect him to return. He had a place in the library to continue his work as an apprentice sage. An entire life waited for him, and one single step in the right direction would do it.

A baby's cry cut through his thoughts, and he was back to the now, standing outside a barn, traveling with two dark elves, and heading on an adventure he could not even fathom.

The goblin baby cried again, and his heart jumped. He slowly turned back to face the barn.

And now this child, he thought, *a child of another race had been dumped into his life.*

The child was helpless. And while his life would be set should he simply turn away, the baby's life was just beginning with no idea of what would happen next.

Make a choice.

He heard the words inside his head. Just like on the battlefield when the golden dragon had spoken. But it was not the dragon that spoke this time. It was his heart. A third cry came from the baby goblin. His heart smote him again.

This is something, he thought, *something I have never felt before. A connection? How is that possible?*

He gawked at nothing except his own thoughts.

Is it possible I . . . I love the child? A goblin child?

Ord slowly started toward the barn, mulling over his own thoughts. The barn loomed closer. Once through those doors, he knew there was no turning back.

While dwarves tolerated some outsiders, they always remained firm as a community against outside influence. Even he, being taller than the others, had been different enough for other dwarves to shy away, all except Findor. Findor had helped him learn to outwardly shrug off taunts from the other dwarves. Neither his parents nor his relatives were as tall as he.

He tried . . . at least for a little while . . . to take Findor's advise. In the end, a good beating, sometimes done by him and Findor, sent most oppressors cowering. Unfortunately, it did nothing to stop the murmurs behind his back.

While Ord was admired for his strength by others, no other dwarf even pretended to be as good a friend as Findor. On top of that, no female dwarf was willing to take the ridicule that would follow if she married Ord. His chances of ever having the family he wanted were very low indeed.

Is that the source of my reluctance about this baby? he thought. *Is it my own insecurity coming out? Even if I took the child in, it would no longer be accepted by dwarves or goblins.*

A baby's whimper came from within the barn, and he heard Jada trying to comfort the hungry child with words.

But there can be no comfort, he thought. *The baby is a goblin. I have killed its kind on the battlefield. Sheesh, I have done it in this very building and for all I know, I could have killed the baby's father.*

He drew a deep breath and stared at the barn's entrance, seeing his own shadow cast inside upon the back of the wagon.

Am I making the right choice?

Ord stepped into the barn and heard Aidan speaking in low tones.

"While I hate to say it, the dwarf is right." Aidan worked at hollowing out a spot on a piece of flat board to serve as a shallow bowl for the child. He tapped the board on the ground to knock out the dust, followed up with water to rinse it, and used a flannel cloth to dry it off. Undoing the folds of a second cloth, he extracted a slice of hard bread and crumbled it into the bowl's depression. "We cannot travel with this baby. It would be a danger to us all."

Jada stared at the wall with her eyes holding a faraway look. "She is here for a reason. There are no mistakes in this world, no accidents."

"I'm not denying your visions. I'm just saying . . ." He glanced over and saw Ord. The light behind the dwarf made him look like a silhouette against the entrance. Aidan speculated, nodding toward the bottles in Ord's hands, "You found the milk?"

Ord slowly nodded. "Don't stop on my account. I did find *milk*." He moved past the wagon and placed the three bottles beside Jada. "But it is not milk. It smells more like yogurt, well preserved. How did you know? Or were you just guessing?" He set one of the bottles near the wooden bowl Aidan had carved.

Jada answered, "How did you know to step out of the circle of protection?"

With one hand, she used her thumb to work the cork loose from the nearest bottle and set the cork on the flat of the carved wooden bowl. Lifting the opened bottle, she sniffed. "Kefir is just as good, probably better." She poured the whitish liquid on top of the crumbled pieces of dried bread. The bread softened and became whitish in color.

"I . . ." Ord thought back. "I just knew. Dwarven intuition, I guess."

Jada held the baby almost vertical and picked up one of the softened pieces.

At the smell, the baby's eyes lit up. Her little mouth opened.

The elf placed the morsel on the baby's tongue. The tips of sharp, little, white, goblin teeth descended having already penetrated through the gums, and Jada jerked away her fingers.

The dark elf giggled. "Ha-ha, no wonder you were weaned so fast." Still smiling, Jada glanced at Ord to answer. "And I say it was something more. You *saw* what was right."

The feeding continued as Ord watched. He was caught up in this tiny life doing nothing but taking the food given to it. It had no cares other than to fill its little stomach. Without convincing, it explicitly trusted the one that fed her. Yet, even as the baby ate, she continued to look toward Ord.

Ord held her gaze, refusing to turn away this time and trying to understand that thing which drew him to her and her to him.

At last, the baby turned away, refusing to open her mouth. Jada laid a linen cloth over her right shoulder, leaned the baby to it, and patted the child gently on the back.

The right door to the barn creaked. Ord jumped and turned around.

The once gentle wind, which had begun to blow off the dirty, brown air, swayed the treetops beyond the barn doors. The loose dirt brought down by the avalanche swirled up blowing to the south. The path, which had been previously covered, the one they had followed to the barn, could be made out among the trees as the dirt lifted.

It never occurred to Ord to keep guard at the door though he should have. With the goblin cries he had heard from the direction of the lodge, it was only a matter of time before search parties came to one of the last buildings still standing, the barn.

"So, gentlemen," Jada said.

Ord turned around to face her.

Jada eyed them both. "What shall we name her?"

Ord jumped. "N--name?" He felt edgy. Though he had decided to step into the barn and not head for home, he had no idea how they would deal with the baby next.

He shook his head. "We can't take it with us . . . Can we?"

Naming a thing gives it permanence, he thought. *In worst case, we need to leave her with goblin parents . . . somehow.*

Aidan smirked.

The smile brightened on Jada's face. "Of course, we can take her.

And we can't very well refer to her as an *it*. She must have a name."

The more Ord watched the child, the more he stepped back.

No matter how I feel, a quest is no place for a child.

The dwarf heard the crunch of hay beneath his feet and realized it was his attempt to increase the distance between him and this new change of events. "*Hey you* works perfectly nice," he finally said, forcing himself to stop.

Jada stood up and rocked the baby. "That's your dwarven life experience speaking. What are you afraid of, Ord?" Her eyes caught his.

Ord fought to look away but could not. The elf's brown eyes drew him in. He remembered the golden dragon and the words the dragon had mouthed in his direction. The smallest of whispers left his lips, "Find the Branwen."

Why did that pop up now? he wondered to himself. *By all the dwarven gods, I need to hear this dark elf story.*

Ord looked to the blue baby goblin. She watched him with intelligence beyond what he had ever encountered in his goblin foe.

Her eyes sparkled. Perhaps it was the light but shine they did. For a moment, a vision appeared in front of him. He saw a blue skinned maiden standing on the edge of a cliff overlooking a vast lake and watching the setting of the sun. Her body was trim, taut, and firm. Delight lay upon her features as the wind rustled the edges of the leather shorts and top she wore. A jeweled necklace hung around her neck. A spear with black feathers near the head was gripped in her right hand. As he watched, her face turned toward him, and she smiled with eyes of love.

He squinted as a word from his dwarven past popped into his head. It was a story about a female, human, protector who had guarded a pass from a troop of oncoming orcs and given the dwarves time to set their defenses.

"Shamira." He glanced at Aidan before coming back to Jada. "Her name will be Shamira."

The smile on Jada's face broadened. "And how do you know that?"

Ord blinked. He raised his eyebrows in disbelief. "She told me."

CHAPTER 4

Jada wrapped the child in a linen blanket while shaping the blanket to form a hood to protect the child's head. This included a flap to block the light from her face.

Shamira cooed, snuggling into the wrappings.

"Ord, you are her protector now. She has revealed to you her name. She has chosen you to be her champion as she grows to be who she must."

Ord gawked, shaking his head in disbelief. "I only gave her a name."

Jada nodded toward the wagon. "If you will climb into the back, I will hand you Shamira."

He pulled at his own beard.

"What are you afraid of, Ord?"

"I am not afraid." He dropped his hand to his side. "I just don't understand what I saw." He swallowed. "Or, why I saw it."

"Life," she stepped toward the wagon, "goes beyond what we can perceive with our five senses. It is more than history recorded in books and our future is yet to be told."

He stepped backward, noting the location of the wagon from the corner of his eye. "That fits what I saw to a T." He shook his head with a sardonic smile. "If life is yet to be told, why did I see her as an adult?"

"Life is instantaneous, happening all at once throughout all creation. For one to know someone's past or future is to merely read the record written in the ethereal of all things. You simply caught a glimpse of who Shamira, though in her baby state at present, will be. At this moment, she is more attuned to the ethereal plane than those of us who are *grownup*, so in her own way, she knows you, too. As I said before, it is called The Sight."

Ord laid his left gauntleted hand on the side of the wagon and looked down at the child in Jada's arms.

Shamira smiled up at him.

She knows me, he thought, *in the ethereal?*

Climbing into the back of the wagon, he sat down facing the rear. With a slight turn of the head, he could see the right side where Aidan normally sat.

He spotted the male elf heading to the back of the wagon and followed him with his eyes until he passed out of the barn.

Thunk. Clatter. Thunk.

Aidan had to be clearing the rocks so they could open both barn doors. Ord turned his attention back to Jada.

"But." He leaned back as he reluctantly extended his arms to receive the baby. His jaw dropped. "But I . . ."

Jada placed the baby in Ord's arms.

He gazed down at it. "But I don't know what to do with a baby."

A smirk formed on Jada's lips. "It's time you learned how to be a father."

He swallowed looking down into Shamira's tiny face. "But I'm not the father."

The child cooed up at him with its big green eyes.

"You named her."

"*We* named her," he declared and then swallowed. "You asked us as a group. I simply knew the name first."

The wagon bounced as Jada stepped up to the seat in the front of the wagon and took the reins.

Aidan opened the second door. The dirty brown air had brightened to a golden filter of dust as the sunlight penetrated much more easily. The light from the outside struck, appearing as rays highlighting the back half of the wagon.

Aidan peered at the horizon moving from right to left, seeing as far as the dust would permit him. "We are not being watched." He turned around and stepped backward to act as a guide, motioning with his hands to show Jada where to maneuver the wagon.

Jada worked the horses back and then forward in small segments until she turned them around to face the barn entrance.

Clang.

From the wooden box secured in the wagon, metal hit metal. Ord glanced into the box and saw Adian had cleaned and stored two goblin axes, one goblin short sword, and one goblin dagger. Ord pulled up some of the linens to allow a separation between the weapons so they would not hit together.

As the wagon pulled out, the bodies of the blue goblins they had defeated lay piled in one corner. And yet, here in his arms was a child, who, had it been grown, may have had the same fate.

Other than the kefir in the bottles, the wooden bowl, and the goblin weapons Aidan had collected, Ord saw nothing new.

At Jada's led, the wagon completely left the barn. The horseshoes of the horses clattered against the rocks as they slowly picked their way toward the main trail. Without the wagon stopping, Aidan placed a foot on part of the wagon's frame and stepped up to the front seat. Their transportation rocked as the horses continued over the stones.

"Careful," Ord tightened his grip to keep the baby still, "she's just gone to sleep."

A quiet laugh came from Jada. "There's no telling when she last ate, but I don't think she's been hungry for long."

Aidan snorted.

Shamira's head bobbed unexpectedly. Her eyelids fluttered, but they did not stay open.

Ord shifted her into his right arm, holding her against his side. It helped to steady her.

As the rocks grew fewer, Ord angled his body to the right allowing the burlap sacks to help support his right arm and to make use of the gentler sway of the wagon to keep Shamira asleep. By turning, it also allowed him to see a portion of the wagon front as well as Jada and Aidan.

The wagon moved past the barren trees to those that still had leaves.

"She's mixed-race, you know," Ord said to everyone.

The wagon wheels created defined ruts in the excess dirt deposited from the avalanche.

He looked down at Shamira, the skin on his brow involuntarily wrinkling.

If Jada is right, he thought, *whoever is searching for us will know we have come this way.*

They approached the road in the glow of the golden rays as the dust clouds above them parted.

Jada glanced back at him. "You saw that in your vision when you received her name?"

Ord soberly nodded. "She's half-human and half-goblin, more than likely conceived when a human woman was taken by a goblin male as a slave. She'll never fit into either world."

"Is that necessary?" Jada asked, her tone assuring it was not.

"Must we all fit into the mold of those around us?"

Ord thought back to his own situation growing up. "There are advantages to fitting in." He made a fist with his left hand. "There is a learned strength by standing apart."

"As with all change," Jada nodded, "sometimes life must point us in the right direction to wake us up, an unexpected direction." She paused, watching the horses as the dust puffed up in small clouds beneath their feet. "It is not easy to change." She glanced back at him. "For any of us."

He listened to her tone and sensed a meaning beyond the words. She was not applying this just to him but to herself as well.

What is Jada's story?

Aidan's cloak lay between him and Jada on the wagon's seat. The male elf had not bothered to put it back on. Jada's dark hair puffed back in the breeze, held in place by her own cloak with the hood down. One by one, small strands whipped out to flow in the wind. Her long, black, waist-length hair could almost reach him in the back of the wagon.

The dwarf felt the turn before seeing the wagon lean to the right. "What are you saying, Jada?"

"Elf, dwarf, goblin," she continued, "they are only names given to those groups with similar physical characteristics. To learn the truth of whom we are, we must go beyond those limited perceptions and see life for what it is, for what it was truly meant to be."

The slope of the road changed to go first up and then down. The wagon bed groaned. The contents of the wooden box shifted as metal scraped against metal. The box lid clacked.

As the wagon rolled downward, the view of the landscape revealed new types of forest details. Groups of oak and ash were growing among the conifers. A slow-moving stream whispered along catching Ord's eye as it paralleled their track to the right side of the wagon.

He considered her words. "Are you trying to imply we should all be mixed-races in order to fit in with each other?"

"Ord, I'm saying we already are." Jada handed the reins to Aidan and slipped the cloak from her shoulders. The breeze caught the rest of her long black hair, allowing it to ripple in the wind.

Shamira squirmed, yawned, and stretched up one of her tiny arms before laying it back down and becoming still.

"That's not possible." The dwarf adamantly shook his head. "I am my father's son, and his father was a dwarf before him." Ord glanced toward the horses over the low backboard of the front seats.

Jada looked sideways and met his eyes. "And yet, you are twice your father's height."

He shrugged. "A fluke of nature, the healers called it."

"There are no flukes in nature, Ord. Only predicted results from conditions set in our past."

Ord tightened his fist, the one not holding Shamira. He could feel his back muscles clench. "So, you think I'm part human?"

Jada said in her same soothing voice, "I'm saying something in your past has influenced you to be who you are. Exactly what happened, I do not know. It is up to you to find out . . . if you want to know the truth."

Ord grunted as the wagon rocked from one side to the other. His eyes dropped back to Shamira.

The child's head shifted to the left, but she did not wake.

He answered, "Or, we can choose to live as we are." He lowered his voice to a whisper and added, "In a lie?" When he glanced at the front, Jada still watched him.

She nodded. "Whichever we choose."

Ord looked down at the blue baby goblin.

Shamira had no more asked to born than I. Yet, somehow, we are both here, an integral part of each other's lives.

Do I honestly believe this? It makes no sense. Instantaneous moments of creation in the ethereal defining what some call The Sight? He blinked wondering why that thought had jumped in. *How could anyone know?*

He looked away to the surrounding countryside. "Where are we going?"

"To a grand city, dwarf." Aidan laced his voice with disdain. "If you get in trouble there, we can't bail you out with an avalanche." The male dark elf chuckled. "We won't be able to get you out at all."

Shamira stretched both her arms. Her tiny facial features squinched in discomfort.

Ord adjusted her in his arm until she stopped moving again.

Jada reached back, touched the baby's wrapping, and peered at the baby's face. "She needs to be changed."

Ord wrinkled his brow. "Changed into what?" An odd odor

reached his nose. He sniffed and leaned back. "What is that?"

Jada chuckled. She reached over and tapped Aidan's shoulder then pointed to the right. The trees formed a curved alcove just ahead. "There, Aidan. Ord needs his second lesson in being a father."

Ord glanced up. "When did I get my first?" He dropped his gaze back to Shamira who he held in his right arm. "Oh."

Aidan snickered. He angled the wagon to the right.

Near the treetops of the alcove, a cliff jutted out forming a natural canopy above the branches. Aidan slowed the wagon to a stop.

Ord panicked inside and quickly said, "I am doing this only until we find a place to take care of the child."

At his voice, Shamira's eyes shot open. Her lips quivered. She began to cry.

"Hush," Ord quietly said, trying to silence his own nervous stomach.

How I can be this child's father? he asked himself. *I know nothing of what to do.*

A wisp of smoke drifted to them on the wind.

Ord warily looked from Shamira to the surrounding trees. To the right, through the branches, he spotted a blackened firepit whose flames had been quenched. Smoke wafted into the air, filtering through the leaves of the trees.

There was only one explanation for such a sight: someone had recently put the fire out. He looked down at Shamira and urgently said, "We must not cry in enemy territory."

For a moment, she stopped and stared up at his face contained within his dwarven helmet, but then the cry grew louder.

"What do I do?" he pleaded.

Jada stepped from the wagon. It bounced despite the little weight she had. Walking past Ord, she went to the tailgate and released the hooks. The metal hinges creaked as she lowered the backboard and reattached the hooks to keep the tailgate level. Her voice remained patient as if no other job existed except one. "Hand her here, and come around."

Ord caught his balance as he stood up in the wagon bed. He put one foot on a stack of burlap bags and stretched forward, placing the child in Jada's arms.

Turning back to climb down himself, he spotted Aidan watching him. The male dark elf's stoic expression could not hide the laughter in his eyes.

Thud.

Ord hit the ground after he dropped over the side of the wagon and listened to the sound reverberate above his head. The curved cliff outcropping acted like a mini-echo chamber broadcasting their presence even louder than it was.

The piece of cloth half-covering Shamira's face shifted so that she could see more of the world around her. She stopped crying. With wide eyes, she appeared to study Ord in his plate-mail armor as he walked up beside Jada.

"Aidan, get a waterskin and cloths from the wooden crate, please."

Aidan opened the lid. As he dug through the contents, the goblin weapons clanged together. The pitch echoed from above them into the trees. He swore, eyeing the forest behind Ord and Jada and then pulled out a waterskin and two linen cloths.

Quietly closing the lid, he hurried around to the back of the wagon. "We should make this quick. This isn't the best time to . . ."

Jada handed Shamira to Aidan.

He shut up, while keeping an eye on the forest as Jada took the waterskin and cloths out of his free hand.

Ord watched Jada soak one cloth with water while holding it off the edge of the tailgate. The excess water hit the ground turning the dirt to mud. She shoved a stack of burlap bags further into the wagon bed and cleared a space to lay Shamira in.

Holding up the second rectangular linen cloth, she folded it over and showed Ord how to lay it out so that he could keep the baby as clean as possible. "When you are done, you will tuck it around her here and here." She pointed at the two folds. "This will help hold the diaper on her."

Taking Shamira from Aidan's arms, she laid her down in the space she had prepared and removed the baby from the wrapped blanket.

"It's very easy, Ord. You'll undo the cloth from around Shamira's bottom like this."

A puff of putrid smell assaulted the dwarf's nose.

The baby gurgled, kicked her feet, and wiggled trying to get off her back.

Ord gasped. "Babbling sewer rat, she stinks worse than Findor when he hasn't showered in three days." He gagged but held it down. "That," the dwarf pointed at the soiled linen, "came from that?" His finger shifted to the baby.

At the front of the wagon, a burst of laughter came from Aidan who had apparently hurried as far from the baby changing lesson as possible. The elf picked up his bow and shook his head while walking away toward the edge of the forest. "Better you than me. I'll take lookout." He chuckled until he entered the woods.

"Coward," Ord shouted after him as he swelled up his chest, but he could not hide the disgust on his face. He grumbled. "I would gladly take lookout myself."

Jada adjusted the new linen on the wagon floor beside Shamira and waved toward the rag wet. "That's to clean her with. Move the rag front to back as you wipe. It's healthier for the baby."

Ord inched nearer. His eyes felt as round as mugs. As Jada stepped out of the way, he attempted to catch Shamira by her two feet. As if it was a game, she pulled each foot away from him.

"You're being too gentle in trying to keep her still," Jada coached. "Hold on to her feet. You're not going to hurt her."

He captured both and lifted Shamira by her legs. Using the wet rag, he did as Jada instructed. "How often does this . . . changing . . . take place?" The cleaning of Shamira's bottom helped to reduce the smell, thank the dwarven kingdom.

"It depends on the eating schedule and the baby," she thought, "anywhere from three to four times a day to once every couple of days. If it is soft and passes easily, it is normal. Although, I must say, I have never cared for a goblin child."

"That makes two of us." Ord cringed at the lingering smell and hunted to make sure he had missed nothing.

As he finished, Jada slipped the soiled cloth away and laid it folded to the side. Folding helped cut the odor, but not by much.

Jada stepped back farther to give him more room to work.

He laid the rag on the soiled cloth to avoid getting the mess on anything else. "Wouldn't it be better to find a stream and dip her in a few times? Not the whole baby, mind you. Just her lower half?" When no one answered, he glanced toward his left. "Jada?"

Flutters sounded in the treetops. Ravens gurgled above him. Ord found he was alone with the baby.

The hairs on his arm stood up, no different than when he was in battle. He cautiously peered to each side but saw nothing to support his gut feeling of being watched. If Aidan was on guard, where was the elf and why had Jada disappeared so fast?

Moving as if he suspected nothing, he tucked the unsoiled cloth around Shamira as best he could and wrapped her within her warm blanket.

All the time, the stiffness of the hairs on his arm grew. His thoughts went back to the smoke he had smelt in the air as they arrived.

Those who had started it must have hidden when the wagon rolled in. They were either afraid or hostile. Afraid meant, more than likely, they would leave them alone unless cornered. Hostile meant they would attack if the conditions appeared in their favor.

He held perfectly still and listened. At first, leaves crinkled slowly in the distance. But then, they increased exponentially in his direction.

He turned, throwing up his left armored forearm. A wooden club rang against it, deflected by his left block, but the force thrust him back. He slipped in the mud created by the water when Jada had wet the cloth. Underneath his raised forearm, he saw the wooly face of a bugbear as he was slammed backward into the rear of the wagon.

A deep growl came from the bugbear's throat. It bared its teeth and raised its club to strike another blow.

Ord hit the creature's large, fur-covered, chest three times in rapid succession with his right fist, letting his gauntlet work as a mallet.

The bugbear staggered back.

Ord reached for his war hammer held in the harness behind him. However, the harness release was pinned between his back and the rear of the wagon. He leaned a few inches away from the edge of the tailgate, released the hammer from its harness, and lunged toward the bugbear. But before he could swing the hammer, the bugbear collided into him, sacking him in the middle.

With the plate-mail armor, Ord felt little of the impact, but both opponents went down.

Ooof!

He hit the ground on his back, the force knocking the breath from him. The hammer hit the tailgate, made it jump, and then landed about a foot out of reach.

The bugbear pummeled down on Ord's helmet and chest.

From the corner of his eye, the dwarf spotted the soiled linen. It had fallen from the back of the wagon and landed near his right hand. Unable to stop the onslaught of fists from the bugbear, his fingers reached out and caught the edge of the cloth.

Gasp.

A blow to his chest drove the air from his lungs despite his armor.

He swung the dirty linen into the bugbear's face.

The bugbear screamed. Retching, the creature jerked back to claw at the linen, smearing its contents even more.

It was too much to watch. With his gauntlet, Ord backhanded the side of the creature's head, striking the bugbear's temple. The blow sent it sprawling where it lay still.

The dwarf snatched up his hammer as he rolled to his feet and spied a second bugbear heading for Shamira. With a dwarfish war cry, he shouted, "Leave my baby alone," and swung the hammer. It collided with the bugbear's chest.

Bones crunched. The bugbear screamed. It staggered back toward the forest.

A dark elf arrow stabbed through a third bugbear while Ord's hammer met the second.

A raven's shrill cry cut through the trees. Dark fluttering birds descended while a fourth bugbear raced toward them through the forest underbrush. The bugbear dropped under the ravens' dark mass before ever making the clearing.

A fifth bugbear materialized from the undergrowth, spied his fallen comrades, and ran the other direction.

Shamira cried out. Ord turned one-eighty degrees to see her.

As if on guard, two ravens walked on the wagon bed beside the little girl. Quiet, gurgling sounds came from the ravens' throats while at the same time the baby tried to imitate them, periodically screaming out in joy.

Shamira mimicked one sound best. "Ba, ba, ba . . ." She screamed again clapping and then gurgled in Ord's direction.

Both ravens flew off.

From one side of the clearing, Aidan hurried from the undergrowth while Jada came from the other side. The male elf never regarded the bugbear bodies though he did watch Shamira, a curious look on his face.

"Playtime's over," he grumbled in a worse humor than he had left and threw a questioning glance at Jada. The wagon bounced as he climbed up on the wagon seat. He laid his bow beside him on top of his cloak.

Jada picked up the cloth used to clean Shamira as well as the soiled diaper. Using a waterskin, she washed out the wet cloth along with the linen the bugbear had so amply worn. With the cleaning, the smell abated, mostly. She placed the waterskin in the wooden box and hung the cloths on the left wagon wall to dry.

Ord stared at both dark elves, fuming, while he dragged the first bugbear's unconscious body out of the path of the wagon. "And that's all you have to say? Both of you?" After removing the body, he closed up the wagon backboard and secured it with the hooks.

Sniffing at his hands, he went to the crate and opened it, pulling out the waterskin. Carefully holding the waterskin, he washed off his gauntlets, the head of the two-handed war hammer, and then scrubbed the war hammer grip.

He huffed. "While you two were trotting through the woods, Shamira could have been hurt." As the rest of the odor abated, he sighed in relief and placed the waterskin back in the crate.

Jada picked up Shamira from the back of the wagon. She eyed the child with a curious light in her eyes. "We need to go." She briefly caught Ord's stare. "It was your test, not ours."

"Enemy territory is no place to play games," Ord grumbled. He climbed into the back of the wagon, resumed his spot, and accepted the baby from Jada. Instead of attaching the hammer to his harness, he laid the weapon beside him.

Jada checked the backboard and then stepped near the road to listen with her head slightly tilted. "We should take the trail less traveled. This road is no longer safe."

"Duh," Ord added louder than he should have and heard the echo above them. "What the rock-runt is going on?"

Shamira whimpered.

He dropped his voice but not his angry tone. "What just happened here? And why are a couple of do-gooder dark elves being hunted, if you are do-gooders, that is?"

Jada skirted to the front of the wagon, climbed up, and took the reins. She did not look back at him. "A patrol. We'll not be safe until we reach the city."

Using the reins, she guided the horses to back the wagon onto the main road and then started forward again.

"Safe from what? What city? First, it's a dark something or another at the barn. Now it's patrols." He turned and glowered at the backs of both elves. His voice hardened. "I think it's more than fair to say I'm the one with a lack of information. On top of that, you kidnapped me." The wagon bumped as it hit a hole.

Aidan snorted. "It's called saving your ungrateful dwarven hide, which we've already talked about." He raised his bow, withdrew an arrow from his quiver, and held it in his lap, eyeing the trail ahead.

The dwarf refused to be distracted by Aidan's words. "And, tell me I caused the avalanche."

Jada nodded and calmly said, "That has been explained."

"No, it hasn't," Ord snapped. "Why the bat-droppings did all those near the lodge have to die? I've no love for blue goblins," he glanced down at Shamira and mumbled, "you excluded." He turned back to the others. "But what you did, Jada, makes no sense. You're hiding something, and whatever it is will get us all killed."

Silence dropped as the wagon rode along the trail.

Jada leaned toward Aidan. "You remember where the side trail is?"

He nodded.

Ord cleared his throat. "Will someone say something, please?"

Aidan directed the wagon toward a parting in the trees. It didn't look like much. The tree branches hung down low. The foliage had grown thick. There was no footpath to mark the way.

"It's been at least a year since anyone traveled this direction." Aidan pointed to the foliage that closed in on the sides of the wagon.

"Well?" Ord iterated.

Jada shifted her hair off one ear. "For the very reason you have a child in your arms," she quietly answered Ord. "You needed to understand that all life has value. If we are to succeed in our quest, it will be a fundamental principle to our success."

"So, destroying a bunch of blue goblins teaches how valuable life is? Huh? Am I the only one that this makes no sense to? And this was your quest long before I was drawn into it." Ord raised his voice but caught it before it rose too loud. "I have half a mind to go home and take Shamira with me."

It was an empty threat, and he knew it.

There could never be a place in my home city for Shamira, just like I know there is no real place for me.

Branches slapped against the wagon sides as it pulled off the main road and onto the hidden trail. They rounded a tall boulder where the foliage was lighter. The forgotten trail showed ruts now, faint from the weather and forest growth, but they existed nonetheless.

"We are all on a quest, Ord," Jada continued. "Most of us just don't realize it."

The words Jada spoke ate at Ord.

Am I on a quest? He bit his lip and reluctantly agreed in his thoughts. *In a way . . . maybe.*

He eyed the back of Jada's head. *And of course, I have a respect for life. Granted, I have never rescued a baby before, but who is to say the mother wouldn't come back? All I have is Jada's word for that.*

The front wagon wheel sharply dropped. Ord kept a snug grip on the small child in his arm. Shamira wiggled but did not open her eyes. He relaxed.

Before he was trained to go to war, life had been so much simpler. He had been a scribe working to duplicate records when he wasn't helping his father at the family forge. From those records in the library, he had learned other languages. Elven, Goblin, it didn't matter. They had all been in the archives. It had been a way to escape from the turmoil around him. It was one of the things his father had held the most pride in--his son becoming a Learned-One, a scribe of the dwarves . . .

The rear wagon wheels climbed another lump in the road.

Clunk.

The back of the wagon hit sharply as the wheels dropped into another hole.

He tried to keep his voice down through gritted teeth. "Can you *please* take it easy?"

Down the rear wheels went again. Before they reached the bottom, Ord adjusted his hold on Shamira.

Thunk.

He absorbed the jar with his body. He rested his arm on the sacks again and drifted back into his thoughts.

. . . And then the war came. Firstborn dwarves, unmarried, always went to war regardless of their position in the community. Other siblings could volunteer unless the firstborn was dead or unreachable in which case it fell to the next in line to fill the position.

If a dwarf was married and required to go under the first rule, there were two possible exemptions: children had entered the picture and the children were old enough to go in his stead or it was the first year of a couple's marriage. In the first choice, a dwarf could send their son to go in their place, although half of the fathers still went too. In the latter case, they were given a reprieve until the year was over, if they wished. All dwarves had the obligation to both fight for their kingdom and build the kingdom from within, i.e., grow the population.

It was an honor to represent your family in the kingdom's defense. He volunteered for the honor without any reservations, though he was not first born, and had made his family proud. When his older brother had been lost before his time to serve, the mantle had fallen to him anyway . . .

My family would have been proud of me, that is, until I woke up in the bed of this dark elf's wagon.

He glanced up.

A dark bird in the sky flew above them, followed by a second. Ravens rose from one tree and fluttered to the next. Their gurgling cries sounded both far away and near.

The ravens reminded him of duck, and duck reminded him of food. His stomach grumbled.

How long has it been since I have eaten or taken a drink?

The very thought made his lips feel dry. He licked them.

A frothy mug of ale would taste great right now.

The longer he dwelled upon it, the worse the hunger and thirst grew. He glanced at Aidan.

Have the dark elves eaten? Did they eat something before I returned with the kefir? He had seen the bread they had unwrapped for Shamira. It would be just like Aidan to hide the food from him.

He licked his lips.

The kefir? No, that is Shamira's. I will not consume the only food she can eat.

He preferred ale anyway, but the water they carried would do if he could reach the crate. However, to get it, he would have to put the little girl down. He shook his head at the idea, but his decision didn't alter the hunger and thirst growing inside of him.

The trail narrowed. Branches scraped against the wooden wagon sides and brushed against his armor. Ord leaned forward in order to miss most of the branches until the trail broadened again. Even with his helmet on, he could hear the ravens' musical gurgling in the treetops towering above them.

He adjusted his position so he could see the back, front, and left side of the wagon. Removing his helmet, he placed it on two half-filled sacks. This way it would not rattle as badly and wake the baby.

Aidan and Jada had slid closer to the middle of the seat. They seemed . . . cozy.

What relationship did they have with each other?

He watched but saw no overt movements other than sitting close.

Good, the focus is off my stomach and onto other things.

His stomach loudly growled.

Goblin babble, why did I have to think of food again?

He looked down at the sleeping Shamira and frowned, the fatigue twirling his thoughts in odd directions.

For the baby's sake, maybe I need to curve my use of dwarven curse words. Would toe-biting sissy be better?

He yawned.

No. If I am going to be a father, I need to clean up my language, especially around her, if for nothing else but respect.

He chuckled.

This is going to make it hard if I ever catch up with Findor.

He squinted at the forest. The shadows morphed into creatures he had never seen before. A simple blink wiped them away like smoke caught in the wind.

He closed his eyes for a moment then lifted his heavy eyelids. His mind jumped to the dark elves and his feeling that there were things they were not saying.

A part of him answered, *everyone has their secrets*, but his logical mind fought his emotional side.

What am I saying? Has Jada already brainwashed me into believing her?

He looked down at Shamira.

I am not her father . . . I am a dwarf holding a goblin baby . . . There is no link, maternal or racial . . . between me and the baby.

His eyelids shook as he struggled to keep them open.

Could The Sight be an illusion . . . created by Jada to . . . trick me . . . into believing what she said?

He closed his eyes allowing his eyelids to droop shut while he fought to stay awake.

Yet, I saw it for myself . . . I knew her name in the vision of Shamira . . . guarding. . . what? A lake? A territory? Their home?

The last one feels right, though I do not understand why.

He shook his head trying to clear his mind of the fog drifting over it.

My home is with my people, even if I am not completely accepted.

He drew a shallow breath.

I will return.

He lightly rubbed his right eye with his left hand.

When my father passes . . .

He rubbed the back of his neck squeezing his eyes shut for a moment.

. . . as tradition states . . .

All thoughts stopped as he sat there with his eyes closed. He snapped them open and tried to scratch the side of his head.

Ting.

His gauntleted fingers tapped his helmet.

But I removed my helmet . . . I must be dreaming.

Struggling to wake up, a strange sound came from his lower right. He leaned toward the sound and realized Shamira giggled.

Am I awake or asleep?

He blinked, realizing his helmet was already removed, but he was still hearing the sounds Shamira made. His distorted thoughts continued.

Half-goblins? Human-goblins? Goblin-humans?

His tired mind continued to toy with the idea.

What racial combination was she categorized as?

In a moment of clarity, he remembered what others had said about him.

Did it even matter?

Without food or water and with the gentle rocking of the wagon, the fatigue of the present day took its toll. Something fluttered overhead, but he no longer cared. He battled to open his eyes as they dropped to mere slits, only letting in the bare minimum of light.

That's it . . . I'll rest my eyelids . . . It will only take a minute.

Adjusting slowly, he shifted around so he could lean his back more comfortably against the inside front wall of the wagon. At this angle, he glimpsed the right, back, and left sides of the wagon before purposely closing his eyes.

He relaxed his muscles. Images flashed in his mind though he tried to ignore them.

It is okay to rest.

He found himself watching a forest as they rounded a corner. The forest was familiar. The destroyed lodge caught in the avalanche came into view with its smoldering red chimney pouring smoke into the air.

Have we doubled back?

Gray smoke rose from the disaster until an image morphed beneath it. Instead of the lodge and the chimney, the red dragon swooped down at his platoon and roared.

Ord jumped awake. He heard himself stop snoring and whispered, "The dragon's alive. The red dragon's alive."

Shamira, still cupped in his right arm, squirmed. He relaxed his arm muscle and felt her stop her struggle.

In complete clarity, he remembered, *The black arrow had snagged the chain on the amulet. The raven had distracted the red dragon during the battle. The raven had dropped the amulet on the red dragon's back.*

Every detail felt crisp in his head.

Why had no one else seen it?

But someone else had, and he suspected two of them were with him now.

How many more saw the event? The betraying dwarf in their campsite? The other dark elves? The golden dragon? Is it because of this event the dark elves called a truce?

Having snapped awake, the fog cleared from his mind. He blinked his eyes.

How long have I been asleep?

The trees above were alive with gurgling, throaty, raven calls. A rushing roar came from a distance. Ord turned his head to the left.

At first as a tickle on the ear, the rushing sound grew until he knew it was pouring down. At the sound of the water, he licked his dry lips.

Surely they will stop for the horses. It isn't only me exhausted.

The wagon slowed but did not halt. Seen through the trees to the north, a waterfall tumbled from high above to descend into a crystal-clear pool some 100 feet below. Even at this distance, Ord could see fish swimming in those clear waters.

"Jada," he said, noticing how dry and rough his voice had become. "Jada, we need a break, all of us . . . and food."

Aidan shook his head, leaning to his right more than he should. "We must get to the city. Every delay means those who follow draw closer."

"What good is this *city*," Ord stressed, "if we collapse before we get there?"

Jada placed a hand on Aidan's arm. She weakly said, "He's right. The dwarf is right."

"He's wrong." Aidan hardened his voice as he sat up straighter. "You saw what happened at the barn."

She shook her head. "They used the avalanche to home in on us. There will be no more avalanches."

The male elf snapped, "And now they are closer in their search." He drew in a deep breath and calmed his demeanor. "All I'm saying is we should think carefully before listening to this dwarf for advice."

Ord shifted around until he could see the back, left, and front of the wagon better. He flared his nostrils as he tried to cover Shamira's ears with is free hand. "I've had about a stomach full of your hypocritical manners, you stone-headed, hanky-toting, weak-kneed elf."

Aidan scowled. "At least you throw out insults better than you do your fists."

"Enough, both of you." Jada slammed her palm against the wooden seat.

The wagon shook.

"We . . . I . . ." Her gaze swept toward the sky as her head wobbled. "I need . . . to rest." She slumped sideways against Aidan's shoulder.

Aidan caught her, grabbing the reins with his left hand to do so. "Whoa."

The horses slowed their pace.

Ord glared at Aidan. "We'll," he said, "who's going to drive the wagon when you fall off, too? *I* don't know the name of our destination."

The dark elf scowled, stopping the wagon. He laid Jada on the seat and stepped off the front, landing on a patch of grass that was crushed under his weight. "Be a good dwarf and guard Jada. I'll find a safe place to camp."

CHAPTER 5

Ord drummed his fingers on the bed of the wagon. There was nothing else to do. He glanced over at the sleeping Jada and listened to his stomach grumble. Though he didn't want to wake Jada or Shamira, his stomach was determined not to be ignored. Rising slowly with the baby in one arm, he carefully stepped around the burlap bags.

The wagon rocked with each step. Though Jada shifted, her eyes never opened, and Shamira seemed content to snuggle into her blanket.

He opened the lid of the crate with his free hand, cringed at the slight squeal of the hinges, and retrieved a waterskin. Using his teeth, he worked the cork out and dropped it into the crate.

Ord drank deeply. The water spun down his throat and washed into his complaining stomach. He lowered the waterskin and sighed. For the moment, the water made him feel full.

Placing the throat of the waterskin between his knees, he reached into the crate. The cork had fallen among some folded cloths tucked in one corner. He counted the cloths, all the right size for Shamira.

This could not have been an accident.

He picked up the cork and pressed it firmly into the end of the waterskin, still considering what he saw.

How many dark elves travel the countryside picking up dwarves and discovering babies while just so happening to carry the cloths needed for diapers?

No doubt Jada would say it was The Sight, but having little experience with such a thing, are they trying to pull something over on me?

He placed the corked waterskin into the crate and, after closing the lid, grabbed the side of the wagon and lightly dropped to the ground. His armor clanked.

He froze, eyes wide open, and watched Shamira's face. The baby's eyelids struggled to open then slowed until she was still once more.

"That was close," he whispered, having no idea if this was normal for a goblin baby.

He slipped Shamira into his left arm and slowly stretched the muscles of his right arm after his tense hold on the little one.

Weightwise, the child wasn't much different than the family hammer he carried, and it was a good thing, too. He chuckled.

The nap had helped, though he had not intended to nap. He worked the kinks out of his right arm, arching his back, and drawing out a yawn.

The green leaved forest lay on both sides of the path, and though the grass had grown up to overtake it, patches of dirt, ruts cut by wagon wheels, and animal prints could still be seen.

Ravens flew from branch to branch in the trees above him. Finches darted among the leaves. A hawk glided over the treetops.

It is the perfect time to hunt.

But he could not hunt. He was on baby duty, stuck at the wagon while waiting on Aidan to return. He paced around the wagon, watching the forest and listening for sounds out of the ordinary. He heard his stomach gurgle, not quite finished with the water but getting close.

My stomach says it is time to eat.

He walked around to the other side of the wagon and glanced through the crate. In a corner, separated from the stack of cloths, he spotted something wrapped. Using his right hand, he undid the string and lifted out a slice of hard bread. He remembered Jada pouring the kefir over the hard bread crumbles.

Was there enough for Shamira?

He counted two wrappings, estimated the number of slices in each, and decided there was.

He bit off a piece, chewed only briefly, and swallowed. It drifted down his throat teasing his stomach until it touched down.

By the piper himself, elven or not, it is delicious.

Taking another bite, he turned to peer through the trees toward the waterfall. Ravens descended and lifted from the rock walls where water splashed filling small holes. However, he saw none of the ravens descend to the pool or the pool sides. They only drank from the stones jutting out beside the falls themselves. The pounding of the falling water obliterated the ravens' gurgles around the waterfall.

He admired the birds' intelligence. To land on the basin edge put them into a potentially dangerous position. Any mammal in search of a quick meal could easily pounce, which meant they suspected danger. But upon the rock wall, the birds had the advantage of height, sight, and a quick getaway.

He bit off another piece of the bread and chewed thoughtfully.

So, what lives near the pool?

Ord stepped closer to the waterfall side of the trail without entering the woods. The waterfall took up one end of the pool. The cliffs around the waterfall covered the north side.

The east side of the pool was rocky but flat. The west side was rocky near the pool but the rocky ground turned into soil and grasses a good thirty feet out. The south side appeared to touch the forest but it was difficult to get a good view of how close the trees began.

He took another bite of the hard bread and heard the crunch as he bit down.

Nothing stalked the outer edges of the pool. If something was lying in wait for the ravens, it was well hidden.

No, this is something else. Something the ravens are cautious of but not afraid.

The raven calls farther from the waterfall were magnified by the curve of the cliff to the northwest. Yet, even there, the thundering of the water hitting the basin drowned out most of the ravens' gurgling calls.

A few empty nests extended from nooks along the rock wall, but not many. Even they had been built a good thirty feet off the ground.

Maybe I should take a closer look?

A flutter of wings came from behind him. He turned in time to see three ravens drop toward the wagon. One of the ravens tapped its beak against Ord's family war hammer.

"You'll not be getting that, my friend." Ord chuckled. "It weighs more than you could pick up, and it belongs to me."

The raven eyed him.

If I didn't know better, he thought, *I would swear the bird understood my words.*

The gurgling croaks of before changed pitch as the three ravens communed among themselves. With a cock of its head, the bird who had first tapped his hammer stared Ord in the eye, expectantly. When the dwarf did nothing, the raven soared back into the trees followed by the two others.

Jada moaned.

Ord stuffed the rest of the bread into his mouth, chewed, and swallowed, savoring every piece. He hurried around to the far side of the wagon and retrieved the waterskin. Using his teeth, he pulled the cork and dropped the plug back on the folded cloths.

The smell of the water made him swallow. He took another swig, savored it as it filled his stomach, and headed around to where Jada lay on the front of the wagon.

Jada opened her eyes but did not seem to see him.

With his right hand holding the waterskin, he shifted Shamira higher up and then touched the water to Jada's dry lips. No more than a few drops met her mouth when her eyes blinked, and she focused on him.

"What happened?" she asked.

"Aidan has gone to find a place to camp," he answered. "He'll be back shortly."

She lifted her body to a sitting position and tried to stand up. Her legs wobbled before she dropped back to the wooden bench. With her right hand, she grasped the top of the seat's back to help support her as she accepted the outstretched waterskin from Ord.

Her dark brown face took on a tint of red. "The circle of protection took more from me than I thought."

Ord raised an eyebrow and teased, "It most certainly couldn't have been traveling all night without sleep."

Jada chuckled. "Certainly not."

She eyed him, wrinkling her brow. "You're looking a little pale yourself."

His chest swelled, if only a little, inside the armor. "I'm a dwarf born of the hardiest stock. Trouble I face with ease. A little discomfort is nothing. And in battle? My foe beware."

Jada glanced to the left of him. "Like that one?"

Ravens descended into the back of the wagon as if the elf, dwarf, and goblin baby did not exist. So many landed, Ord couldn't tell what they were trying to do. The burlap shacks were tied shut. They seemed uninterested in the open crate or the kefir bottles. However, they all hovered around his hammer.

Granted, he couldn't blame them. It was shiny and bright, the perfect eye-catcher for a raven, but nothing nest-worthy. Those small branches they used would crumble under its weight.

The ravens' gurgling grew louder. More ravens dropped darkening the sky over the wagon. They slid the hammer around.

"Hold it right there, you little thieves." He waved his free hand to scare them off.

They ignored him, the fluttering wings and calls so loud, it almost drowned out his own voice.

"What do you think you're doing?" he continued, trying to peer through the mass of dark feathered birds. Through the momentary gaps of the hordes of ravens that descended, he realized what they had done.

The thick black cloak he had woken to find over him, when he lay in the bed of the wagon, had been scooted underneath the two-handed war hammer. That meant they had lifted the hammer to do it, if only temporarily. As his mind grappled with the impossibility of what they had done, ravens on all sides, grasping the edges of the cloak, rose into the air.

"That's my hammer," he hollered as the weapon lifted off the bed of the wagon.

Shamira opened her eyes staring up at all the ravens. A smile formed on her lips. She imitated the gurgling of the birds.

Ord reached out with his free right hand but missed his grab for the side of the cloak by an inch. He hurried around to the rear of the wagon as the cloak lifted higher into the sky with ravens on all sides gripping the edges.

He jumped but missed again.

Jada's voice shrieked, "Ord!"

The pitch was so sharp, Ord glanced back toward her.

"Not with the baby."

Without a word, he dashed to the front of the wagon and placed the wide-eyed Shamira into Jada's open arms. He glanced into the wagon and spotted his helmet. Snatching it up, he dropped it on his head and searched the sky behind the wagon. Already the war hammer had risen beyond his reach. The best he could do was to keep it in sight.

He raced after the hammer, staying to the wagon trail until he was forced to follow the ravens into the forest. He dodged trees and skirted brambles. The birds' flight evened out barely beneath the lower branches, once more out of his reach.

Shrill birdcalls grew louder as he followed. Ravens, not helping to carry the weapon, swooped by him. The birds then curved their flight path to dart in the direction the hammer was being taken. The ravens' musical notes escalated at the brink of a small stream.

Thinking quickly, he spotted a log and several large stones stationary in the water. The downward bank gave him momentum. Ord jumped from log to stone to stone until touching the other side.

With a scramble up the acquired bank, he plowed down a trail he could barely make out, shoving brush aside. Fifty feet from the stream, he emerged into a clearing.

Weather-beaten boulders many times his height blocked his way. Though he could no longer see the black cloak with the war hammer carried upon it, ravens darted overhead following the border of boulders and appeared to vanish into the northern rock wall.

He rushed closer, studying the ground, and noticed the unevenness of the soil at the base of what had appeared to be a solid rock wall.

No, the ravens did not vanish into the rocky boulders. They traveled down a corridor camouflaged by the surrounding texture of the stone.

He stepped past the optical illusion and found himself standing on a path five foot wide. The squawk of ravens and the sound of breaking rocks echoed from the other end.

Ord slowed his advance, noting that the ravens did the same.

Cracking stone reverberated toward him. Heavy stomps shook the ground. Rock fragments splintered as a smaller boulder, maybe ten feet in diameter, bashed into the cliff wall above the height of his corridor creating dust and falling debris.

The trail emerged into a larger corridor that ran perpendicular to the one he was on. The larger corridor tracked along the base of the rocks that formed the foundation of this side of the mountain range. Keeping as quiet as he could, Ord peered beyond the end of the trail.

The creature he spied was taller than he by a minimum of five times, broader by three times, and determined to accomplish its goal. With its four fingers on each hand, it lunged at the raven nests scattered throughout this area of the rock wall face. The sharp, knife-like nails at the end of each hand, sliced at the woven nests, scratching gouges into the cliff wall despite the hardness of the rock.

Green, olive, and blue eggs, spotted with brown, bounced and tumbled, bursting on impact with the ground and revealing deep orange to red yolks. The ravens dove incessantly at the beast, but it would not stop its assault on their homes.

Thud.

Ord's family hammer dropped a few feet from Ord. He glanced up and saw the ravens leaving with the black cape still clasped by the edges in their talons.

The massive creature, attacking the raven homes, sniffed. As it turned to glare at the dwarf with narrowing eyes, Ord knew it from the stories he had heard as a child.

It was a stone troll with hide so tough a dagger could not penetrate and arrows, unless they hit directly, would not even stick. And now, it had his scent.

Ord dodged for the hammer and snagged the handle. But before he could duck back into the safety of the corridor, a large boulder crashed into the mouth of his exit.

Rocks shifted as they fell in, filling the five-foot area until his way out was blocked.

Ord staggered away from the blocked opening despite his armor. The debris from the collapsed mouth of the corridor pelted against his armored back, driving him toward the enormous stone troll.

As the dust settled, he heard a distinctive showy growl directed straight at him and smelt the stink of bad onions and garlic.

Ord coughed and tried not to breathe through his nose while attempting to clear the dust with a wave of his left hand. His nose wrinkled even more at the additional stench of stinkweed, knocked loose from the crevices of his demolished exit, aired upon the wind.

He sneezed and then inhaled the air. The bad onions and garlic was stronger than before as the dust cleared. Turning to the side, he looked up into the face of the troll, about a foot from his own.

It stood hunched over him, eyeing him as it shifted its great head from side to side. Moving a few inches, the troll sniffed, wrinkled its nose, and turned away to stomp toward the ravens' nests.

The birds wheeled through the air, covering the sky, attempting to drive the troll back. They struck at the troll's face and hands with their beaks and claws but never left a mark upon the troll's skin.

From the corner of his right eye, Ord spotted a human female stroll toward him.

"Hello," she cheerfully said as she watched the troll jump at the ravens' nests, which were out of reach, for he had already destroyed those lower down. "Don't worry. He doesn't eat dwarfs."

"For a moment . . ." Ord watched rock crack when the troll slapped his palm against it. Part of a raven's nest ripped apart with the broken rock. An egg teetered on the edge of the damaged nest ready to fall. ". . . I was sure he thought about it."

"He did." She soberly nodded. "But in the end, he figured out you weren't a human/human but a really tall dwarf/human." She extended her hand and grinned at him. "I'm Frida."

"I am not a human." He spoke between clenched teeth.

"That's what I said." Frida tilted her head as she watched him. "Sore spot, huh? I meant no offense. She brushed dust from his left armored shoulder. "There now. Better?"

Ord eyed the thin blonde-haired girl. For a human, she was quite fetching, but for a dwarf, she needed a beard and some more weight. Her form-fitting outfit had a skirt that came below her knees.

She turned from him to watch the massive troll work, but her gaze darted back to Ord for a moment. "Like what you see?"

Ord stammered, trying to get his voice. "Er . . . no." He quickly turned back to watch the stone troll. "I mean, shouldn't you be afraid of the huge stone troll?"

She tilted her head. "Why would I be afraid of my cousin, Vindr?"

Ord glanced back with a squint and caught the swish of a tail behind her. Now he knew exactly what she was. "You're a Hulder, a female troll."

She winked. "Please, step to the left. Vindr's about to work closer to our area next."

The section of the sky above them darkened with ravens. Ord glanced up at the birds and then looked back to the troll.

"Stop," he demanded as he purposely stepped in the way, attaching his hammer to the leather strap on his back.

The huge troll froze in place. Apparently, Vindr, the troll, took it as a command.

"You can't go around destroying ravens' nests." Ord moved closer to the wall and held out his arms as if to protect it.

Frida huffed and raised her eyebrows. "And why not? We were here first."

Ord held his ground. "You're killing the next generation of ravens."

She tilted her head toward the dwarf. "Better them than us."

The ravens noticed the pause. Though some still dove at the troll, their cries were less frantic. Others swooped down and snagged eggs, which had fallen but not broken. Those ravens, which did score against the troll's thick hide, could not get a bite or claw to scratch, although it did not stop them from trying.

Ord blinked, shifting his gaze between Frida and Vindr, mulling over her words. "How are the ravens killing you off?"

Sadness rippled across her face. "Until several months ago, humans would journey around these mountains. Not as many as a year or so back, but still a few. It was the fastest way to the City of Taika."

She grinned. "I picked out a few mates. Our family ate the others. Never too many." She shook her head at his growing frown. "We weren't greedy. But when the ravens began to multiply, that all stopped."

Vindr, the huge stone troll, looked like he was about to cry as his lips drooped at the corners.

Frida moved forward and patted him on the leg. "There, there, we'll get rid of those nasty little birds."

She turned back toward Ord. "Without the humans as our main course, most of my relatives moved or passed away. Pickings had been slim for a while, and the cave spiders can scurry into holes we cannot reach.

Now, we are the last two. Why, only this morning we realized this. Before we go, we want the ravens to understand the terrible thing they have done."

"But," the dwarf held his palms up imploring them. "The ravens didn't do this. The goblins did."

She lifted one of her eyebrows as she watched him. "Goblins?"

He nodded. "Blue goblins invaded the human settlement in these mountains." It dawned on him he didn't even know what mountains these were, but that was beside the point.

Yet, she did mention Taika, so if I remember my geography correctly . . . he mused to himself and said, "The goblins killed or ran off all the humans, not the ravens."

She narrowed her eyes warily watching him as she said, "Why?"

He had no idea how to answer. "Uh. . .Territory? Greed? Maybe they didn't like each other?"

Steeliness settled into her eyes. "Now, I know you're lying. The blue goblins have lived in peace with the humans for generations. They had no reason to war. Trade was a big deal between them. Why, I personally have found many treasured goblin artifacts in the human's baggage. They were among the items taken from those who joined us for lunch." She waved to the right, bordering on exasperation. "I can show you if you wish?"

Ord spotted where her hand pointed. There was a bend farther down among the line of boulders against the mountainous cliff side. He suspected there would be a cave opening beyond that point where the trolls lived.

"No, no. That won't be necessary." He swallowed. "The point is the ravens did not run off the humans."

She drew a deep breath and folded her arms. "How do I know you're telling the truth?"

"If you don't believe me, ask the dark elves I travel with. They will confirm my story."

Frida tapped her lips with one finger. "Dwarves are not normally given to lying. That is a human trait."

"Perhaps not so much a human trait as a personality trait?" he suggested.

She tapped her lips again. "And I do like you. So . . . I could give you the benefit of the doubt."

Frida took a deep breath, exhaled slowly, and then looked up at her cousin. "Hmm. Vindr, what do you think?"

The huge troll grunted and looked down at his cousin.

"Go to the cave until I return," she said, keeping eye contact with the stone troll. "I'll get to the bottom of this."

Vindr whined but nodded. As he walked away from the nesting area, the raven calls grew less shrill.

When the massive troll passed around the bend Frida had previously shown Ord, many of the great black birds settled, landing on ledges and checking for their unborn. Other ravens reached the ground and tucked their heads in mourning staring at the splattered eggs.

Ord stepped away from the area just in case his presence might make the ravens nervous about finding their eggs. It helped. Soon, the unbroken eggs were all gone, all except one blue egg with brown spots.

Frida turned back from watching her cousin, Vindr, leave and studied Ord instead. Her arms did not cross, but a wary look remained in her eye. “We are not unreasonable trolls. But do be warned, if I am not convinced you are telling the truth, Vindr will be back to finish what he started.”

Ord kept his voice firm. “If I were not convinced, I wouldn’t have brought it up.”

An outbreak of birds launched into the air. The single blue egg with brown spots remained with sparse few ravens still checking the grounds. Ord remembered the echor Jada had given him and wondered if this was its purpose. With no raven parent to claim the egg, the egg would surely not mature.

He waited, but none of the ravens approached the egg. One by one, the last of the raven parents left the ground to either return to their nests or fly somewhere else.

Perhaps a parent lost it and didn’t realize it had survived the fall?

“Give me a moment,” he said to Frida.

Ord walked closer, noting the number of eggs that had broken. He knew ravens were also scavengers. Yet, none of them approached any of their own broken eggs.

He reached down and picked up the blue egg with brown spots. It was warm to the touch. He held it up, remembering how the ravens, which had carried off his hammer, seemed to understand his words.

“One of you has lost an egg. Will none of you claim it?”

They answered him in gurgles and shrills as his voice echoed off the rock walls and boulders. Yet, not one of the ravens approached.

What if the parents had been hurt by the stone troll’s attack? What if they didn’t know of the attack and had not come back yet to see their nest destroyed? How would I feel if I lost my own child?

He thought about Shamira.

I barely know the baby, and yet, I couldn’t have left her behind either. Jada had known that. This raven’s egg doesn’t deserve to die.

Opening the mouth of the echor, he slipped the egg inside. It vanished into the darkness, the bag remaining just as flat as if nothing was within. He had no idea what he could do to hatch the egg.

If nothing else, perhaps Jada can help me find a parent to take it in.

Spotting Frida watching him, he frowned. "Maybe we can still save this unclaimed egg. Perhaps the magic my bag holds will keep it safe until a parent can be found."

Frida tilted her head at him, and then dropped her gaze to the echor hanging on his belt. Her sweet smile returned as her eyes seemed to view him in a softer light.

"Well then, shall we take a stroll?" A sparkle flashed in her eyes. "If they are innocent, then saving the egg is a just fate."

He nodded, all his senses alert at the abrupt change in her demeanor. Despite her intention to see if he was telling the truth, her expression, the openness of her hands, the position of her feet, the slight flush to her face all told him . . . *She likes me.*

Ord glanced back at the ravens. He couldn't let Vindr destroy them, but there was no way he would get in a relationship with a hulder.

I am a dwarf, raised by dwarves, not a human.

But first things first, he had to save the ravens.

How did one amble with a hulder? he asked himself.

Hesitantly, he extended his arm. After all, she did want to stroll, and he was raised with manners.

With a bright smile, she took hold of his arm. "I'm sorry the path you came by collapsed, but perhaps it is for the best. This way, we'll have more time to talk."

They sauntered down the rising bluff walls. Sparkles caught Ord's eye embedded in lines of the solid rock. Veins of minerals ran thin to thick in all directions. With a good eye, any dwarf knew what those were. "Gold?" he asked.

"Yes," Frida waved it away. "Truly, we have no need of it, but there are those of my kind who hoarded it."

Ord squinted. "Did the humans know about it?"

"Of course," she smiled whimsically. "A few even dared the deeper part of these mountains to set up mines. I found some of my best mates that way. Those I didn't want, well, Vindr enjoyed as meals." Frida giggled. "It was a very agreeable situation for the both of us."

Though not so agreeable for the humans who were eaten, Ord thought.

He wasn't sure what to think. Here a female hulder enjoyed his company with casual conversation about eating humans as a meal.

Not that he had any human friends, but still, there was something about the mention of it that sent shivers up his spine. With her portrayed friendliness, he hoped this wasn't a trick.

Vindr might find me a tougher meal than a human.

As Ord walked beside her, she prodded, "Have you ever been to Eurig?"

He blinked. "Is that a city?"

That was a stupid response, he thought. *Of course, I know of Eurig. I am just too preoccupied in my own thoughts to think about what she is saying.*

"It's this territory, silly," she teased. "It spans from the beginnings of the Rin River in the north, to the start of the Enaid River where three streams become one. The city of Taika is at its southernmost point before the mountains slope toward the hills. The Havilah is northwest of here."

The details of what she said made perfect sense to Ord, and he now knew exactly where he was.

I am in the south east corner of Eurig along the Eirwen mountains, the fabled mountains of gold. The Eirwen mountains entered the Awen territory to the east and the Durgan territory to the south.

Ord could not help but smile, impressed by her knowledge of the area. "You certainly know your geography."

Come to think about it, he continued his thoughts, *I should have known my approximate location at the mention of Taika, though she had undeniably put it into perspective.*

Frida beamed. "I have a good teacher." The sides of her lips drooped, wiping her smile away. "Had. Had a good teacher." Just as the brightness of the smile had made her shine, the sadness of her thoughts rained like clouds. "It was one of the humans I had taken for a mate that taught me of our geography, but he has passed, too."

They had come to a passage between the boulders. It lay to Ord's right, and he nodded toward it. "Is this the way?"

"Oh, yes!" As if lighting a candle, her sad thoughts faded away. Her smile returned as they walked up the path. "But let's talk about you." She lowered her voice, speculating, watching the ground as they walked. "Do you have a special someone at home?"

An involuntary swallow occurred before he could stop it.

I hope she didn't hear me do that. Ord felt sweat trickle down the side of his head inside his helmet. *How good was a hulder's hearing?*

He cleared his throat, noting the end of the path. "Uh, well, it depends on your definition of," he tried to loosen his gorget though he knew it wasn't possible, "someone special."

She giggled. "I take that as a *no*?"

Her tail came up and lay on his shoulder. Though armored, he could tell it was there. It was rumored hulders could be immensely strong when they wanted to be. He did not want to find out in person.

In a playful voice, she asked, "Want to stop by my place before we go to yours?"

Ord coughed. Frida tilted her head with worried eyes. "Are you okay? Did the dust of Vindr's attack hurt you?"

His hand waved it away, though he did walk faster. She easily matched his stride.

"It's nothing, really." Ord tried to take a deep breath, all the while running through scenarios to speed up the walk. Frida was friendly enough but getting into a relationship with a hulder wasn't on his bucket list. "At our wagon, there's some water. Let's hurry."

The trees around him were familiar, but Ord could not remember his exact location. The croaking of the ravens had never gone away, although they did seem more distant.

Thankfully, a raven swooped in, circled him twice, and darted off to the right, passing between a group of trees. He followed.

Frida eyed the raven, speculative curiosity on her face. "Are they friends of yours?"

He couldn't read her expression beyond that. "I'm not sure *friend* is a good definition. The ravens have helped us for sure." Moving around an unusually large bramble, he held a part back so she could pass.

Her eyes brightened, and she curtsied. "Thank you."

It wasn't the effect he was trying to elicit. He was purely being polite. Although, he was glad it wasn't the opposite reaction. Hostilities now could mean doom to the ravens that lived on the mountain cliff.

At the stream, no easy way existed to span the waters. Brambles lined their side of the brook. They would have to press through them to get to the water.

They could always follow the stream to the west until they found the other crossing he had used. The log and stones there would be enough to get across. However, the meandering stream could go on for a while. Fighting their way through the brambles here might be quicker followed by a short plunge into the water.

He peered beyond the brambles.

The stream doesn't look deep.

Ord pushed through. The brambles scratched against his plate-mail armor while he slid part way down the bank to the edge of the stream. Picking up a stick, he poked it into the water a foot from the bank, and then holding it angled, he poked it into the stream again about three feet out. Had he been the height of his brethren, it might have been a problem. However, he was not.

"As long as the mud isn't too deep, it looks safe enough." He stepped down into the flowing water.

The current thrust against him, but he planted his feet and kept his ground. A cold chill climbed his legs, filling his boots. However, his body quickly warmed the water that flowed into the joints of his plate-mail armor.

The thought of the water being this close made his throat dry again. The slice of dried bread he had eaten was wearing off, and he licked his lips as his stomach complained. Ignoring it all, he extended his hand for Frida.

She glowed as she took his hand and allowed him to help her to the other side.

A nagging feeling kept telling him he was doing all the wrong things.

But until the truth of the ravens persuades her and her cousin to stop attacking the ravens' nests, what choice do I have?

With Frida safely across, he rinsed his gauntlets off in the stream and then lifted water to his lips between his cupped armored hands. Water raced between his fingers and ran down his plate-mail armor, but he managed to drink some.

It was so much easier to drink from the waterskin.

Satisfied for the moment, he worked his way closer to the other side and climbed from the water up the dirt bank. The liquid ran in rivulets out the cracks in his metal armor. His boots, still wet, turned dirt into mud weighing down his feet. He cleaned them as best he could on rocks near the water's edge.

Thankfully, his armor was not designed to rust. Any dwarf who knew his stuff created his armor well using a composite of metals. Training in the art of blacksmithing occurred at an early age in his family, whether you were going to choose it as a profession or not.

Frida extended her hand to help him up the steeper part of the bank. Her grip was firm.

In a blink, Ord was at the top. With wide eyes, he extended his elbow once more. She held it as they walked.

The path came quickly. The trail the wagon had followed, while unused for some time before them, showed the ruts the wagon had traced.

Ravens ran tag making sure he knew the way though he had no doubt where he was or where he was headed. How he had befriended these birds made no sense to him. While he understood ravens tended to live around human habitats, he wondered if they had mistaken his identity, for never had ravens chosen to live among the dwarves.

As the wagon came into sight, he spied the back of Jada and Aidan. The black cape the ravens had used to carry his great hammer away now lay partially draped over the wooden crate in the wagon bed.

In earnest, Aidan paced back and forth in front of the horses. Ord could not make out the words that Jada spoke in soothing tones to Aidan. However, whatever she said did not seem to matter. The male elf continued to glare at the ground as he walked.

Still a hundred feet from Aidan, Jada, and Shamira, the male elf abruptly spun toward Ord and Frida with an arrow nocked in his bow. He pointed the arrow directly at Ord.

"Where have you been?" Aidan shouted. His eyes appeared to darken as he turned his gaze from Ord to Frida. "I told you to stay with the wagon, not collect strangers!"

Frida's grip tightened on Ord's arm. Ord could hear her tail nervously whipping in the air behind them as they approached the wagon's backboard. Two ravens dropped onto the saddle of one of the horses and paced while both birds' gazes darted between Aidan, Jada, Ord, and Frida.

"This is Frida," Ord announced. He kept his composure calm, gently removed Frida's hand from his arm, and stepped forward using his body to partially hide her. "There was a misunderstanding between her, her cousin, and the ravens of this place." He crossed his arms. The metal of his gauntlets rang as they tapped together. "It needs to be clarified."

Frida stepped to his left side, chin forward, making herself completely visible once more. "Tell me truly, are the humans gone from this land?" Her eyes fell to the blue goblin baby as Jada turned to face her directly. "Do the goblins rule?"

Jada's eyes met hers. "They do. We rescued this wee one who had been abandoned. You are the first human we have seen."

Frida looked from Jada to the sleeping Shamira. "And why would you help the goblins?" she questioned, and then she tightened her jaw. "Did you aid them in driving the humans out?"

"Why would we not help a child who had lost her parents?" Jada asked. "War does bad things on both sides. We fight for a nobler cause."

Frida met Jada's gaze and then looked away toward the forest floor considering Jada's words.

Ord watched both noting Frida's reluctance to accept what she knew to be true.

"Listen to your heart, Frida. You already know the truth," Jada said. "It is easy to take our frustrations out on another, to blame someone else for our circumstances. But it is a magical gift, indeed, when we take responsibility and alter the course of our life."

She walked around the wagon closer to Frida. "I perceive you have the heart of a friend and are looking for others who will give that friendship as well."

The female hulder looked slowly back at Jada. Her shoulders slumped. "Then what you've said is true." She turned toward Ord but would not meet his eyes. Instead, she stared at the ground. "It was not the fault of the ravens."

Ord said in a low voice, "No, it was not their fault."

A look of horror crossed her face. "And we have killed so many." Her tail whipped from behind her in a nervous twitch.

Aidan pulled back, centering his arrow on the hulder.

Jada lifted Shamira higher up into one arm and held out her free palm toward the male dark elf. "Aidan."

Aidan pointed the arrow toward the ground away from Frida but kept it ready.

Ambling toward the back of the wagon, Jada rocked Shamira and said, "It is a pleasure to meet you, Frida. I would offer you something, but we are rather limited now. We plan to setup camp for the night, if you would care to join us."

Aidan cleared his throat. Jada kept her face pleasant despite his unspoken objection.

"I," Frida said quickly as a tear raced down her cheek, "I need to talk with Vindr before he thinks I have been gone too long."

She turned and ran.

CHAPTER 6

Ord started to follow Frida, but Jada slipped closer to him and touched his arm. "Let her go. You did the right thing by bringing her to us."

One of the ravens took to the air, rising above the treetops and heading toward the nesting wall. The other continued to pace turning its head side to side, watching them all.

"No," Aidan's face grew red, "no more." Taking one of the horses by the bridle, he started the wagon forward. "I will not allow you to add another race to this group. There are too many additional complications already."

The remaining raven peered at Aidan from the back of the horse as the wagon moved. Ord kept pace with the wagon, pushing the black cape so it slid into the wagon bed. He reached into the crate and pulled out the waterskin. Keeping one eye on their direction, he drank greedily. The water helped. His stomach stopped rumbling.

"Aidan, you're missing the point." Jada hurried to catch up with the elf.

Shamira stirred. The female dark elf rushed a few steps and then was forced to walk. Ord put the waterskin in the crate, dropped back to Jada, and took the baby.

"What is the point?" Aidan growled. "We were told by Anryulong to bring one. One." He spun around to face her and shook his index finger as he walked backward. "It's going to be hard enough getting the dwarf inside without watching eyes knowing everything. Now we have a baby goblin and a hulder, too?" The elf turned around just in time to avoid colliding with a tree. "And who put that there?" Aidan forced the horses to go around, shoving at the animals.

As Ord listened, he could hear what Aidan was saying under his breath. Though Jada did not seem to pay attention to what Aidan mumbled, when Ord glanced at Shamira, Ord felt his ears grow red.

The language was no surprise for Ord. His platoon would have been impressed. Oddly though, after his decision to tailor his curse words in front of the baby goblin, he found himself more sensitive to listening to it.

Ord mumbled under his breath, "Wait 'til you meet Frida's cousin."

The wagon rolled into a clearing west of the waterfall. The waterfall was on Ord's right. Though most of the noise from the falling water was muted due to the curve of the mountain wall, the splash of the water created a calming feel as if telling them it was the perfect place to rest.

Shamira opened her eyes. Round balls of delight took in everything she could see, but the first thing they centered on was Ord.

His heart melted. The smile on the baby's face caused his knees to be weaker than they were. In that moment, nothing else mattered: not their location, not the circumstance, and certainly not the dark elves' quest.

How could someone this tiny do that to me? It makes no sense at all.

Taking a few steps, the raven jumped from the back of the horse's saddle to the wagon seat and gurgled.

Jada walked up beside the front of the wagon and nodded at the bird.

The raven took off with a flutter of wings, following the mountain wall toward the partially viewable waterfall. It soared over the pool, whipped around in a quick turn, and vanished into the trees of the forest.

Ord's questioning glance at the raven's actions was met by no response from Jada. He shrugged and turned Shamira around to view the source of the water's noise, the waterfall.

As he strolled closer, the frothing liquid of white dropped from a hundred feet above and crashed into the pool below. Walking around the part of the mountain that formed a partial barrier between their camp and the waterfall, tiny mist droplets pelted them.

After a moment of wonder, Shamira blinked her eyelids and softly whimpered. He walked her back toward the others, his boots still squishing with the water he had yet to get out from crossing the stream with Frida.

Aidan, still muttering under his breath, dug a small firepit. The elf seemed to ignore them all now, including Jada, though Ord was sure that was just pretense.

With the bluff to the north and the rock face jutting out between them and the waterfall to the east, the only two directions they would have to keep watch on were the front of the camp that faced the forest, south, and the open side as the mountain curved back away from them, west.

It was a decent, makeshift camp, all in all. Still holding Shamira, Ord looked around to see what he could do to help.

He spotted Jada working her way toward the waterfall's pool picking up stones and placing some she selected in a bag. Each stone she collected was about the same size and shape. However, more than once she rejected a stone though it appeared to Ord to match the previous stones' characteristics.

Walking over, Ord checked for any other features that might make one stone stand out from another.

If it is physical, I am not seeing it.

He ambled beside her gently rocking Shamira. "Shouldn't you be resting?"

Though weariness laced her features, when she looked at him, her eyes shone with a warm feeling of friendship. "Your concern is appreciated, Ord, but I have enough strength to do what must be done."

Picking up another stone, she held it in her free hand, shook her head, and placed it back from where it came.

Ord leaned closer, inspecting the bag. "And you're doing what?"

Three ravens dropped down, two to Ord's right and one to Ord's left. They matched the pace of Jada and Ord.

Jada smiled. "Not all protections require me to focus directly with my magic. I am empowering these stones to work as our shield as night falls."

He raised his eyebrows. "May I hold one?"

Pulling the top one out of her leather bag, she placed it in his free gauntleted hand.

It felt no different to him. "How do you tell if it can be empowered?"

She reached over and closed his fist around it. "Touch it lightly. Listen to your body. What do you feel?"

"It's hard, roundish in shape, and not exactly smooth."

"Feel it," she stressed. "Stop using your logic to analyze it. Use the heart."

Ord wrinkled his brow as he tried to concentrate. He stopped and shook his head. "I can't feel anything."

A smile crossed her lips. "Never fear. When it is time, you will know." She glanced up at nothing Ord could see. "And that time is coming."

The mist from the waterfall touched Ord's face, and he realized they were making their way to the edge of the pool. He adjusted the cloth above Shamira's head to help keep the mist out of her eyes. With a sigh, he placed the stone back in the leather bag.

The two ravens on Ord's right gurgled at each other, periodically fluffing their wings to shake off the water. They both studied Jada. The raven to Ord's left eyed Shamira.

Jada glanced up at Ord as they reached the pool edge. "You have something to say?" Instead of looking for more stones, she reached into her leather bag and placed the first stone on the ground about a foot from the edge. She pointed at the water. "We can use the pool as our eastern line of defense."

The raven to Ord's left bobbed its head as if in agreement.

Ord slowly nodded mulling over his own thoughts and watched her place the stones two feet apart as they headed back toward the camp walking the outer perimeter. He finally said, "Aidan mentioned the name Anryulong. You did, too, before. Why does this dragon want me brought in?"

One by one she continued to place the stones creating a dotted line to divide their camp from the edge of the forest. "Anryulong is the guardian of all magical worlds. She is the heart and soul of the city we go to."

Aidan glanced over at them as they moved past the firepit. A pile of tinder sat on the ground next to a small stack of branches he had found in the forest. Using two rocks, he struck a spark in the firepit. A flame burned upward consuming the dried grass, bark, and leaves. He stacked more of the smaller dried branches around the flame.

The conversation with Frida came to Ord's mind. "So," he said, "you mean the city of Taika?"

Jada raised an eyebrow at him and gave an amused grin before placing the next stone. "You've learned quickly where we are."

One of the ravens on the right launched into the air and landed on a perch on the rock wall above the campsite appearing to keep watch.

Ord thought back to what happened in the battle with the red dragon. He hesitated and then asked, "Has our world been altered?"

Smoothing out a place on the ground, she blew on it three times. Satisfied, she continued with the stone placement. She speculated with a whimsical tone in her voice, "Why would you say that?"

"Because of what happened in the battle. Because of what no one else could see," he paused, thinking of his friend Findor, "or remember."

She smiled. "Did it ever cross your mind that you might have dreamed it?"

The raven, standing by itself, ruffled its feathers and turned its head sideways at Shamira and Ord while it gurgled. Shamira reached a hand toward the raven.

A sheepish smile spanned Ord's face. He shrugged. "Any sane dwarf would . . . However, I know what I saw." He looked her in the eyes as they reached the western edge of the camp and followed a curved path toward the mountain wall. "Did. I know what I did. And I had help in doing it."

The corners of his mouth dropped creating a frown on his face as he remembered his wounded friend.

"Do not fret." She shook her head. "Your friend Findor is safe."

Shamira imitated the raven's gurgle and laughed at her own sound. Her tiny fingers touched and released the warm cloth she was wrapped in.

Ord's mind leaped in the direction Jada had led his thoughts. "And the other dwarves at the encampment?"

"They were not the objective of the hunt."

Shamira cooed. She played with a corner of the warm cloth that had been tucked around her. The raven on the left cooed back.

Ord watched Shamira as he contemplated Jada's words. "Was I?"

Jada chuckled. "What would you think if I told you *no*?"

Ord wrinkled his brow. He slowly answered, "I would say, then, why am I here?"

"This is what Aidan seeks to understand from Anryulong," she said in a faraway voice.

The dwarf stroked his beard, noticing her distracted answer. "Why am I here or who is the person that was hunted?"

She placed the last stone precisely two feet from the mountain wall and smiled.

"Both," she said. Siting with her legs folded under her, her back to the mountain, she closed her eyes and mumbled inaudible words.

A shimmer jumped from stone to stone, starting from the one beside Jada and running back along the dotted line to the pool of water. She said in an elven whisper, “May only what we need be drawn this way, so the path we take will save the day.”

Her eyes slowly opened. Contentment drifted across her features. After tying the empty leather bag onto her belt, she started to rise. But before she could complete the process, she sat down again, her lungs heaving with the effort. “It *is* time to rest.”

Ord reached out his free hand. She grabbed hold of his larger one with her smaller ones, and he lifted her feather-light body until she stood on her feet.

He blinked. “Are you all right? No one can weigh this little and be alive.”

Jada smiled at the startled look on his face. “With my power goes mass. For most, it is not noticeable, but for me it means I must recharge.”

As he helped her toward the firepit, he eyed the mountain guarding their north side. The slope of the semi-sheer mountain at the back of their camp angled up until it reached the sparse grass above their heads near the top. There were trees up there, too, though he could only see a few branches.

Near the firepit, Aidan had placed three rolled up sleeping mats. Each roll stood on one end, all leaning together and forming a pyramid between the rock wall and the firepit.

Beside the sleeping mats, a small satchel sat with its top open. Inside the satchel were additional rolled up cloths, obviously for the baby.

Ord raised an eyebrow. “This fact about dark elves and magic, that mass is used when magic is used, I have never read about.”

A slight smile crossed Jada’s lips. “It is a condition of its consumption, not a general characteristic. Each race is affected in a different way by their use of magic. It is the price dark elves pay just like running a marathon will make a person eat more food for energy to maintain their bulk.”

“If I were to guess,” Ord ventured, still helping her to the sleeping mats, “this expending of magic is how they tracked us to the barn.”

Beside the satchel, unwrapped bread sat on the flat piece of wood that Aidan had carved out a shallow bowl from on one side. A kefir bottle had been fetched. Aidan had added more kindling beside the firepit with a spit setup for turning meat. The fire burned as coals with periodic flames bursting out in unexpected moments. Aidan could not be seen.

Beginning to lose the struggle against sleep, Jada closed her eyes. Her head nodded forward. "We must continue this conversation later."

Ord snagged one of the rolled up mats from the pyramid. The pyramid collapsed, the two unused rolls hit the ground and bounced. He unrolled the mat he had taken with one hand and helped Jada to it.

Sitting down sluggishly, Jada focused on the ground. "Ord, I'm sorry we have not been more forthcoming with information." She sighed. "There are some things you must experience to understand. Speaking of them beforehand could taint how you respond. I . . . I know it's not easy. I . . ." She bit her lip. "I wish I could save you from what you will endure."

She frowned up at him, a dark foreboding in her eyes. Her emotions, those she hid so well, hit him like a hammer without any further words.

He took a step back. "Rest," the word tumbled from his lips as he fought the desire to flee those emotions.

What in the world is happening to me? I have never felt this type of connection to a complete stranger.

And yet, something told him she wasn't a stranger.

But that is impossible. I have never met her before. No dark elf would dare to be caught within the confines of my home city. It wasn't permitted.

Jada lay down. Even as Ord watched, Jada's chest rose and fell in sleep. Whatever magic she had used creating the circle of protection in the barn and forming the dotted stone line at their existing campsite had certainly drained her.

The baby in his arm shook.

He looked down to see Shamira's lips tremble as if she had felt the elf's emotions, too.

"Hey there," he gave the child a big smile. "What's that all about?"

She gazed up at him in wonder, her quivering lips forgotten as a smile took over.

Ord glanced at the bread sitting on the board.

How long has it been since the baby ate? For that matter, how often do they eat?

He sat down beside the bowl. Water poured out of his boots mixing with the dirt and sand. The dampness of the padding inside his armor, water and sweat combined, felt mucky against his skin.

He eyed the firepit. If things were quiet for a while, it would be a great time to at least dry it out if not find a way to bathe . . .

Ord looked away from the fire and laid Shamira down beside him. He pulled off each boot and watched the lingering water dribble to the ground as he held them one at a time upside down.

Once each appeared empty, he wiggled his toes, which were still inside the wet stockings. Water squished out of the stocking material. With a sigh, he pulled both boots back on.

There was no help for it. Unless Jada and Aidan had brought along a change of clothes for him, all he owned was on his back. And unfortunately, this was no safe place to take off his armor.

From the corner of his eye, he caught Shamira's expectant gaze as she spoke to him in oo's and ah's that he had no idea how to translate. Taking the hard bread in hand, he broke it up into the carved depression of the bowl and poured in the kefir on top. Tilting Shamira up, he placed a piece of the kefir soaked bread to her lips.

She snapped up the food, barely giving Ord a chance to get his fingers out of the way. For a goblin, she definitely had a dwarven appetite. She would make any dwarven dad proud.

When she finished, he remembered Jada had patted her on the back, causing the child to burp.

Nodding to himself, he got to his feet. "Better done standing up."

He certainly did not wish to add more odors to his armor so he pulled one of the cloths from the satchel, laid the rest of the hardened bread on the flat part of the carved bowl, and positioned the cloth on his shoulder.

The cloth was small, but if he could aim the child right . . . Picking up the wrapped Shamira, he placed her head as close to the small cloth as possible. With his left gauntleted hand, he patted the baby's back through her wrapping.

Thump, thump, thump.

Nothing.

Thump, thump, thump.

Still nothing.

He held Shamira in front of him with both hands. "Is something going on that you are not telling me? You did it for Jada so easily."

Shamira flayed her arms at him babbling more nonsense.

He held her up once more and used his left hand to pat her on the back.

Thump, thump, thump, thump.

Burp.

"There now," he brought her from his shoulder with a smile, "isn't that better?"

He sniffed, wrinkled his noise, and spied a strange mix of kefir and stomach acids running down his shoulder armor.

"Shamira, did you miss the cloth on purpose?"

She cooed and smiled happily.

Switching her to be held in his left arm to minimize getting the liquid on her, he held his right arm as still as possible trying to decide the best way to clean it off before it seeped into any armor joints.

He grunted. "And why does it smell so bad coming back up?"

He eyed the pool, glanced at his arm, and looked down to Shamira. "We need to go for a walk and a wash." A smile crossed his face. "Yeah, that's what we'll do."

Not bothering to remove the smelling cloth, he strolled to the pool, talking to Shamira.

"Come to think of it, a whole lot worse than baby burp has run down my armor, and I and the armor have endured. War is never pretty", he told her. "You do what you must to survive."

In battle, goblins liked to spit. Dragons sometimes drooled, and if the dragon was performing a flyby, they dropped their drool on you from the air. Not to mention the splatters caused by a war hammer as it bashed into an unprotected body.

"I can handle this. I can," he told her.

He wrinkled his nose.

"Hopefully, not for long."

At the water's edge, he laid Shamira on the ground. Dipping the cloth in, he rinsed it and cleaned off.

The odor dissipated in the waterfall mist. Shamira blinked as the droplets descended. She reached up to feel them on her face.

He adjusted her wrap to protect her eyes though the droplets continued to build on her arms and hands.

"What am I to do with you, Shamira? Other than hold you and feed you?"

He cringed.

"Change you and burp you? How did your mother have time for anything else?"

Adjusting the flap of the wrap so it would help keep the mist better from the little girl, he picked her up and ambled around the pool, studying how it met the side of the mountain.

He took in every detail. A dark hollow stood out behind the waterfall higher up the rock wall. However, the distortion caused by the falling water made it difficult to tell how deep it went. He continued to trace their mountain backdrop with his gaze until it turned from north to east.

On the far side, almost directly opposite of his location, he spotted Aidan. The elf had a pole in his hand to which was attached some type of twine. Attached to the twine, floating on top of the water, was a small piece of bobbing wood.

The bobber jerked downward. Aidan heaved back on the pole. The pole in his hands bent until Ord was sure the wood would snap. As the elf pulled the string from the pool, a fish wriggled on the end.

Ord's mouth watered. His stomach growled. Fishing was what he should be doing if he expected to fill his belly tonight. Otherwise, that satchel of bread might be the best he could do.

Detaching the fish from the end of the twine, Aidan held it up. The water creature attempted to wriggle from his hands, but the elf's nimble fingers held it firm. Even from this distance, Ord could hear Aidan's words on the wind.

"Mother Lucasta, we accept this life for us to live." He placed the fish on a large flat stone surface and struck it with a fist-sized rock. The fish went limp. Pulling his knife from his sheath, he carried the fish downstream from the pool. Here, the pool overflowed toward the boulders where Ord had found Frida and Vindr.

With precise cuts, Aidan separated the head from the body, trimming the tail and fins. Using the edge of the knife, he scraped the outer skin to remove the scales.

Finally, he slipped a small leather bag from his pouch and walked closer to the stream. He dipped the leather bag into the water. The leather bag expanded until it was full. Stepping back to the bank, he brought the bag to the fish and poured water over the area, cleaning up the blood. The washed blood absorbed into the ground instead of flowing into the pool.

Aidan raised his head to glance at the sky. "We thank thee gracious mother."

Ord watched him circumnavigate the pool, away from the waterfall. This time the elf crossed the stream and stepped out of sight into the woods. It was the first time Ord had ever seen a dark elf hunting ritual. Until now, he had only read of them in his studies.

The dwarf's stomach growled, reminding him, again, he had not eaten. Though the hard bread of the satchel might work in a pinch, he would prefer meat, and that would involve fishing or hunting.

"Is it possible to hunt with a baby?" He looked down at Shamira. "You would certainly make it an interesting challenge."

He placed a foot near the edge of the pool, watching the waterfall crash into the clear pool water. Fish darted in the depths, catching bits of food that splashed down from above the rock cliff.

He said to Shamira, "A prayer of thanksgiving for the food one ate? It isn't a bad idea. But whom would I pray to and why? If there is food given from a friend that is one thing. Thank them. But otherwise, I have always been taught the food I catch, kill, and skin is my own responsibility."

He stroked his beard watching Shamira play with the edge of her wrapping.

"There are those in the dwarven community who believe in the gods. I don't disbelieve, and yet, none have ever shown themselves to me."

Leaves rustled on the far south side of the pool, and Aidan's image materialized from the shadows, striding from the forest, now, on this side of the pool. The elf stepped gingerly over the stones Jada had placed, careful not to disturb them. Ord watched the elf move to the spit and secure the fish to it.

Flames danced up through the kindling as Aidan placed more wood on the fire. The firelight, despite the daylight, cast a red/orange glow on Aidan's face. Based upon the portion of fish the elf had brought, Ord guessed, Aidan had no intention of sharing.

"The whole thing would barely make half a meal anyway, right Shamira?"

She peeked at him from beneath the flap and giggled.

Ord squinted at Aidan.

"And I'll not be owing to a pompous dark elf either."

His stomach loudly grumbled.

Shamira's eyes widened.

Had she truly noticed that?

"Well," he looked down at the baby in his arm, "I had better figure out something to do with you before I go hunting for myself."

He glanced up at the waterfall.

"But where should I put you to keep you safe? Jada is asleep and Aidan would never agree to help."

He eyed the hollow behind the waterfall.

"Maybe up there? It is up high, protected by the downward fall of the water on one side and a wall of rock on at least two of the others. But how do I get there?"

He walked closer to the left side of the waterfall. Thin ragged lines, more shaped than natural, distorted by weather, came into view the closer he approached. At one time, someone had taken great care to cut a path from the mountain to the hollow. However, the pits and depressions on the top of each carved step showed neglect was taking its toll. The steps did appear to be the only way up, forming a ragged path leading along the west rock wall and curving to follow its contour.

He nodded. "It is certainly worth a try."

The mist from the waterfall gathered in the small depressions on each step, reflecting the sky in blue and yellow light. The depressions became more frequent the closer he climbed to the hollow.

Due to the s-type shape of the cliff above, he wove his way past the absence of periodic rock borders that had at one time guarded the climber from falling off the stairs. The trail wove onward deceptively tall until the entrance to the hollow abruptly showed itself.

The passage was wider than expected, like large double doors. It was hidden by a thin glaze of water redirected from the waterfall by holes cut into the rocks above it. The water poured down into a three-foot gap between the end of the last step and the landing in the cave. With the hollow three stories above the ground and Jada's stones guarding the primary route up, it appeared to be a near perfect spot to safely leave Shamira.

Covering the baby by leaning forward, he stepped through the sheet of falling liquid. Water dashed down his back and ran around the curves of his armor as he stepped over the three-foot gap between the stairs and the cave. A shiver took his breath, but by angling his body, Shamira and her wrapping stayed dry.

The hollow, indeed, had only one outside entrance, although, he did notice the back wall, the north side, held a darker patch of shadow. Quiet whispers came from beyond the darkness, more than likely the wind coming up from cracks in the earth. It was a common occurrence in his mountain city home.

On the east side, an eighth of the floor had collapsed. He walked across and peered over. The rock had dropped away to the pool beneath the waterfall, but the rest of the floor seemed stable as he looked for signs of structural weakness.

He turned back and spotted a dry, shallow, depression in a carved rectangle rock three feet tall on the west side of the hollow. A maiden with her arms upstretched had been chiseled into each side of the rock. At one time, it had served as some type of large bowl lined with lime, probably for a ceremonial ritual.

He stroked his mustache. "And now it would serve as a safe place for Shamira to stay."

She fit perfect with no possibility to accidentally roll off. He turned back to the falling water on the south side of the hollow.

With cupped hands, he reached out, caught some of the downpour, and drank deeply. Once more it ran through his gauntlets and down his plate-mail armor, yet he managed to drink his fill. The water was cold, pure, and fresh. What slipped through his gauntlets spun around the curve of his armor and dripped onto the rocks in muffled droplets.

He licked his lips. "I have never tasted water so good." His voice echoed behind him.

With his thirst quenched for the moment, he turned back to investigate the hollow. Once more, he spotted the veins of gold interlaced within the rock. If he ever got word to Findor, there would surely be an army raised to drive the goblins out.

The thought pleased him. He might even have a town named after him, and if it grew large enough, a city.

Ord City?

He laughed.

No, they'd need to go by my first name, Steredenn. The city of Steredenn would be just fine.

Tracing the wall toward the dark patch at the back of the hollow, he spied a hole, wider than his shoulders. The quiet whispers grew the closer he approached the hole. There was no evidence of anything inside.

It was probably formed by the wind when this place was no longer used.

Just to be sure, he hefted a large rock.

Boom.

The sound reverberated around him as he jammed the rock into the hole, blocking it tight. It would take chisels and hammers to get that rock out and a lot of dwarves to boot.

The whispers dropped though they did not go away. He listened for a moment noticing the way the sounds repeated in intonation and were monotonous. Convinced it was nothing more than the wind moving through an internal cave system, he turned away from the blocked hole.

"It is enough. If I am going to be your father," he said to Shamira, "I must figure out how to do things on my own with you."

Turning back to the front of the hollow, he watched light play across the falling water. Darkness was coming faster than he'd like. He stepped in front of Shamira, reached down, and touched her tiny hand. "I'll be right back." Ord stepped through the waterfall.

Twilight was descending. His dwarven dark sight kicked in as he made his way down the stairs.

The question was how to hunt. He had his hammer, but it wasn't a long-range weapon to bring down an animal, and traps would take a while. Ord could always make a fishing pole as Aidan had, but with the light fading, unless he could use a lantern, which he didn't have, he would have nothing to draw the fish.

Water was still an option. He didn't *have* to eat tonight. Truly, he had drunk enough to make the hunger go away. Although, given a short time, it would be back.

The more he thought about it, the more he realized hunting was out of the question. He was a dwarf after all. A few days of no food he could handle.

Changing direction by the pool, he started up the ancient steps toward the hollow. In the dimming light and shadows, the decorative nature of their construction revealed itself. Though old and roughed from age, the stones were carved from the strata of rock forced together by some cataclysmic occurrence when these mountains were first made. Carved faces, worn down by weather, could barely be seen in the vertical part of each step.

Giggling came from inside the hollow. Shamira's voice rose, echoing from the gaps between where the water fell and where it did not.

Ord hurried up the rest of the stone stairs and pushed to get through the sheet of water guarding the entrance.

The water pushed back as the torrent increased. His leg muscles strained against the downward pressure. With a low growl, he heaved forward, barely able to plant his feet over the three-foot gap and forced to his knees as he reached the inside of the hollow.

Near the waterfall on the south side, the translucent image of an adult female stood. Water filled her shape as perfectly formed curves. In her arms was Shamira. The water lady seemed to be communicating with the child though Ord heard no sound except for Shamira's giggles.

The water female turned to face him and demanded, "Why have you stolen this child?"

Chapter 7

Ord had read of these foul water sprites in the dwarven library. They would draw in beings to drown in the depths of their domains. Though he never believed all the myths he read, he nonetheless had heard them.

He slowly rose from his knees. "Don't hurt her."

He thought back to Aidan who had fished in the pool beneath the waterfall.

Nothing had disturbed his fishing. Jada had indicated no danger when she had collected the stones. Where had this creature come from?

Ord stepped cautiously toward the water sprite. "Look, I don't know who you are, but this child was not stolen." Though almost transparent, he could see the distortion of the curves that made up the sprite's body.

The eyes of the water nymph followed him. The pupils of the watery creature stood out against the backdrop of the waterfall like tiny magnifying glasses. It said nothing but continued to stare at him.

He swallowed and continued, noting how she held the child. "We found her abandoned. By who, we don't know. Her mother was gone."

The whispering voices at the back of the hollow formed familiar patterns, now, like a language though the words were not clear.

The water creature adjusted the baby in her arms and gazed down at the baby's face. "With no mother, what does she have to live for?" She walked backward, away from Ord, toward the drop-off between the falls and the floor's edge. "Your life would be less complicated without her."

The dwarf stepped forward but stopped at the decisive look in the water sprite's eyes. "Please, stop."

Ping. Ping. Ping.

Tapping came from the back of the hollow like picks chipping away against stone.

The water nymph continued. "I heard your wagon as it traveled along the road. I have listened to the dark elf who does not believe the child should be with you." The water creature held Shamira a little closer to the edge.

Shamira laughed as she reached out touching the water as it fell.

"A child such as this should not be allowed to endure without love," said the sprite.

Ord's voice rose. He pleaded, "Don't hurt Shamira."

The nymph brought her back a few inches. She curiously asked, "Why have you named her?"

The dwarf dropped to one knee and held out his hands in supplication. "Because she is my child. Though not born of dwarves, she is bone of my bone, flesh of my flesh. She is my heart and soul. I don't understand how this can be or why, but I do not care. Please, do not harm her."

The whispers from behind them filled the hollow with echoes. And the echoes made a language though Ord had no idea what words were being said. Yet, he felt to his core the meaning behind the words that were expressed by the very intonations that reverberated around him.

They do not believe me.

Tap. Tap. Tap.

The tapping against stone became louder, like chisels sculpting a rock, not unlike one honed by dwarves, such was the power of each strike.

Ord glanced back to see cracks forming on the rock's center, the very one he had used to plug the hole. Something unseen worked to free it from the other side.

The water creature looked up as if listening to the language Ord could not translate. She slowly regarded Ord once more. "How well can a dwarf care for a goblin child?" The nymph wrinkled her brow. "Would you defend her to the death?"

Without hesitation, he said, "Yes."

"Then prove yourself, dwarf," she answered. "My protectors want to see if you are telling the truth."

The stone he had placed in the hole burst inward into the hollow. Tiny bits thudded against the walls and floor. Two, hairy, spindly, front legs gripped the sides of the hole as the creature they were attached to revealed two red eyes glowing in the darkness. It pulled its black body through the opening, compressing down and then expanding into a massive spider.

Ord rose from his knee, pulling the hammer loose that hung upon his back. "What are you doing?"

"Your dedication to this child, the child you claim is yours, the child you say you will give your life for, is being tested."

The dwarf caught sight of a second arachnid as it slipped smoothly through the hole at the back of the hollow to join the first. Standing to its full height, Ord gazed at its enormous fangs. "Why?"

The water nymph's voice became cold. "You have violated the Temple of Tajita. You have stolen its fish and entered its sacred cave. You have placed your child on the altar of sacrifice."

The fangs of the spider slowly extended. A liquid dripped from the ends.

Ord glanced at the rock beneath his feet. The ground was firm although in places there was soft soil. He studied the slant of the ground. He stood on the lower slope.

The advantage lay with the spiders. But that wasn't what bothered him the most. Even if he succeeded in stopping the arachnids, the water nymph might still cast the baby into the pool. He needed to understand the situation better. "We had no idea we were trespassing. Give me the child, and we will go our way. I will warn others of your sacred shrine."

The water nymph pointed a finger at him as she turned. "It is too late. Words are not enough."

The whispering voices rose louder for a moment and then became an impatient murmur.

She hesitated and then slowly said, "You may leave unharmed, and we will keep the baby." The nymph raised an eyebrow. "They'll even let you warn your friends."

The last sentence echoed in Ord's head. He tightened his grip on the hammer. "And if I win?"

She paused consulting with the whispers. "You and your child may go free."

"And how can I know you will keep your word?"

The spiders twittered in the darkness.

"He has that right," she said, bristling at what the whispers spoke to her. She turned back to Ord. "Do you know of the power in a water sprite's name?"

Ord nodded. "To know the name is to control the water sprite."

"I will give you a single part. While you may not be able to control me with it, it will bind my word in this holy temple. You may call me Cy."

He remembered the giggling Shamira had done before he entered the cave.

If the water sprite is truly evil, would the baby not be crying out?

Ord addressed the water sprite. "If the spiders need proof of my intentions, I will give it to them." He adjusted his hold on his hammer, gripping it with both hands and raising the hammer head above his right shoulder.

The spider leaped but its jump was restricted by the height of the hollow. As it sprang into a second hop, the dwarf dodged. The spider's fangs jabbed through the air where Ord had been. The fangs gouged out bits of rock from the hollow's floor.

Though larger than the other dwarves, Ord's speed had not suffered. Using the added seconds to his advantage, he slammed the hammer down on one of the spider's back legs.

A squeal rose as he ducked under the back half of the arachnid's body. It spun toward where its struck leg had been attacked, giving Ord time to aim again.

He shouted to the nymph, "What do you owe them?"

The spider listened, quickly turning to the left to locate the dwarf by his voice. But Ord had already moved, keeping an eye on the position of spider's head. The spider's fangs dripped with venom.

The water sprite adjusted her stance to study Ord more closely. "Owe them?"

"They are your masters, are they not?" Ord slammed down his hammer on another back leg before the spider could track his new position.

The spider screeched. It jumped away from Ord, managed to turn around, and sprang back, headfirst, before Ord could hide.

Its fangs struck against the chest armor the dwarf wore. Black ichor ran down the dwarf's plate-mail. Had his armor been made of leather, the sharp fangs would have pierced right through.

The blow knocked Ord backward. As he hit the ground, his metal armor screeched across the rocky floor. The arachnid sprang away, quivering.

"So," the dwarf said, "you don't like that sound?"

Rising as fast as he could, Ord glimpsed the ground under him. Points on the rock had scraped against the back of his plate-mail armor. Shifting his hammer into one hand, he snagged a loose stone and scratched it against the metal armor of his chest.

Screech.

The pitch the scratch produced made him cringe, but the arachnid scampered farther back.

"Interesting," he said. Slowly advancing, the dwarf kept the spider in sight. "Well, nymph? What bargain have you struck with the spiders? Your temple has been in ruins for a long time. I would dare say it has been abandoned for a hundred years."

The spider started toward him. He pulled the rock across the surface of his armor.

Screech.

The arachnid leaped back.

Cy answered Ord's question without emotion, "Those who would use my basin . . . the spiders dispose of. As a result, they have meat."

"But it's lonely, is it not?" Ord watched the spider for any dip in its body's position along with the shuffling of its legs for another jump. "For there are no exceptions."

"None." She looked down at the baby. "That is the bargain."

Ord inched closer to the spider. "Then perhaps it's time for the agreement to change." The dwarf raked the stone against his plate-mail.

Screech.

The spider leaped back and hit the wall then tumbled forward. The second spider hurried farther away.

Dropping the stone, Ord grabbed the handle of his hammer with both hands and swung toward the spider's quivering body.

Two fangs stabbed at him, striking the side of his armor.

He was knocked sideways, unharmed, but the spider's hit had been enough to make him miss his mark. He staggered trying to get his balance.

The spider pulled itself up to stand on its feet and pounced.

Ord lost his footing and slammed into a boulder to the left of the hole at the back of the hollow.

The arachnid struck three times, but each attempt hit Ord's plate-mail.

A white sticky substance accumulated at the spider's rear. Using its working back legs, the spider pulled a shiny strand out and attached it to the side of a nearby rock.

The dwarf knew better than to go near those sticky strands. He slipped out of sight, using the boulder as a shield.

The spider scooted toward his last position beginning to form a web, a cage for a dwarven fly, blocking of one way by which Ord could escape.

Spying out around the edge of the boulder, which was taller than he, Ord leaped out and swung his hammer. The hammer hit and scored against a third spider leg.

The arachnid raised its wounded appendage off the ground, shaking it in pain. Now operating on five legs, it ominously chittered. The chitter echoed in the hollow louder than what Ord had managed with the stone's screech.

Splash.

Through the air, a dark shape with feathers whizzed by. It had burst through the waterfall and soared into the hollow.

Splash. Splash. Splash.

Three additional ravens streaked through the wall of water. They spread their wings and glided through the air, following the inside hollow wall. They repeated the sound of the screech the rock had made when Ord scraped it against his armor.

The spider hit the wall trying to get away from the racket, bounced back, and fell into its own partially created web. The second spider pulled back toward the hole but did not exit the hollow. It hunched down as if waiting for the ravens to leave.

While the first spider fought to untangle itself from the sticky web, Ord climbed to the tallest of the boulders in the cave. He leaped into the air with a blood-curdling war cry and swung his great hammer down with a very precise aim.

The arachnid struggled to free itself while cringing from the ravens' cries but only managed to increase its tangle.

Ord slammed his forefathers' hammer down on the spider's head.

The exoskeleton crunched. Pale blue liquid splattered as the body of the spider collapsed.

Ord roared again as the spider lay still. Lungs heaving, he pulled the war hammer from its crushed skull. The pale blue liquid dripped from his hammer, forming puddles on the ground.

The ravens circled until finally landing on the spider's broken body. They dove into a hefty meal, dipping their bills into its blue ichor. The longer the ichor was exposed to the air, the stronger it smelled like dead decaying fish.

Movement stirred in the brief silence that followed from beyond the hole at the back of the hollow. The clicking of many spider feet upon rock echoed through the chamber.

Dark wiry legs reached through the hole as a third arachnid pulled into the hollow. It spied the ravens and shied back to the left of the hole to stand beside the second spider.

Four more spiders climbed out with beady red eyes burning at Ord. And though Ord did not understand the words, the meaning was quite clear.

"No," Cy shook her head, eyeing the spiders, "he has defeated the champion. The rules were one spider to face one dwarf."

The whisperings rose and fell in a broken angry song.

The water nymph glared. "The deal was struck. They must be allowed to go."

The spiders shifted again as another arachnid slid out of the darkness from the hole into the hollow bringing the live count to seven.

Ord kept his gaze on the spiders as he tightened his grip on the great war hammer. "I take it the deal is off?" He glanced back at Cy but quickly refocused on the seven spiders.

Their whisperings turned into higher pitched twitters as they continued to watch both the ravens and Ord.

Cy's eyes were laced in remorse as she looked down at Shamira. "You have earned the right to live, little one. I am truly sorry."

The dwarf snorted. "That the spiders broke their deal? I could have told you they would not keep that agreement." He adjusted his stance to see both Cy and the spiders.

The water creature shook her head. "For what I am forced to do now."

The water sprite lost her shape, merging into the waterfall and allowing the baby goblin to fall.

"No," Ord bellowed, reaching out with is free hand as he started into a sprint toward the south side of the hollow.

The spiders sprang forward. Their pounce cut short by the limits of the hollow's ceiling and their numbers.

Ravens took to the air calling to each other and echoing the screech Ord had made by using the stone on his plate-mail armor.

Ord had almost reached the south edge of hollow, where the waterfall poured down, when the hairs on his arms stood up. He swung his hammer back with only a glance as the first arachnid reached him.

Something snapped, but he had no time to see. The ravens dived amongst the spiders zipping over their bodies.

Screech. Screech. Screech.

The spiders scattered from the ravens. Some hunkered down like statues until the ravens soared past only to take a few quick steps again before the ravens winged their way back around.

Ord silently thanked the ravens for those precious seconds he needed.

In three steps, Ord leaped off the edge and plummeted toward the pool. His only thoughts were to see where the baby had fallen.

Loose stones tumbled after Ord as the spiders scrambled to keep from stumbling off the same brink. A muffled twittering echoed from the hollow above Ord.

Splashes pierced the waterfall above him. The dwarf spotted three ravens winging down behind him just beyond the falling water's touch.

Taking a deep breath, Ord hit the surface of the pool. A huge wave went up adding to the turmoil of the churning water.

The ravens curved their flight to sweep across the surface of the pool and headed toward the forest.

Ord was tossed through the water, thrown around as white bubbles rippled in scenes of a painter's unsteady brush. Up and down lost meaning. The force of the water drove him in spirals until he dropped deep enough to be below the tossing water.

He trembled, the chill of the depths absorbing into the wet soaked pads beneath his plate-mail armor. The water above him filtered out the light from the surface the deeper he sank. With his war hammer gripped in his right hand, he awkwardly swam, struggling to move fast enough to keep from sinking to the bottom too quickly. His dwarven dark vision kicked in when he viewed the bottom and out when he looked toward the surface.

There was no sign of Shamira. His heart began to sink.

Had the water sprite truly done it? Was Shamira's lifeless body now lying caught in an unknown depression forever lost?

He refused to believe it. The child had been unafraid of the water sprite, and Cy had shown great fondness for the child.

And I remember the stories . . .

Toward the center of the pool, he spied a particularly large outcropping submerged beneath the waves. The outcropping appeared to glow at the edges, catching light, not from the surface but from a source farther down.

It was too far to swim in a direct route. He would have to go to the surface several times for air. And the more times he went to the surface, the more apt it was that he would be seen by the spiders.

A school of fish zipped past. Fresh water plants on the rocks beneath him curved over where the current was the strongest. He stroked toward the current.

The current shoved him into a horizontal sweep. He pushed off a rock formation to keep from slamming into it sideways. It rushed him through a weaving maze of rock outcroppings, near misses, and scraps against his armor.

He struggled to slow down by using both his arms to swim against the current. When Ord was to the left of the light source, he dove.

The glow from below lit the sides of the other boulder-sized rocks around the central formation, sending up bright sparkles as he drew near from composites that made up the stone.

He snagged a rocky formation with his free hand and held it long enough to shove his great hammer into the leather holder on his back.

It worked, but he could feel his need to breathe building. In a pause of indecision, the muffled thunder of the waterfall hitting the surface above him sounded louder in water.

He eyed the surface above. Twilight had descended. With the loss of natural light, the clear pool became a murky dungeon, despite his dwarven sight.

Fish zipped out of his way. Plants waved as he dove deeper. Only one thought remained: he had to find Shamira and Cy.

The light from below grew brighter the closer to the bottom he came. Muffled sounds and voices became louder as he approached. And then, he heard a baby giggle.

Shamira was alive!

Listening intently, he searched the dark gray waters following the sound like breadcrumbs on a path through the woods, focusing of nothing else. The closer to the light he came, the more Ord realized how little air he had left, but he refused to stop. Grabbing the edge of an outcropping near the bottom, he pulled himself around and stared with round eyes.

Iridescent rocks reflected the light of a glowing crystal. Shamira floated in the arms of Cy. The baby gurgled and played as if nothing was wrong. The dwarf moved closer but dared not open his mouth to speak for fear he would drown.

His lungs had reached their limits. He could feel the heaving as they fought to make him breathe in air.

I can't turn back. I must save Shamira.

Within touching range, the water sprite cupped Shamira in one arm and placed a hand on Ord's shoulder. "Breathe," she commanded.

Unable to keep it contained anymore, Ord blurted out, "But I can't."

Sweet air filled his lungs. Despite the sensation, Ord gawked at his hands as he moved them around as easily as he could on the surface. He shook his head, trying to believe what he could not deny.

I am dry, completely dry, floating in the depths of a water basin.

These types of things had been recorded in the myths he had read in the library but never had any dwarf that he knew experienced such a thing. However, only one thought stayed in his mind.

He growled. "My daughter, please."

Cy sighed watching Shamira play and then gave a single nod. "She is yours. I will fulfill the agreement, despite the actions of the spiders."

Ord grasped the child to him, holding her with both arms. She was such a tiny bundle of cloth in such a precariousness situation. His own circumstances were not lost to his mind. All Cy had to do was remove her hand from his shoulder, and he could drown along with the child.

"Thank you." He said, still wary and biting back his anger.

The water sprite simply nodded in understanding.

He hesitated. She was not his enemy. His enemies were the spiders. "Since the spiders did not agree, what will they do now?"

"There is a second entrance to the spider caves along the top of the cliff," she said. "You must return and warn your friends. Once the arachnids realize you did not die, they will come for all of you more quickly."

"Now," the water sprite warned, "take a deep breath. When my hand is gone, so will the air leave from around your body. You must swim to the top as quickly as you can. If you stay toward the left side, under the shadow of the waterfall, you may reach the surface and your friends in time to save them."

The dwarf slowly nodded, considering her words. "Wait. What of Shamira? I know to hold my breath, but she may not."

The water sprite smiled. "To the baby goblin, I have given the gift of water-breathing. It is something someone can receive only if they can suspend their disbelief."

Ord swallowed, tightening his close hold on Shamira. He looked at the water around them. Though the outcroppings in the pool could be used as stairs, none went high enough on this side for him to reach the surface.

What choice do I have but to trust her?

Despite her assurance, he squinted at Cy remembering the stories he had heard as a child. Sprites were known for their deceptive words and misguided directions. They were never known to benefit those they offered to help. "How do I know you're telling the truth?"

"See for yourself." The sprite of the water removed her hand from his shoulder.

Ord's heart leaped into his throat as the water closed in--cold, heavy, and wet. In moments, the padding in his armor was soaked through, and he found himself weighed down to the floor of the pool.

There was no change in Shamira. He could hear her coos and gurgles as she waved her hands and watched the fishes swim about. He relaxed, but only a little.

Realizing his air was limited, he gave the nymph a nod and stroked the water using his one free arm to lift toward the surface. Though he rose a foot off the bottom, he sank far too quickly. He tried again, but the plate-mail bore him down. Even if he could use the outcroppings as stairs, he would never make the surface in time. He turned back to see Cy watching him struggle.

A slight smile crossed her face. "Your armor is too heavy. You will need to leave it behind."

Ord shook his head as the water sprite placed a hand on his arm. Words tumbled from his mouth as the air returned. "There has to be a different way."

"I could guide you." Cy frowned. "However, they will know that I have aided you. It will be seen as an act of defiance against them. The pact between the spiders and I will be broken."

He looked into her thoughtful eyes. "Isn't it time? What good is a sacred place without the people to come and worship?"

The frown on her watery face became more defined. Her eyes narrowed as she stared at nothing and then said in a faraway voice, "There was a time when children came to dance among my sisters and me. When men were drawn to be husbands to nixies who served me." She sighed. "But that time is long past in these waters . . ."

"The campsite is in danger," he said. "I must warn them before it is too late."

The water sprite nodded. "Agreed. Yet, my aid to you may assure their demise."

Without the ability to rise to the surface, he had no choice. "Please, help me."

Cy looked up at the surface with a wrinkled, watery brow. "As you wish."

Bubbles erupted around him. Ord felt lighter. Calm settled over him. The water did not push away the air, and he breathed normally. He floated without even swimming, lifting toward the surface.

Above him, a rolling reflective mirror of the underside of the water's surface gently rocked. Though he could see the depth changing as he ascended, it felt like he wasn't rising at all.

They burst through the surface of the water, and though it shifted in waves around them, it did not make him feel wet.

The water sprite towed him to the side of the pool using currents that spun around him. Irregular rocks became awkward stepping stones. This granted him a path from the murky liquid to the land near the bottom of the steps that led to the hollow. What little light shone to guide his path came from a crescent moon shining above them in the sky.

The dwarf stepped up on the side of the pool and found Shamira dry and warm. The pads inside his armor were dry as well, there was no water in his boots, and the smell of battle was gone. He turned to spot the water sprite, her body from the waist up visible as her transparent form caught the moonlight giving her a slight glow.

Shamira waved her hands in the waterfall's mist, and though it touched her skin, she did not appear to feel the cold nor did the droplets bother her as they touched her face.

The water filled air from the waterfall descended upon his beard, creating tiny sparkles of moonlight. He nodded toward Cy. "Thank you."

She paused as if considering something and then said in a warm voice, "You should hurry to the others." She slipped beneath the water and became part of the pool.

"The others," he said to Shamira, turning toward the campsite. "Are we too late?"

Ord rushed to get around the protruding edge of the mountain and sped on until the bluff's angle changed and the mist from the waterfall was blocked. The reddish-yellow glow of their campsite fire reflected against the cliff face in the darkness.

Aidan met his hurried steps with a sneer but did not look up from what he was doing. In a quiet voice he said, "Don't you think it's a little late for a walk with the baby?" The horses anxiously neighed as Aidan unhooked the driving harness off the first horse in the pair.

Relief swept through Ord at seeing Aidan by the wagon and Jada on the sleeping mat. Yet, at the same time, he knew it was the calm before the storm.

Ord did not keep his own voice quiet. "Be ready." He moved to the farthest edge of the west side of the camp and traced the stones Jada had set to protect them, checking for any which might be out of place.

The obscure forest of trees and shrubs beyond the campsite had eyes of its own. Small animals, from foxes to mice, skittered away through the brush. Larger animals, deer and elk, dashed through the forest to distance themselves from the campsite. His dwarven sight picked up slight variations in the dark terrain and even slighter movements in their direction as long, straight, branch-like legs opened and closed creeping through the forest toward the camp.

Leaves shifted in ways the wind could not account for. Tree limbs dipped in unexplained directions. His ears could not hear anything, but he knew they were there. Holding Shamira away from the perimeter, he stepped backward toward the wagon as hundreds of beady red eyes opened to catch the firelight and then appeared to vanish.

Ord bumped into the side of the wagon. "We are about to have *friends* over."

A slight twitter came from the outer edges of the forest. Twigs snapped in the darkness. Dirt sprinkled down from somewhere above the cliff face.

Aidan huffed. He looked up from the horses and toward Ord. Placing one hand on the horse he had been removing the driving harness from, he steadied the horse's abrupt nervous stomp. "I told you, no more friends. Why can't you get it through your thick dwarven brain?"

"Listen," Ord growled, "your stupidity has already cost us. Just pay attention."

With the rising of their voices, Jada stirred. Startled, she blinked away her sleep and sat up with a puzzled look on her face as she took in her surroundings. "What's happening?"

Dust sprinkled down on the camp from the edge of the cliff above them. Bits of plants landed in the fire, smoked, and then burst into flame.

Ord gazed up, but whatever moved on the cliff had already shied away from the edge.

Jada coughed and dusted out the dirt and grass that had fallen into her hair. She gazed at the mat she sat on as if reorienting herself, and then she looked to Ord and Aidan.

"Ord is what is happening," Aidan said with a snarl. "Not only does he think something is about to attack us, but he made enough noise to wake you up."

The twitter grew louder still. Even the crickets stopped to listen. Aidan frowned, turning his head to listen better to the forest beyond the protective barrier and reconsidering his own words.

With her eyes, Jada followed the smooth stones from the east side of the camp by the pool to the west side of the camp where they touched the mountain. In the darkness, their faint glow had brightened.

"Only those things we need can get through," she said. Despite her calm voice, she stood up and peered at the forest beyond their camp.

Ord threw a nod at Aidan. "Perhaps you'd like to have a closer look?" He pointed at the forest. "Be my guest. But I suggest you take your weapon and stay near. We may have to save your skin."

Aidan's face took on a tinge of red. He snatched up his bow, readied an arrow to the string, but did not draw back. "If it will help put your mind at ease, milord," he gave Ord a mock bow, "but of course I will scare away the phantom monsters."

He walked toward the line of stones and raised his foot to step over the line.

"Wait." Jada pointed to the trail they had come through to the campsite. One dark image followed by two followed by many worked their way in a line walking closer to the border of stones that she had laid. The moving of their legs, legs almost the same color as the darkness, made it difficult, even with Ord's dwarven vision, to see how close they had progressed toward the camp.

From the forest beyond the campsite to both sides of the trail, the red eyes Ord had spotted before appeared two by two reflecting the yellow glow of Aidan's firepit.

The arachnids in the darkness chittered. The chittering, whispering voices created similar sounds Ord had heard in the hollow under the waterfall. A shiver went up his dwarven spine. He didn't have to know the meaning to understand what they wanted.

Attack, subdue, and take alive.

Two spiders leaped from the gloomy forest toward the camp. They reached the edge of the stones Jada had so carefully placed and slammed into her invisible magic wall, their front two legs crumping as the middle of their body bent from the unseen protection.

Other spiders pounced in behind the first two spiders, now more wary, and tested every angle by varying the height of their leaps. But in each case, they tumbled back to the ground unable to get above the barrier.

The horses attempted to jerk away from the spiders. But with the wagon harnesses still partially attached and the yokes firm around their necks, with the mountains' bulk in front and no easy way to turn around, they had no direction to go.

They struggled to turn with their noses an inch from the cliff face. The wagon creaked. The horses neighed, lifting their heads in terror with eyes wide open.

Aidan dropped the arrow he held into his quiver, shouldered his bow, and placed a hand on the horse beside him while reaching for the part of the driving harness he had removed.

The horse shifted, stomping its feet.

"Whoa." He patted the horse nearest to him while hurriedly buckling the driving harness back in place.

Spiders continued to leap at the camp even knowing the invisible barrier was in place. They stacked upon each other creating a living, squirming pile that grew ever higher as the arachnids searched for a limit to the barrier's height.

Ord, still holding Shamira firmly to him, even more so now, stepped closer to Jada. "What do we do?"

"Nothing," Aidan snapped as he finished reattaching the driving harness.

Though still with wide eyes and throwing glances at the spiders' pile beyond the campsite, the horses struggled less against their bonds as the onslaught seemed to be at bay.

Aidan stared in disbelief, pulling out the arrow he had placed in his quiver. "They can't get over. It's a wall of magic, not brick or stone. The higher they climb, the taller the wall becomes." He looked toward Jada, the corner of his eyes wrinkling in concern. "You are not rested enough for this."

"We all do what we must," she answered, drawing in slow breaths. "They are a relentless foe. A wall will not be enough. I sense . . ." She glanced toward the pool. "They are controlled by another. We must end this quickly."

Though the spiders were on the other side of the invisible magic wall, their presence sent a ghastly tremble through Ord's body, which he prayed Shamira did not feel. He had faced only seven in the cavern, and it was through the ravens' help he had escaped.

The spindly legs of the piled arachnids shifted in a living mass. They used each other to reach up higher into the air, flowing in a curved pattern like a vine growing up a house wall. The base thickened but not as quickly as it should. When the living spider vine became too tall to balance, the arachnids crashed down.

Legs snapped. Bodies broke. Those not damaged from the fall climbed again while the spiders that could not climb became the base of a whole new, thicker vine.

"They're not giving up." Ord tightened his jaw. "They'll find another way."

A soft sound, out of place among the spiders' attack, drew his attention. He turned toward the campsite's east side, where the waterfall fell into the pool, and strode that direction.

The mist coated his armor in glistening tiny dots as he realized the soft sound was made up of low tapping echoes. He took in the edge of the pool with his gaze, and slowly looked up. Thin spindly legs attempted to thrust through the water's downpour that hid the hollow's entrance at the top of the stairs. The roar of the waterfall seemed louder to his dwarven ears than when he had first heard it during the daylight hours. However, none of this explained the tapping.

They are determined, he thought. *They will find a way.*

He stepped farther from the waterfall until the mist could no longer reach him and caught the orange glow of the firelight reflecting from the side of his armor.

Bits of rock peppered down from the cliff that guarded the back of their campsite. The rock bounced from small ledge to small ledge sprinkling on the horses. Despite Aidan's presence by the front of the wagon, the horses nervously stomped the ground.

Near the hollow, a loud twitter came from the top of the stairs. Three spindly black forms thrust two-thirds through the portion of the waterfall that protected the hollow's entrance.

The falling water rumbled in a way Ord had never heard. The protective torrent of water, gleaming in the moonlight, frothed. From above the hollow, a large wave struck against the cliff wall bringing down loose dirt and rock to mix with the water.

The rock pelted the bodies of the spiders, striking at their legs, abdomen, and eyes, before sweeping them down the waterfall where they plunged into the pool. The last vestige of the spiders vanished into the water's depths.

The whispers became louder above the camp. Against the starry night, thin reflective strings appeared as if from nowhere while dark spidery shapes leaped from one location to the next.

Ord hollered toward the campsite. "I hope this barrier has a top, too."

CHAPTER 8

Jada gazed up, lifting her hands. She moved her lips, but no sound came from her throat.

Aidan eyed the sky above them with bow in hand, arrow nocked. The whispering voices of the spiders came from everywhere. Drawing back his bow, he released the string.

Twang.

A spider squealed above them. He spotted Ord on the east side of the camp in the direction of the waterfall and glowered at him. He raised his voice to be heard over the spiders' twitters. "Don't say it."

Ord shook his head and stepped sideways toward the middle of the camp while watching the sky above. "If we live through this," he chuckled, "you can thank me later."

With his free hand, Ord reached back and pulled the hammer from its place on his back while keeping Shamira tucked close in his other arm. The metal of the hammer's shaft felt comforting in his gauntleted grip. The weight of the weapon was balanced. But never had he fought with a child in one arm.

He meant to only glance down to check on Shamira, but his eyes locked with hers. Those big round eyes that seemed to know more than what she could possibly understand.

She belongs in a nursery, not on a battlefield.

He swallowed.

By all the gods, she will not die today.

Shamira continued to stare up at him with her wide eyes. Not a cry left her lips. Not a nervous shiver went through her body.

What can this possibly mean?

Even with the crazy situation of the water sprite, she had seemed to have known about Cy's good heart and not been afraid.

Did she discern something else about this situation, too? Who is this human-goblin child?

Jada gasped and Ord broke eye contact with Shamira to take in the rest of the camp.

The female dark elf raised her hands higher. The ring on her right hand caught the firelight, the same ring he had noticed before. She chanted faster, continuing to move her lips without sound.

The squirming spider wall toppled beyond the invisible barrier, yet this time as the spiders fell, their legs snapped, and their bodies stuck the ground like boulders. It was as if each spider weighed at least ten times their own normal weight.

A glowing sheen rippled through the invisible barrier, and Jada staggered though she remained on her feet.

Aidan shot his bow. A spider screamed. He aimed up into the darkness and launched another arrow toward the dark sky.

The spiders that had survived the fall regrouped. More chittering voices came from the forest. Multiple spiders crunched through the leaves as they no longer tried to hide their numbers. Thousands of red eyes reflected in the firelight.

To the immediate east, none of the spiders attempted to circumvent Jada's invisible wall where it touched the pool. To do so would have required them to walk on water.

But there was another route, a longer route. It was the one Aidan had used to get to the other side of the pool beyond the basin.

A small path circumvented the water basin under the waterfall. A narrow trail, it traveled toward the ravens' nesting location and skirted between the edge of the basin and the foot of the mountain. After seeing what the ravens had done to the spiders with their calls, the chance of the spiders coming that way seemed slim to Ord.

But slim is always a possibility, he thought.

He glanced down at Shamira. "It's up to you and me to help guard the east side."

Ord walked toward the east and picked a position which would allow him to watch the campsite, the waterfall, and the hollow.

Another arachnid thrust through the water that poured down to guard the hollow's entrance. Its front legs reached farther than the others, but before it could get its footing, in a froth of spray, water, and rock, it tumbled down into the pool.

The trail seemed safe for the moment, but he could not allow the spiders to get out of the hollow. With his hammer and Shamira still in hand, he hurried to the foot of the stairs and started up, clenching his jaw.

I will let no spiders get through.

The mist of the waterfall felt cooler than before. The stairs were laced in shadows. Even without his dark vision kicking in, he could see them reflecting distorted moonlight.

A third spider lurched into the falling deluge from the hollow's mouth. It clung to the rocks as the liquid beat upon its body.

The spider's front legs trembled. Its body shook. But gradually, it pulled forward, sliding through the downward force and onto the top of the stairs. While it still recovered, Ord swung his hammer.

The spider lurched back to avoid the first swing and whisked its two front legs like bats at Ord's head.

Ord ducked, swerved too close to the edge of the stairs, and skated away from the drop-off, catching a glimpse of the pool far below. As the spider's right front leg recoiled for another strike, he cracked his hammer against the spider's exoskeleton head.

The spider staggered. Blue ichor oozed from the hit. It swung again at Ord, but its aim was drunkenly off, straining to keep upright.

Ord swung a second time, breaking through the exoskeleton.

Crunch.

The arachnid's legs collapsed. Part of its body slipped backward into the falling water. The friction caught the spider's body and dragged it down. The pool depths swallowed it whole.

Squealing echoed from beyond the wall of liquid, which guarded the hollow. Dark spider images scampered both toward Ord and away. A spider, at least twice the size of the others, rose in the blackness, its image distorted by the water as it fell.

Twittering followed. The smaller spiders left one by one. With its red eyes, the larger spider continued to face the stairs, adjusting its stance to always face Ord.

Ord swallowed. An uneasy feeling rippled through his spine. He stepped back, eyed the larger spider, and listened for the others.

The distant shuffling sound of many legs faded away. The whispers in the hollow fell until they barely existed at all, yet the image of the larger spider remained, unmoving, staring at him.

The ground he stood on momentarily shook, and then the shaking subsided once more. Still watching the large dark spider through the curtain of water, he leaned back against the rock wall with hammer ready. The moment his back touched the wall, his armor vibrated from his torso to his gauntlets.

He stood up straight and then slowly leaned back. The vibration happened again.

What were these spiders up to?

He glanced up at the cliff edge some fifty feet higher. No glowing spider strands caught the moonlight. No dark spider bodies appeared checking over the edge.

He looked nervously back at the large spider beyond the wall of water. It stood there, unmoving, waiting.

But waiting for what?

The vibration in his armor stopped but tapping began, and that tap came from inside the mountain.

Ord put down the hammer and placed a hand on the wall beside the stairs.

The tapping is definitely from within the rock wall.

Leaning closer, he placed the side of his helmet to the cliff wall. The metal helped amplify the sound for his ear. Slowly moving, he placed his helmet against the wall time and again as he walked backward down the stairs, trying to identify the direction of the tapping.

Stopping about the middle of the stairs, the sound took on a fuller composure. It came from this side of the waterfall, it did not originate as an echo, and it was very close. Based upon his conversation with the water sprite, Cy, there was no telling how riddled the cliff was with spider passageways.

The tap grew louder the longer he waited. The frequency of the tapping increased. He remembered what had happened to the large rock he had jammed into the hole in the hollow, tightened his jaw, and spotted his hammer he had left above him on the stairs.

Ord rushed up the rock steps, splashing in the puddles of water formed by the waterfall mist. With every step he distorted the reflected moonlight like an omen. Snatching up his war hammer, he turned and held it ready, torn between guarding the hollow and stopping the terror that was about to be unleashed.

Fractures formed across a ten-foot diameter of the rock wall along the middle of the stairs. At the same time, a large crack raced in a jagged circle around the fractures.

The watery figure of the female sprite, Cy, flowed from the waterfall and took shape beside him. "You must flee. I will deal with these."

Shaking his head, Ord said, "They will know you have broken your agreement."

The nymph smiled sadly, looking back at the large spider contained within the hollow. "The situation was known when I let Shamira drop into my pool. I had simply ignored what I already knew to be true."

Ord pursed his lips and said, "You cannot hold them all back alone."

"Go to your friends." Her voice softened as her eyes drifted to Shamira. "Your concern is touching, but I *will* deal with the spiders from the east side. You and your friends must deal with those that approach from elsewhere."

The dwarf nodded and said, "Thank you."

He hurried down the stairs. Before he reached the bottom, a chip flew from the fractured wall and bounced into the pool. A second chip followed, striking the stairs before bouncing down to land near Ord's feet.

After the third chip, the tapping echoed off the rock cliff wall across the pool despite the waterfall's turbulent voice. As the fourth chip fell, a spider poked its leg through, withdrew, and a ten-foot diameter of wall collapsed.

Rock tumbled behind Ord, bouncing from step to step as if racing to see which of them could make it to the bottom first.

He leaped the last three stairs, landed firmly on the ground, and heard a large splash as he turned the corner into the camp. The mist of the waterfall fell away replaced by the glow of the firelight.

Ord caught sight of the others. Aidan shot arrows up into the air at spiders descending on strands of reflected moonlight.

Jada had her eyes closed. Her brows were furrowed in deep concentration. A slight tremor shook her uplifted hands. Even in the moonlight, he could tell her body was paler than when she had woken.

Aidan glared a dark eye toward Ord. "I take it the east side *is* secure?"

Ord didn't like the dark elf's haughty implication. The dwarf growled back, "It is covered."

Jada, though her eyelids remained closed, rasped out in a high-pitched whisper, "Load the wagon. At the first opportunity, we *must* break through."

Aidan and Ord spoke at the same time, "To where?" They glanced at each other.

She sighed, all the weariness of the moment playing at the edges of her concentration as the tremors in her hands grew, but she said nothing more to them.

Aidan turned toward Ord before letting another arrow fly. "That means just do it. It will explain itself."

Ord blinked. It was the second time Aidan had spoken halfway civil to him in a distracted moment. Ord could see the concern written upon Aidan's dark elf features.

The male elf nocked another arrow. As if snapping out of his brief courtesy, the disdain returned as he said, "And since I'm rather busy, it looks like you get the job, dwarf."

Aidan's bow twanged. A spider screeched. Aidan drew another arrow.

The jump between Aidan's temperaments made Ord wonder what was going on. He checked the wagon. Most of their items were still within.

Turning to the sleeping mats and satchel, he slipped his hammer into the leather harness he wore on his back and eyed the surrounding area. There were no spiders, and Aidan was keeping those that descended at bay.

He placed Shamira on the ground and reached for Jada's sleeping mat. With both hands, he rolled Jada's mat, secured it at the ends, and tossed it toward the wagon. None of the other mats had been unrolled, so a quick pitch had them land in the back as well. He picked up the satchel, walked it over, and dropped it into the wagon bed near the secured wooden container.

The dwarf spotted some stiff bread he had forgotten to throw into the satchel but ignored it. Instead, he grabbed Shamira's wooden bowl, and spun it toward the wagon.

Thud. Thunk. Bounce.

Sure he made the throw, he said, "Loaded up."

Aidan swore. "Watch out."

Crash.

Sparks of flame jumped in every direction. Ord spun around. The firepit was gone beneath the body of a spider with an arrow sticking out through the spider's head. The legs wiggled in its death throes, but it did not stand up. A silver strand from its tail end caught the moonlight and floated to the ground. It shriveled from the heat of the firepit.

Smoke issued from around the spider's body, and the stench of its burning carcass seeped across the camp.

Shamira wailed from above them.

Ord darted over to where Shamira had been, but the baby was gone. He glanced up and for a precious second forgot to breathe.

In the grip of two powerful front spider legs, Shamira was held by a spider clinging to a moonlit strand. The spider used its back four legs to work itself up the silver thread toward the top of the cliff.

Ord reached back and snatched the war hammer from its harness. Eyeing the speed of the spider's climb, judging the weight of the great war hammer, he slung the hammer into the air using both hands.

It spun end over end, the head and the handle of compensating weight, center balanced as all proper dwarf weapons should be. It hit the spider's tail segment and broke the spider's grip on the silver thread.

Spider, baby, and war hammer plummeted toward the ground. The war hammer was a few seconds behind the spider, and as gravity conquered the hammer's upward thrust, it started to fall.

Shamira no longer wailed as she fell through the air. The wrapping that protected her head flapped in the wind. The spider stretched out with its two most forward front legs and attempted to snag her, but she was inches beyond the spider's grasp.

Ord snatched Shamira out of the air with the spider's body only moments above him and ducked the swipe of the spider's two front legs. With no time to run, he leaped from beneath the spider, tucked, and rolled despite his heavy armor.

Bang.

The spider's front legs lashed out with a glancing blow to the back of Ord's plate-mail armor.

Thud.

The spider hit the ground on its eight legs managing to absorb the impact without breaking an appendage.

Twang.

Aidan's dark elf arrow stabbed through the spider's brain with enough force to drag the spider's body to Ord's right.

Thud. Crunch.

Ord snatched up his war hammer from where it hit the ground and slammed it into the spider's head. The spider went limp. Above them, its silver thread whisked away in the wind.

"Hurry, Ord," Jada shouted. Sweat ran in droplets down the sides of her temples. Her arms trembled. Her eyes were still closed tight. "The time is now."

Rocks tumbled down by the basin. Water flowed about an inch deep around the corner into the camp picking up dust and dirt, sand and pebbles, like a piece of flypaper. The chittering of the spiders grew louder as a cluster of drenched arachnids rounded the east rock face and picked up speed toward Jada, Aidan, Ord, and Shamira.

Aidan exclaimed furiously, "I thought you said it was covered!" With jaw clenched, he swung the bow horizontal and let loose three arrows. None missed their mark, but they were so few among so many.

The words had barely left the male elf's mouth when a huge wave of water rose from the basin to the east behind the charging spiders. It lifted higher than the stacks of spiders kept out by the invisible magic barrier to the front of the camp, crested in frothing white, and plunged toward the land.

Ord turned his shocked gaze from the wall of water and dashed toward the wagon. "Incoming!"

Jada twisted at the waist to face the flood and tripped as she turned back to run.

Aidan rushed around the rear of the wagon trying to reach Jada in time.

The water hit. Arachnids swirled, sucked in by the liquid. The spiders rolled along with the loose dirt, caught as if trapped in a thick tar.

Fish struggled against the current, thrown alongside their unwanted eight-legged guests. As the flood enveloped the east side of the camp, just as it reached within ten feet of Jada, the water lifted toward the sky once more.

Spiders, fish, dirt, and rocks swept upward caught in a watery world that seemed separate from the laws of nature as Ord knew them. Curving once more in the air, the wave dropped backwards. The frothing end slammed into the basin taking everything it picked up with it.

A roar came from the forest beyond the stones of protection. Wood snapped. Tree trunks were slammed aside.

In the forest to the front of the camp, Ord could see the dark spider bodies thrown left and right, crashing against tree trunks or becoming impaled by large limbs.

Still hurrying to Jada's side, Aidan hefted his bow upwards at the next descending spider. "What now?" He skewered the arachnid that hung by its silver thread. "Jada?"

"I'm fine. Keep watching the sky above us." She got to her feet, staggering slightly, and raised her hands once more. A thin smile crossed Jada's lips. "Now is our way out."

The large bulk of Vindr appeared at the forest edge. He roared at the wall of spiders, raised both large fists and crunched the arachnids unlucky enough to be caught against the ground.

Blue goo covered both his hands and the earth. Most of the spiders tried to flee. Of those that did not, he snatched one in each hand and slapped them together. Light blue spider ichor shot both directions.

Frida stepped from behind the stone troll swinging a massive club. A rucksack lay upon her back. She smacked one of the spiders Vindr had missed, nailing it to the ground as its exoskeleton crumpled.

The spider went still.

With bright eyes, she beamed at Ord. "Thought you might need some help when we heard all the commotion."

Jada's voice cut through the tumult before Ord could respond. "To the wagon. Everyone, now."

The moment Jada dropped her hands, a clutter of dark spider shapes started their descent from the top of the cliff above the camp. Aidan's bow twanged, arrow after arrow, clearing the area above the others, the wagon and the horses, allowing Jada time to get to their transportation.

Arachnids touched down on both sides of the encampment.

The horses attempted to rear up but were held in place by the driving harness and straps.

Ord swung his hammer taking his stance on the east side of the wagon, breaking spider legs and heads, keeping Shamira tucked tight in his other arm.

Aidan shot his bow, steadfastly striding to the west side of the wagon. Taking aim at the dark descending opponents, he fired his bow with deadly accuracy.

Vindr scooped up spiders and crushed them together, paused only momentarily to lick his fingers, and grabbed another set. He grumbled some words at Frida in the troll tongue Ord was not familiar with.

Frida bashed the head of one spider after another, the large heavy club looking odd in her dainty hands. She shouted up at her cousin answering his spoken question, "Not until after we finish. Then you can eat all you want."

The blue ichor flowed like a rising river mixing with the soil and creating dark brown globs of mess. The strong odor of dead decaying fish, the stench of the spider blood, rose to the west and east of them carried by the winds like a massive cloud.

Gurgling came from the sky above. It grew louder by the second. Silhouetted against the stars and the moonlight, ravens dived, screeching at the same pitch that had driven the spiders away in the hollow.

Twittering spiders scampered back. Those that froze in place Vindr and Frida crushed. The screech of the ravens drove the remaining spiders to flee backward, bumping into the mountain's surface only to be smashed, crunched, or shot by an arrow.

With the ravens came the calm. Ord felt his lungs burn as he gulped air to fill them and gagged at the smell of the spider blood. Satisfied that the retreat was real, he laid his hammer beside him ready to grab it up once more.

Frida turned to Vindr. "Let's see how many we can gather for your dinner." She grinned and led him back into the forest.

Jada took her time climbing into the wagon, pale in the moonlight and holding on to give herself support. Using the back of the driving seat to steady herself, she slowly turned, gazing at the scene of dead spiders and blue spider blood, until she spotted Ord leaning against the side of the wagon.

"Let me guard the child," she said. "There is something you must do." She extended both arms for Shamira.

Ord hesitated. "I almost lost Shamira twice this day, and you are in no condition to watch a child."

Yet, it was more than these two things that cluttered his thoughts. Jada's abruptness and urgency bespoke of something too dangerous for the baby to go along. He warily watched the dark elf.

"What do you have in mind?" he asked.

"I need you to go to the pool." She reached into the crate and withdrew an empty waterskin. "Dip this in and bring it here." She laid the waterskin over the wagon side.

The dwarf shook his head. "We have caused enough harm to this place. We cannot take from the water sprite again. We owe her at least that."

Jada met his gaze. "There will be no harm," she assured, shifting closer to him and placing a hand on his shoulder. "Only peace for what has been disturbed. Recompense for what has been done."

Ord looked down at Shamira, remembering the spider that lifted her up into the night sky. His insides hurt. His heart beat faster.

"Trust me, Ord," she soothed. "What happened here was meant to be."

But how well do I really know you, he thought. *Can trust you're on my side and Shamira's?*

He glanced at Aidan who still watched the south and west sides for anything resembling a returning spider.

Either of you? he continued in his thoughts. *To be frank, I feel more comfortable with Frida.*

The realization shocked him. Ord looked to the south, the front of the camp, but saw no sign of Frida or her cousin, Vindr.

"How can I trust you," he said, "when you aren't completely honest with me?"

Jada looked away. "I would rather you be safe in ignorance . . ."

Ord bristled.

Removing her hand from his shoulder, she held it up asking silent permission to finish. ". . . for the moment. There will come a time when you will understand it all. Just . . . not . . . now."

Jada looked deeply into his dwarven eyes. "As I told Frida, listen to your heart and you will know the truth. We are not lying, Ord. We are not hiding anything that would be for your benefit." She glanced at Shamira. "Or hers."

He fought to separate his fears from his feelings, a kaleidoscope of textures all forming a picture that made no sense. The strange knowing that he should trust her was there, and yet, something was amiss. A dark spot in the kaleidoscope's colors trying to stay out of sight.

Leaning back but with arms extended to receive the baby, she quietly said, "Trust me or not, it is your choice, but getting the water will be so much easier without Shamira. This I know."

"Why?" he asked. "If this Sight thing gives you so much information, where is the rest?"

"It gives what it must. That is all one can say." Jada looked up at the stars. "You will understand in time."

"You keep saying that."

But she was right. Despite the blanks, she had never been wrong yet.

He slowly placed Shamira in her arms.

She held the child close, smiling down at the baby. "Time is short. You must hurry."

It doesn't make sense, he thought. *How could destroying a person's home, violating their sanctuary, and corrupting a way of life be meant to be?*

A glimmer of something crossed his thoughts. Not a feeling exactly, but an assurance of what he had to do.

I need to dip the waterskin into the Cy's pool but have no idea why.

"Hurry." Jada looked at Ord with wide eyes.

Aidan launched an arrow at a spider while it leaped from one crevice to another in the side of the cliff above their camp. The spider jerked to a stop and then slowly fell backward off the mountain until it smashed into the ground on the east side of the campsite. "We don't have all night, dwarf," Aidan said. "Until we are out of here, the battle is not over."

"Well said, elf." Ord turned back to Jada and pointed to Shamira. "I will be back."

He turned toward the east and started into a jog, avoiding the arachnid bodies that had fallen from the sky. Black arrows of elven origin stood in their unmoving corpses. Crushed heads and broken legs littered the ground like a dwarven obstacle course. He grinned.

The ravens will be feasting in the morning.

Reaching the edge of the water sprite's home, he leaned over the side of the pool. Dark spidery shapes walked beneath the waves across the basin's bottom.

The spiders are contained but have not drowned.

He swallowed.

Can these live underwater?

The thought made him shudder. The idea that everything the water sprite had done to help them might have been in vain made him feel even worse inside.

We have destroyed her home.

The crystal light of the water sprite that once shined in the midst of the basin was gone.

What had the water sprite given up to free them? Had it been her life?

He dipped the waterskin into the basin, allowed it to fill, and tried to make sense of Jada's request. It still felt like sacrilege to him after what they had done to Cy's home.

Was this a ritual? An apology? How could any of this make better what had happened?

The chittering of the spiders had stopped after the ravens had descended, but he felt their presence near even though he could not see them. He eyed the edges of the forest as the waterskin filled. He glanced around at the mountain tops.

They were watching, but after the ravens had screeched, they had been driven to wait in stealth.

As the waterskin expanded to full, Ord hefted the load and closed it with a cork. His stomach loudly grumbled. His arms felt weighty. With the loss of the adrenaline of battle, the mass of this one bag felt heavier than the hammer he had been swinging.

Regardless, it is time to go.

Rising, he took one last view the stairs, which led up to the hollow.

Is the large spider, who had watched from the hollow, looking upon me even now?

The shadows shifted. A glint of moonlight struck a round disk-like gem glistening at the foot of the waterfall. Ord peered closer.

The round gem moved silently toward him from the darkness. The moonlight that struck it made him realize it was not a gem at all but part of a much larger creature whose silhouette took shape before his dwarven eyes.

An enormous black shape with eight hairy legs materialized from the shadows, towering above him. Despite its size, there had been no warning: not a tapping of its feet upon the rock or a single splash of water. In a whispering voice, it accused him, opening its red eyes, "You. You have killed my children."

Ord tightened his grip on his war hammer, but before he could blink, the spider jumped.

Oofff!

He exhaled as his body slammed backward against the ground, breaking his grip on the waterskin. The waterskin flew from his hand, bounced twice, and landed where he could not see. By his fingertips, he barely clung to his family war hammer.

The spider jabbed at him with its thick lance-like fangs, fangs that were immensely larger than what its children had used.

He rolled to his right side as he scrambled to walk his fingers up the war hammer grip and caught sight of the basin a mere three feet from him.

The spider jabbed the ground behind him, its fangs cutting into the earth. It pulled back, spitting dirt from its mouth.

Ord firmly grasped the handle of the great war hammer.

Clang.

The spider knocked him from his side to his back, a glancing blow, but enough to jar his bones.

Ord parried the fangs with his war hammer held horizontal to his body as the spider struck a third time.

Clang.

He shifted from block to attack, but the spider used its legs to lift its body out of reach even though it was directly over him.

The spider angled the attack. Like two fencer's crossing blades, the hammer in Ord's hands and the fangs of the spider rang together. But before Ord could parry again, the spider jabbed at him with a downward death thrust.

Bang.

Ord's armor rang with the spider's strike. His ribs ached as the jarring vibration transferred through his body to the ground. Though the spider could not pierce his armor and the padding inside his plate-mail helped absorb the shock, he felt like a turtle in a shell trapped on his back. In a momentary lull between the spider's attacks, Ord tried to rise.

Bang.

The spider knocked him against the earth taking his breath with the strike.

He struggled to inhale allowing his gaze to sweep the area for any other advantage. The pool was within two feet this time. He rolled toward the basin.

Bang.

The spider jabbed downward and almost succeeded in separating Ord's helmet from his body armor despite the strap that held it on. One fang scraped along the helmet's left bottom edge, jerking the helmet cockeyed and pulling the leather strap tightly across Ord's throat.

He gasped before the pressure released as both fangs rose and then plunged into the ground on either side of his neck.

Clang.

The enormous spider slammed its left front leg against Ord's chest, forcing him from his side to his back.

Ord stared up at the spider's underside noting with his peripheral vision that he could reach the pool with his right hand.

Hissing, the mother of the arachnids used one leg to keep Ord from getting closer to the pool while the other rolled him away from it.

He tucked his arms near his body, holding his war hammer close, waiting for a place to strike, and playing dead.

After rolling him about ten feet from the pool edge, she whispered in the common tongue, "Playtime is over."

He swung his hammer with his left hand to hit the spider's leg, but she pinned his left arm cutting off the motion and jarring the war hammer out of his grasp.

Ord kicked but she remained out of reach, taunting him. His shoulders ached. The pain increased as she shifted her weight on his arm until he had no choice but to lie still.

Using her back legs, she pulled a milky-white thread from her body and extended it toward him. Her whisper rose in volume until it sounded like a cackle. "You will be the food for a whole new set of spiderlings."

Frida's voice chimed in, "Wanna bet?" She swung her club above Ord's head.

Crack.

It connected with the closest spindly leg, the one pinning Ord's left arm. The whole appendage vibrated but did not move.

"Silly troll," the huge spider hissed. "Your kind exists in these mountains only by my will." It clacked its chelicerae together. "You will be next."

Releasing Ord's left arm, the spider flicked the leg, which had been holding Ord, out at Frida.

Frida leaped back swerving to avoid the appendage as it sliced the air in front of her.

Ord rolled to his left side and stretched toward his war hammer in his right hand.

Thud.

The spider pinned him, this time with his front facing the ground.

He gasped despite the plate-mail as the vibration of the hit stabbed through him. Gritting his teeth, he grunted through the pain and grabbed the handle of his weapon.

Frida sneered as she strode toward the giant spider. "It'll take more than that, pitiful wench."

The arachnid raised her whispering voice and said, "You mock me?" She lifted her body on its back legs, trembling in anger.

Ord rolled to the left as the spider's front leg released its pressure from his back.

The spider scoffed eyeing Ord's movement as if it was no concern. "I will have you both."

Her front legs descended with one leg set to crunch the dwarf into the ground and the other aimed at Frida.

Ord dodged, already on his feet because of Frida's distraction, while Frida ducked in the other direction.

Boom.

The arachnid's legs struck the empty ground on both accounts and sent ripples across the water.

The mother spider screeched as she leaped toward them, the front four legs on both sides of her body striking at Frida and Ord.

Ord struggled to keep his balance as he dodged out of the way. Frida weaved, bashing at the spider's leg each time it came close. Breathing heavily, she bellowed, "Now Vindr!"

Frida jumped sideways, away from the arachnid. Ord, seeing the huge stone troll step from around the mountain's outcropping, which led to the campsite, dove for the ground just beyond the spider's reach and landed inches from some blue ichor splattered across the ground.

Vindr stomped, his foot landing a crushing blow to the spider's pedicel, where the head of the spider met its abdomen.

Crack.

Light blue ichor sprayed in all directions as the back of the thorax and the beginning of the abdomen flattened. Luckily, the spray shot past Ord and Frida.

In its death throe, the spider wrenched sideways toward Vindr but much too slowly. A second stomp crushed the mother spider's head.

Amplified squeals came from the area inside the hollow. Skittering feet sounded against the rocks as the spiderlings frenzied.

"Come on." Frida hurried near the dwarf and extend her hand.

Ord gave her a broad smile as he finished standing to his feet, rolling his shoulders to work out the pain. "Thanks, I'll be right there."

Frida's bright smile waned. She glanced at the stairs near the hollow. "But they're coming."

He grinned. "I know. You've helped me." He caught her gaze with his own. "Now, please help Shamira and Jada. I need to know they are safe."

With wrinkled brow, Frida slowly nodded, the confusion plain on her face. She said to her cousin, "Vindr, we need to guard the wagon."

Vindr grunted. Reaching a hand down, the massive troll picked up part of the mother spider's shell and crunched it in his teeth as he turned away. The blue ichor ran down the sides of his chin and dripped upon his chest.

With her club in hand, Frida ran behind him toward the dark elves and the wagon.

Ord watched her go before taking a deep breath and . . . gagging. In the heat of the battle, he had forgotten about the blue ichor that dotted the landscape and the reason for him being here came back.

The waterskin, it could not be seen. He walked around the gigantic spider to the place where he had filled the waterskin and traced the steps of the battle to the spot where the spider had pinned him down.

The spider had . . . he turned, remembering the sudden strike that had nailed him to the ground and shivered. He had never encountered a creature that fast. At the mere thought, he could feel the ache in his back that had followed. His abused muscles needed a rest.

Looking to the west, he eyed the potential trajectories of which the waterskin could have flown from his hand and followed them one by one.

He spotted a bulge under some of the pale blue liquid. Had he not retraced every possibility, he might never have realized where it was. Ord slipped the war hammer into its sheath and gingerly picked up the covered bag.

It hadn't busted, and the cork was still tight. It had to be an odd twist of fate for that to happen.

Why does Jada want this? When is she going to tell me all the truth?

The decaying fish smell of the spider blood reached Ord's nose. He almost retched. Stirred by the lifting of the bag, the putrid spider blood smelled worse than ever.

Gurgling came from above as a raven soared near in the moonlight. Ravens were not usually nocturnal birds but had been known to hunt when the moon was full. Yet, there was another connection here he could not quite fathom hidden at the edges of his mind.

Why do they keep coming to my aid?

He forced his stomach down, fighting to ignore the smell of the blue ichor. Fortunately, what he found disgusting was quite agreeable with some of the other races, animals, and birds, trolls included. Already ravens dropped from the sky to feast on the delicious snack Vindr had so graciously provided. The cleanup would not take long.

Moving swiftly to the basin, he washed the waterskin off in the water. It cleaned the bag but cast a muddled look to what had already become a murky pool.

As the taint of the spider's blood drifted deeper, water currents hurried the blood along. Fish swam from it. It coated the rocks darkening their texture. It reached the dark spider silhouettes still at the bottom of the basin.

The spiders trapped there frenzied. Like a dog tracing down a scent, they creeped along the bottom of the basin to gather on the west side below Ord and attempted to crawl up the slippery sides.

Some climbed higher than others but all slid down to the bottom. After repeated attempts, they scrambled on top of each other rising toward the surface of the water.

Ord retrieved the bag and raced to the wagon, which had been turned around in preparation to head toward the road. He spotted Vindr, standing with his head visible above some of the lower treetops just past the forest edge. Near the base of the trunks, Frida pointed right. The tree limbs shifted. The leaves rustled. Vindr moved. Twittering grew louder.

Squeal. Crunch. Silence.

Ord was certain he heard Vindr chewing.

Aidan had the reins to the horses though his bow was near on the seat. The elf scrutinized the area around them. It seemed the trolls and the ravens had done an excellent job of driving the rest of the spiders from the campsite.

Jada held Shamira while mumbling words without a voice. She watched, ever vigilant, and searched the forest. She spotted Ord first as he hurried to the wagon. With a nod of her head she gave approval of the waterskin in his hand.

Ord climbed into the wagon bed, rolled over the sacks, and dropped into his space. The bedrolls he had tossed in, he stuffed between two burlap bags. Shamira's wooden bowl he placed in the crate. Positioning himself to face the rear and sides of the wagon, he leaned against the left inside corner and held up the waterskin he had filled, a question on his face.

Jada said, "Please place the waterskin in the crate."

"I hope it was worth it," he answered. Ord placed the waterskin in the crate and then extended his arms for Shamira.

Jada handed her back. "It is for the benefit of everyone." She took the reins from Aidan and with light tension said to the horses, "Wealayu"

The horses started forward behind the trolls.

Aidan raised his bow, searching the forest to each side. The wagon rocked. The boards creaked. After a prolonged silence he asked, "How many dwarfs does it take to get water?" He leered back, "Oh, wait. It doesn't. It takes two trolls."

"Ha," Ord said. "Next time, when I tell you there's trouble, you will listen." He glanced over his shoulder at Aidan and saw the elf's cheeks turn a shade darker under Ord's dark vision, and Ord knew Aidan's face had flushed. The dwarf pushed his point a little more. "And on top of that, you ate her fish."

Aidan glanced toward him. "No one owns the fish. All fish are a gift from Lucasta."

"They were the water sprite's fish." Ord huffed. "You stole in the name of your religion. Had you left the basin alone, none of this would have happened."

Jada shook her head. "That's not entirely accurate, Ord. You entered the hollow above the stairs."

Ord raised one eyebrow. "That wasn't the cause." He blinked. "But how did you know?"

She chuckled. "I saw it in my dreams. You are both at fault whether you like it or not. But in this instance, it was meant to be for all involved."

Ord grunted. "Including the spiders? Like the avalanche?"

She nodded with certainty. "Just like that."

The wagon passed around a tree. The road appeared closer through the tree trunks. The twittering of the spiders sounded farther away as Vindr's stomping took out another two or three.

The dwarf fought to keep the irritation out of his voice but did not succeed well. "If you knew there was going to be an issue, why didn't you warn me?" He glanced at Aidan, reluctantly. "Why didn't you warn us?"

Jada sighed. "I told you. You have to . . ."

Ord growled and then interrupted, ". . . learn on your own. You know I am raising a child, and that child's life was put in danger." Even as he finished the words, the words caught him off guard, and he paused, thinking, before continuing. "So, I would kindly appreciate being informed of any future events."

The wagon wheels rolled over the leaves crunching them. Vindr smashed another spider. Frida's club connected to the top of a spider's head just to Ord's right. With a glance toward the front, Ord spotted Aidan snicker and a smile form on Jada's face.

Jada said, "Raising a child? Why Ord, I do think you have become a real father."

For Ord, time stopped at Jada's words.

He thought, *Have I? Is this what it means to care for a child?*

Ord sighed and chuckled. He looked down into Shamira's face. In a quiet voice, he whispered, "Maybe I am. Maybe I have." Extending his gauntleted finger to the little girl, he watched her as she oohed and awed. "You know," he examined her face, "you're not bad at that."

A smile crossed the baby's face. A smell hit Ord's nose.

He cringed. "Please, let this be gas."

Both the dark elves burst out laughing.

Jada halted the wagon right before they intersected the trail.

Vindr stood on the trail in front of them chewing on a spider's exoskeleton. Blue ichor dripped down his chin. Though the smell was not as bad as in the camp, Ord hoped Vindr stayed downwind.

Frida ambled up to the side of the wagon closest to Ord. Her club casually swung in one hand as she strolled to a stop. Sniffing the air, she glanced toward Shamira with knowing eyes before pointing at the trail with her club. "Which way?"

As the laughing subsided, Jada caught her breath. She continued to smile. "To the right."

Frida raised her voice and said, "Vindr."

The huge troll glanced down from watching three ravens, which soared above the treetops and circled above the wagon.

"Hold up and let them pass." She nodded toward the left. "We'll guard the rear."

Vindr rumbled something, not in any language Ord knew. The troll stepped to the side, out of the wagon's way, looking thoughtfully toward the campsite as he swallowed the last of a spider's exoskeleton.

Ord suspected that after all the spider crushing the troll had done, it was thinking about more food.

As Jada turned the wagon to the right and started the horses down the road, Frida's cousin lumbered behind them.

As the wagon bounced, Frida tossed her club into the back of the wagon. It landed on a burlap sack and rolled into a crevice between two bags.

Jumping up on the back, she climbed inside the wagon and slid the tied sacks around until she created herself a spot across from Ord, next to the secured wooden crate at the front.

Sitting, the hulder smoothed out her skirt keeping it prim and proper. Her tail rose and fell as if it had a mind of its own.

"So," she asked, eyes bright, "the baby is yours?" A pleased smile crossed her face.

The wagon swayed as it followed the path. A squeal sounded behind them as Vindr pegged a spider trying to track their progress. Crunching followed.

Fighting a grin, but not too hard, Ord gazed down at Shamira. "It turns out she is, although I had no idea it was going to happen."

Frida snickered. "Most guys don't think it will and don't take responsibility when it does. I'm pleased you do."

He raised his head and stared at her with wide shocked eyes, chin tucked slightly. "No, not that. I'm a dwarf not a . . . a . . . I don't know what to call them. Anyway, that's not who I am. I'm true to my dwarven kind."

The smile on Frida fell away.

Ord watched it go. Swallowing, he amended, "Not that I don't like you. I just . . . I mean." He drew a deep breath and let it out slowly. "Look, you're a hulder. I am a dwarf. What type of life could evolve from that?"

Frida's voice took on an edge as she said, "Shamira's part-human, Ord. And, so are you. Don't you think I can tell the difference?" She touched her nose. "Trolls are very good at smells. It is how we hunt."

All the taunts of his boyhood came rolling back. He tightened his jaw and shifted his back straighter. "I am not human. Just because I am taller than my brethren does not mean you have to insult me."

Shamira stirred, yawning.

He glanced down and caught her round eyes staring up at him with a hint of fright. He forced himself to relax.

Shortly, she closed her eyes.

Ord glanced up at Frida and said, "I'm sorry." He wrinkled his brow while staring at the wagon floor. "That's a sore spot from my childhood. I don't appreciate people playing those kinds of games by challenging my heritage."

Lowering her voice, Frida said, "Ord." She reached forward and touched his outer leg armor. "I didn't mean to hurt your feelings." She sniffed, wrinkling her nose. "And I do believe that child needs to be changed." She held out her arms. "Would you like me to do it?"

Ord blinked. "In a moving wagon?" He gazed at the bags around them. "How are we going to wash off the . . ." He shivered. ". . . stuff?"

She smirked. "Surely, it's not as bad as all that?"

His eyes became round as he studied the female troll. "You don't know this baby. I shoved its soiled linen into the face of a bugbear. It was none too pretty."

Frida gave a cynical smile. "You hit a bugbear with the baby's diaper?"

He nodded, his look so straight-faced, she grinned.

As the amusement danced in her bright eyes, Frida asked, "Why?"

He blushed, a little embarrassed, and glanced away. "It attacked us. I felt bad, really bad, though, after I did it." A serious frown dropped over his face while his eyes grew large and round. "I had to knock it out to end its misery. Of course, I am sure it suffered more after it woke up . . ."

Frida closed her eyes and fought not to laugh. However, the more she struggled against it the more tears crept to the corners of her eyes.

When Ord thought about what he had just said, a tickle started in him, too.

A strange sound came from behind the wagon where Vindr walked. It went from a low rumble to a full fledge shake as the stone troll drew multiple sharp breaths. Vindr swayed struggling to keep his balance.

The dwarf pointed at the enormous troll. Between the jostle of the wagon and the laughing he could not stop, it was hard to focus. He took several deep breaths and finally managed to say, "What's wrong with him?"

Inhaling, Frida fought to stop laughing. Between attempts, she got out, "He's chuckling at the bugbear."

CHAPTER 9

Aidan said in a gruff voice, "What is going on?" He glanced at the back of the wagon.

Like children caught in a mischievous act, all outward noise abruptly stopped including Vindr. However, the tone of Aidan's voice could do nothing about what was happening inside them.

"Well?" Aidan glared. His eyes caught the swaying Vindr. "Tell your pet were supposed to be incognito, not alerting the countryside as to where we are."

That sobered Frida some but not completely. "He's not my pet," she stressed each word. "He's my cousin," she said more pleasantly with a hint of pride.

Ord fought to control his own laughter. He reached over with his free hand and tapped against the dark elf's traveling cape. It was still draped over the middle of the driving seat between Aidan and Jada. "It's okay, Aidan. Vindr's just laughing."

"He's exposing us more than necessary," Aidan snapped. The elf narrowed his eyes. "Calm him down, now."

Ord sighed and rolled his eyes. Frida saw the roll and chuckled again.

Aidan's countenance darkened. "I said, now."

The very real arrow in Aidan's bow told Ord what would happen if they didn't do something. Not that Ord thought the arrow could hurt Vindr, it would probably bounce off. However, the hostile feelings that might form after the dark elf acted out could hurt everyone in the group. On top of that, he genuinely liked Frida's and Vindr's company.

Ord sobered some, though a small tickle continued in the depths of his stomach. He looked to Frida. "Please." He winked and felt the laughter try to surge.

Frida giggled but swallowed hard before it went out of control. Her face became stoic although her eyes betrayed what was going on inside her. "Vindr," she said struggling not to smirk. She cleared her throat. "Shh, we must be quiet."

The stone troll covered his mouth. The vibration stopped . . . somewhat. After a moment, only the blowing wind whistled as it mixed with the clops of the horses' hooves and the creaks of wood as the wagon rolled down the unlevel road.

In the absence of their laughter, Ord detected a second sound. Gurgling croaks came from above them. Three ravens glided along in the moonlight over the tops of the trees keeping pace with the wagon.

After a glance at Aidan, Frida kept her voice low and asked, "Ord? The baby? Change?" She held out both her arms again.

Despite his aversion to the smell, Ord suddenly felt selfish.

Am I crazy? I should be jumping at the chance.

However, other words came out. "I--I think I should be the one."

Frida dropped her hands to the top of her knees and leaned back with a smirk. "Let me at least help." She looked around the bed of the wagon. "Where's the linen?"

The dwarf pointed to the wooden crate. Frida opened the lid, spotted the linen as well as the skin of water he had retrieved from the pool. She reached for both.

"Not that waterskin. It belongs to Jada. Grab another, please." Ord nodded toward a waterskin at the other end of the crate. "One of those will be fine."

She placed the waterskin from the pool back in the crate and picked up one from the far end.

The wagon bounced.

"Can we slow it down a moment," Ord called toward the front. "I don't want to hurt Shamira."

Aidan scowled, but Jada tapped the dark elf on the arm. The horses reduced their speed though the wagon continued to shift as it rolled.

Laying the baby goblin on the wooden floor in front of him, he undid the blanket. It wasn't the best position. His armor, while well-fitted, was not designed to let him touch his toes easily. He grunted against the straps holding his armor in place while trying to maneuver. However, by the time he found a good position, his helmet played against him, blocking part of his view due to the chin strap. With a sigh, he removed his helmet and set it on a sack beside him. "Better."

Frida brightened. "Nice beard braids. Are you sure you don't want any help?"

The dwarf lifted his chin. "I've got this." Inside, he steeled himself. With the bouncing of the wagon, the last thing he wanted was to end up like the bugbear.

"Actually," he gazed at Shamira, "I think I'm beginning to get the hang of . . ." He unwrapped the soiled cloth and gasped. "By all the gods, Shamira, what have you done?"

Shamira stared up with an innocent smile. She slapped her hands against her moving legs.

The dwarf choked. He caught one of the baby's feet but had to trap the other to get them both. Lifting the baby's legs by one hand, he looked away as he used his opposite hand to fold the soiled linen enough so he could clean her without everything getting messier. Ord reached out a hand to Frida while keeping his eyes half averted from the . . . mess. He rasped, "Cloth for the floor."

Frida chuckled. "Shouldn't you clean her a little better before using a new one?" Instead of placing it in his hand, she leaned forward, her long hair flicking across front her blown by the wind, and laid it under the baby.

The ravens gurgled above them.

Shamira gurgled back matching their tone and pitch.

Finished, Frida smirked as she leaned backward, pushing her hair into place over her shoulder.

Ord held up a pointing finger. "Do you think I'd take any chance of getting that nasty stuff on the wagon floor? *We* have to ride here." He focused his wide eyes on the messy baby and begged, "Wet rag . . . please."

Using the waterskin from the crate, Frida doused a cloth, folded it, and placed it in his open palm. "It is my privilege." She winked at Shamira.

With a wrinkled nose, he cleaned up the child.

Shamira squirmed and attempted to roll. Ord turned her back over. She grabbed hold of a burlap bag and tugged. Ord laid down the wet rag and caught her right leg before it slipped from his grasp. He picked up the wet rag but then dropped it beneath her as her left leg struggled to free itself.

He growled. "Shamira, will you please hold still."

She froze and stared up at him with her big wide eyes, but the spell only lasted a moment. Her body began to turn and twist once more as she struggled to get to her stomach.

Frida raised an eyebrow toward Ord. "Let me help." Before he could respond, she leaned forward and said in a soothing voice, "Shamira. Shamira." She let her hair dangle above the baby.

Shamira giggled clapping her hands. She reached up for the long blonde strands of hair and wrapped them around her fingers.

Frida glanced up at Ord. "Go while you can."

"You don't have to tell me twice," he said and finished cleaning her in record time. Lowering the baby's legs, he recalled how Jada had showed him to wrap and tuck the linen around Shamira.

Frida wiggled her fingers to draw Shamira's attention and gently loosened the baby's hands from her hair. She then took the wet rag from Ord and rinsed it over the side of the wagon using the waterskin. The smell wafted toward the back of the wagon as the poo dissolved. She did the same to the soiled linen.

She held up the soaked cloths, eyeing each one. "We'll have to get some lye to clean it well."

Ord watched her closely. "Have you done this before?"

"Why Ord, is that a proposal?"

Ord felt his cheeks turn red.

Above them, one of the three ravens turned back the way they had come leaving two dark feathered birds arcing across the sky beside them. Of the two ravens left, one descended to land in the back of the wagon on a burlap bag. It cocked its head to watch Shamira with first its right eye and then its left. The raven gurgled at Shamira.

Shamira repeated the gurgle.

The raven changed the tone and pitch.

Shamira paused as if closely listening and then matched it exactly.

The raven said in a low voice, "Ba, ba, ba, . . ."

Shamir joined in matching the sound.

Aidan glanced back at them, a finger going to his collar and a frown on his face.

The raven stopped and looked up at Ord as if expecting him to repeat the sound, too.

Shamira waited for the raven to continue. When it did not, she resumed making the raven's gurgle, clapping her hands as she did.

Aidan looked down at Shamira. "Are you certain you want your daughter sounding like a bird before she even says 'daddy'?"

Ord narrowed his eyes. "If she's good enough to repeat them, what's the big deal?"

He folded the clean cloth around the baby goblin suddenly aware that both Frida and Aidan were watching him. By using Jada's little tuck and tie trick, the cloth held firmly enough not to fall off. Wrapping Shamira in her makeshift blanket, Ord held her up and looked into her pretty little eyes. His voice soothed her as he ignored his audience, "Better?"

The smile she gave made him forget about everything: the dark elves, the trolls, the wagon, and even the soiled cloth.

Well, almost. He wondered if parents could ever forget that horror. He lowered her down and let her play with his finger.

"Ord," Frida quietly said.

He looked up.

Frida's smile brightened as he looked at her. "Do you have a family?"

The wagon hit a sharp bump. The horses picked up speed as the wagon rolled down a hill.

Behind them, Vindr continued to follow, but so were other things. A second raven had joined the one in the sky. The one in the wagon rose into the air as the two ravens above them descended to land in the wagon bed. The two in the wagon paced on top of the burlap bags as if guarding the contents of the wagon. The raven left in the sky circled just above Vindr's head, periodically resting upon the stone troll's shoulders while gurgling louder than before.

Ord tucked Shamira in the nook of his left arm, leaning on the same sack that his helmet rested upon. He remembered Frida's question. With narrowed eyes, he looked off into the distant trees and said, "I have a family."

She tilted her head and raised one eyebrow. "I mean a wife and a child. You know."

He glanced back at her, remembering the flirting she had done earlier at their meeting. The reality of what she asked hit him. In an intentionally uninterested voice, he said, "I'm not married."

The female troll looked down at the linen she cleaned, apparently oblivious to the clue he had given through his voice inflection. "But you do have someone you care about?"

It was time to leave this line of questioning. The baby jumped into his thoughts. He held Shamira a little closer and could not help but smile. "She's right here."

Frida's voice rose. "Good."

The pitch of the wagon sharply altered, tilting forward. Ord glanced toward the front, but his view was blocked. Scooting toward the front, he peered between the two dark elves.

Moonlight reflected upon the few clouds in the sky. To the right of the path, the brightness illuminated a large rocky outcropping in the shape of a humanoid figure holding a sword. Well above 300 feet tall, part of the figure's base jutted out over the road twenty feet above the ground.

The wagon creaked on as its wheels rolled ever closer.

Ord caught the familiarity of the stone figure's shape as the moonlight played against the shadows. It was not entirely a dwarven character, the figure's portions were taller than they should be. And yet, there was an undeniable sense that dwarves had created this monument.

But why here? It is so far from my dwarven home.

Above the trail, the brilliance of the moonlight caught the bottom of the natural overhang in brief flashes of light. The closer they approached, the brighter the light became.

As the wagon followed the curved path under the overhang, beyond the left side of the trail through some sparse trees, Ord spotted a sparkling sight in a valley quite some distance away. Shaped like a six-pointed star, filled with tiny, colorful, bright lights, a city glowed in the night.

Frida gasped in wonder and said, "It's so beautiful."

"The magic of life lain upon the open palm of creation," Jada whispered, "or so the legends say."

Ord looked closer. The dark expanse in which the lights shined was made up of many trees glistening in the moonlight. But more than that, he picked out other specific things: reflective metallic domes and stained-glass windows. Some areas changed color in a way that he had no idea how it was done. Remembering Frida's talk about geography, he asked, "Is that the city of Taika?"

Frida nodded and inhaled slowly as if drinking in the beauty. "It has to be. There is no other city this direction in Eurig."

Jada kept the horses to the trail but stole glances to her left, taking in the view as the path curved farther from the mountain's edge. "We are on the north side still some distance from the valley. By morning, we will encounter Halvardor. If all goes well, we will arrive at the city of Taika in two and a half days . . . if we keep a steady pace."

Ord caught the tremble in her voice. "You think we may not be able to?"

"She thinks," Aidan interrupted, "there are things here that are not as they should be. And she is right, dwarf."

Smack. Clunk. Rumble.

Small rocks tumbled down, bouncing across the road. When Ord glanced back, he spotted Vindr rubbing his forehead as the stone troll gazed toward the distant valley. He ducked below the overhang that supported the monument.

Frida gawked at the light. "Some of my family headed this direction." She touched her lips with her index finger. "I wonder . . ." She looked to Jada. "Could they . . ."

". . . have found a home there?" Jada continued without turning around. "Perhaps. Of all the places in Eurig, Taika would be the most accepting of the troll race."

Aidan huffed.

Jada ignored her companion. "Taika is made up of beings from all walks of life. Because of that acceptance, great magic has been gathered here. With the magic has come good fortune. Excessive wealth followed. These things have attracted many who would like to see it plundered."

Aidan cleared his throat. "In other words, stay close, don't stray, and don't draw attention to yourselves. At first glance, they will not think you are outsiders, but if you give yourselves away like some awestruck country bumpkins, they'll pick you out in a minute."

Ord raised an eyebrow. "I don't understand. If people are from everywhere and it is as big as you say, why should there be an issue?"

Both elves went quiet.

Jada tapped Aidan on the arm.

Aidan put up his bow and took the reins. The wagon rattled as the ground became a mixture of more rock than dirt. The trail grew broader. The city of Taika appeared to disappear behind a thick forest of trees.

The female elf removed her hood. With pursed lips, she turned to face Frida, Ord, and Vindr. Her grave, dark gaze took in each one of the adults until she looked down at the baby, Shamira. "We are here to answer that very question. Things . . . have changed since . . ." She bit her lip. "Since the new council took over control of the city."

Ord watched Jada's lips struggle not to frown. He asked, "I take it those *changes* are bad?"

"For as long as I can remember, the city has always been a safe place for any who wish to enter. Now . . ." She shrugged. "Economic gain seems the only drive of those who lead. People as individuals are rarely considered important, except to pay the council's taxes. And every benefit to the people is simply a new way to legally extort more tax money or worse, slave labor."

Ord grunted. "Sounds like some human cities I have read about." He nodded to himself. "Dwarves deal with a local council, which reports to a higher council under the jurisdiction of the king. Each region makes their own rules. The king only does what is necessary to protect the kingdom while staying out of local politics and decision making."

"In the city of Taika, the council reports to the high councilor," said Jada. "Only the council members can vote on who is elected to that position. Once office is given, they keep it for life."

"While this is great tavern dialogue," Aidan glanced back shaking his head, "I see no point in this discussion. The fact remains that something has to be done to change the rule in Taika, whatever form of government they have."

"So, you're taking about a coup?" Ord pressed back from the two dark elves. "I'm not here to start a revolution. I'm here to save my people from a war." He caught Jada's gaze with his own. "Is this coup why you have brought me here?"

Jada held up her hand. "Anryulong will be able to explain things better."

"So," Ord blinked at the mention of the dragon's name, "I will be meeting this dragon, Anryulong, in person? And what does he have to do with overthrowing the rulers of Taika?"

Jada opened her mouth to speak but Aidan cleared his throat.

She glanced over at him and then turned back to Ord. "Only Anryulong knows the reasons why we must stop the council, and it is unclear whether you will meet the dragon of all magic worlds.

Perhaps you will, if you are found worthy. She has picked each one of us for a reason."

Ord bristled. "And what if I don't want to meet him?"

"Anryulong is a *she*, Ord," said Jada.

"Slip of the tongue," he said as he thought back to his vision of the golden dragon and their previous conversations. "I knew that."

Aidan leaned toward Jada. "Something approaches."

The female elf covered her head and took the reins from Aidan. As if by magic, Aidan's bow appeared in his hands, arrow nocked and ready.

A single glow loomed ahead swaying as in an amble. Ord stared, puzzled at the familiar sight usually found in the dwarven kingdom alone. "A dwarven lantern held on the end of a hooked staff. A sage draws near."

"Not even I can see that far, dwarf," Aidan chided. "What makes you *so* sure?"

Ord stiffened. "How do you know it's not?" he snapped.

Shamira stirred.

Can she feel my mood?

He calmed himself for her sake.

Whatever Aidan's problem is, now is not the time.

"I know my kind." Ord nodded toward the glow ahead of them. "What doesn't make sense is why they would be here. We have record of any scribal monasteries established in this region."

"Dwarves have scribal monasteries?" Aidan sneered. "What is the world coming to?"

Ord snorted and started to come back with a response, but when he saw Shamira's face, he stopped.

Jada reduced the speed of the horses. Vindr slowed his walk.

The glow in front of them became brighter, pushing away the night's darkness a hundred feet on all sides. Trees and brush beside the path took on a bluish white light. It streamed above them as well as to the sides, struck the burlap sacks and reflected from his armor. With his helmet still sitting on a bag, the light caught the top of his helmet.

The glow the lantern cast was not the only source of the light. It came from a translucent aura surrounding the traveler. The light washed away any shadow the sage might have cast in a normal fashion as if the sage wasn't there at all.

Within the aura as they drew closer, Ord could make out a winkled hand gripping a dwarven staff. The old hand attached to an arm that vanished under the sleeve of a dark blue cloak with a hood. Gold embroidery bordered the cloak about a thumb width from the edge. Beneath the hood, no part of the face showed despite the light. The sage appeared to be as tall as Ord himself. Within thirty feet of the wagon, the figure stopped.

Jada halted the horses at twenty feet from the stranger. Vindr stepped to the south side of the wagon and stared with his trollish, unreadable, expression. Shamira opened her eyes, gazed up at Ord, and then reached her tiny fingers for his helmet.

Silence fell as nothing but the wind, trees, and ravens could be heard with the occasional horse neigh.

An old voice emanating from beneath the blue robe's hood said to them in deep, well-defined tones, "You have traveled far?"

No one in the wagon responded.

The hood tilted up, but still the face remained hidden. "Yes, far indeed. A collection to meet the need?"

The hooded figure sniffed. "And I sense some of knowledge among you."

The figure turned his head as if to listen better with its right ear. "Well, let him draw near. It is tradition after all."

Aidan started to rise with bow tightly gripped, but Jada laid her hand on his arm.

"Wise are you, dark-haired one." The traveling sage nodded. "You must teach the male elf more manners if he is to survive long enough to help Anryulong's cause."

Frida cut off a chuckle. Vindr gave a snort.

"And I see there are others with you as well." He looked up as if listening to something no one else could hear. "Well, tradition has yet to be met. Why do you keep an elder waiting, dwarf?"

Ord gradually stood.

"Yes," the blue-robed sage with the staff continued, "you do know who you are."

Shamira shifted her gaze as if she saw something near the sage, which the dwarf could not. The child's lips quivered. She reached for Ord's helmet again.

Ord tucked the blanket around her to confine her hands as he prepared to exit the wagon bed.

Ignoring a soundless scowl from Aidan, he climbed over the side of the wagon and stood on top of the right front wagon wheel while keeping Shamira cradled in his arm. He caught the worried expression on Frida's face as he dropped toward the ground.

As he landed with both feet, Frida nodded toward the baby.

Is that fear I see Frida's eyes? Are her troll senses telling her something is wrong?

Ord met her gaze. At the same time, something spoke at the back of his mind. Just as he knew Shamira's name, he could feel it was right to bring Shamira with him.

But is that the safe thing for a father to do? he thought.

He bit his lip before silently mouthing to Frida, "Thank you . . . ," and looked away from her as he tried to figure out how to explain his decision to keep Shamira with him. He had no idea who this sage was, only that he appeared to be traveling well outside the dwarven kingdom. For this to happen meant something was truly amiss with the dwarves.

Since the sage mentioned the name Anryulong, he must know of the quest we are on, too.

He continued to silently mouth at Frida, "But, I think . . ." He glanced at the sage.

The sage appeared to watch the horses, which were attached to the wagon, as he waited for Ord to commit.

Ord continued to Frida and in silence mouthed, ". . . I think she is supposed to go with me."

Frida whispered so quietly he barely caught it. "He is not what he seems." She tapped her nose.

Ord narrowed his eyes, remembering how she had said Shamira was only half goblin and he was half human.

How good were Frida's instincts, really? I mean 50/50 isn't bad, but it is nothing to bet your life on.

He looked into the bed of the wagon and spotted his helmet.

Shamira, on the other hand, is a different consideration. Did Shamira sense something, too, or had his helmet simply caught the light?

Although he detected no threat from the sage, he remembered Shamira had reached for his helmet at least twice. He picked up the helmet, placed it on his head without buckling it, and turned toward the sage on the road.

The sage carried the right dwarven staff and the correct lantern. The blue robe was appropriate down to the detail of the embroidered gold along the borders.

Why is this sage so far from home?

Although confused by Frida's revelation and Shamira's persistence about the helmet, he slowly walked to the figure in the dark blue cloak. Taking the traditional pose, which all dwarves where taught, Ord went to one knee before the sage and paid homage.

"Elder Learned-One," he said. "I am Steredenn Ord Hammersmith of the house of Ferg-het."

"So you are." The old sage chuckled and placed his free hand on Ord's shoulder.

At his touch, a strange blue energy rippled down Ord's armor. It crackled and snapped, stretching out and forming connections as if fashioning a net all around Ord's body.

Ord slowly stood up, disconcerted yet unable to back away from the sage.

Shamira felt it, too. Squirming one arm out of the wrapping, she poked her hand up. The blue energy created a pattern across her tiny fingers.

"Steredenn Ord Hammersmith, you will come with me."

The world surrounding Ord waved like leaves fluttering in the wind. The stars above winked out. The lighted trail faded. From a great distance, he thought he heard the call of the others. The smell of the woodsy outdoor air slipped away to be replaced with the odor of mildew, rot, and decay.

From the darkness of the nothing, light formed again. No longer on the path to Taika, a circular, gray, stone room took shape around them.

Candles burned on glim mounts connected to the stone walls. A single heavy wooden door stood barred to Ord's left. Separating the glim mounts, bookshelves lined the curved, round room.

In the center of the room was a large, round table. Carved upon its surface, names covered its circumference.

Ord knew of this place, but only in the dwarven legends. The moment the old dwarf with the staff released him, Ord gasped for air. "How long have I been holding my breath?"

"Who says that you have?" the sage answered the question with a question.

Shamira struggled to wake up as she pushed open eyelids that fought to remain closed.

Ord glanced down, not sure why the sage had not noticed the baby Ord carried.

She hadn't been asleep before we left the trail, he thought, looking back at the sage.

"I am Visdor Odenash, Keeper of Mundgurun, and you have been expected, Ord."

Using one hand to slide along the top of the round table as he walked, each name Visdor's hand touched glowed orange for a few seconds before fading. The sage followed the edge of the round table away from Ord until he turned back to face him on the opposite side.

Removing the hood, Visdor looked in Ord's direction. A white film covered the sage's eyes as if the pupils had vanished. No beard adorned his face. Gray hair lay upon his head. And the body-build was wrong for a dwarf.

The more Ord studied him, the more he realized this person was no dwarf, but a man.

Ord cautiously touched the edge of the round table. His thoughts reeled as he fingered the rim. "This cannot be real. It was destroyed when the Guardians fell."

The description of the place where Ord stood matched the legends he had read, though the details were relatively few: stone walls, stone floor, books of knowledge on shelves that lined the chamber, and the Mundgurun, the round wooden table showing the Guardians' names. Little else was known about the chamber for when the Guardians passed so did the secret of its access.

The golden dragon's warning came back, "*You must find the Branwen to know the path home. Seek the true Guardian of the Mundgurun . . .*"

But a man, not a dwarf? How could Visdor be the true Guardian of the Mundgurun?

"This is the Mundgurun . . . itself?" Ord asked in a skeptical whisper. His thoughts swirled. "How can this be?"

He gazed down at the wood carvings on the table and read the names inscribed there. None were familiar, but he knew what was supposed to be on it.

"The sages of the times before." He touched them lightly, reverently. "The names of the Guardians." He turned in a circle gawking at all the books on the shelves that lined the room. "But it was destroyed."

Shamira tried to wake again. She managed to open her eyes only halfway before they closed.

The old sage shook his head. "Not destroyed. It was preserved. The secret knowledge is kept from those who would use its wisdom for their *personal* gain."

"But you're not a dwarf." Ord turned his gaze to Visdor, shaking his head. "This is dwarven knowledge. It does not belong to mankind."

Visdor sighed and said with great patience, "There was a time, Ord, when all species were one. We existed without corporal form. We were greater than the gods."

Ord coldly said, "That's not in our book of creation."

The sage smirked. "It was stricken from it long before the Guardians were created."

Ord shook his head. "This doesn't make any sense."

Ting.

A light metallic tap caught his attention, and he looked down.

Ting.

Shamira kicked his gauntlet again. Her eyes were wide open now.

Ord thought, *How could a child this young show such concern in her face?*

He tucked her foot back under the makeshift blanket from where it had escaped.

"Prove to me who you say you are," said Ord.

Holding up a hand, Visdor nodded. "Simply listen. It is critical to what you must face."

The man took deep breaths and let them slowly out three times. Each time, a glow flashed above him as if igniting from an unseen force. On the third release, a brief torrent of wind swept the room and fluttered the candle flames mounted to the walls.

The sage continued, "The gods tricked us, Ord. Magic used wrong changed us. By its power, we took material form, but there was a price to be paid, a separation from who we all were. Instead of being one with all, we became individual parts of the whole with few physical commonalities. The longer we incorrectly used the magic in our corporeal forms, the more we forgot our origins. Partitions were created. Entire worlds separated. The gods in charge fed upon the warmongering, bathing in greed, lust, and power all to keep us from understanding who we really were. Eventually, we had no memory of where we came from."

Visdor waved his hand at the room. "This place is under threat, the last remaining knowledge of the old world. It is tied to the city of Taika. If that city falls into the hands of the defilers, of those who would keep us separate from our ethereal forms, so will the Mundgurun and our only chance of finding our way home.

You must not let this happen, whatever the cost. Do you understand?"

Ord listened, not just to the sage's words, but to the strong emotions forming inside him. The words and the emotions did not see eye to eye as his own internal battle took place.

Something is amiss, he thought.

"If what you say is true, there is little hope left, for all have accepted that the Mundgurun is no more."

"Hope, love, and peace, all these things live as long as one person chooses to hold them tight," the sage said. "You are the candle burning in the void. Do not let the light go out. You must be the next Guardian of Majik. All worlds *must* be one again."

The man flicked the fingers on his right hand. Tiny lights sparkled at the ends. "You must help me fulfill our destiny."

Visdor's last words echoed from the circular walls, swirling around Ord and coming from every direction. They struck against his plate-mail armor, passed through, and reverberated inside his skull.

If Ord didn't help in this man's fight, those words would suffocate him. The feeling of expediency surged up inside, touching his very core. He could think of nothing else but the man's request. Ord said through hazy thoughts, "How can I help?"

Visdor waved at the round table. "The wheel is almost complete. Only a few spaces are open. Place your hand on one that has not been taken, and the next Guardian you will be."

Ord swept the table with his gaze, still hearing the words *You must help me* echo in his mind. The tabletop appeared distorted now, waving as if unsteady. He blinked trying to get a clear view.

There were many names, but he spotted a place to the right that appeared to be blank. Visdor was correct. Only a few spots remained.

What does that mean? he thought. *Once it is filled, what will happen next?*

His hand hovered over the blank spot.

Ting.

Shamira kicked him.

He looked down, his vision oddly distorted. Even as he focused on the child, the haziness of before cleared.

I am no Guardian. I don't even know what a Guardian does.

He looked back at the round table, eyeing the spot over which his hand hovered.

This is signing a contract. If that is so, I want to read the fine print first.

He tightened his jaw, growing more determined by the moment and said, "I need to *think* about this."

Ord had copied too many contracts in the dwarven library to rush into them himself, and the sage's reaction was not logical, not for a Learned-One.

The expression on Visdor's face changed as the sage's jawline became defined. He leaned menacingly toward Ord and said with a deep, demanding voice, "There is no time. He *must* be found."

Ord pulled his hand back and stepped away from the table. "Who is he?" He searched Visdor's face, aware of the hostility between the sage and whoever he sought. His gut twisted as if in a knot. "Who do you despise that much?"

Visdor remained silent though his face turned red.

Ord said, "Then, the answer is *no*."

Staring straight at Ord, Visdor's face swelled in rage. Eyes bulging, nose flaring, the sage separated each word of his next sentence. "You--will--sign."

The little goblin baby giggled.

Visdor screamed, "Who's there?" The old sage turned about glaring in every direction, unable to locate the source of the sound. "Where are they?"

Ord took another step back, shifting to the right.

Surely the man can see the baby in my arm.

Hitting the table, the old man exclaimed, "Tell me who's here."

Two words popped into Ord's head as he remembered the white film across the sage's eyes. "You're blind."

The man screamed, "Tell me."

Ord thought back. "It makes sense. You stopped before the wagon was upon you. Somehow you knew about the elves, but not about Frida and Vindr. Possibly you heard Jada and Aidan talking in advance or had some foreknowledge of their coming. And what Frida said makes more sense now."

The dwarf tapped his lips. "But how did you know to put your hand on my shoulder?"

Ord nodded. "That's right. I came close enough for you to hear. Your other senses have grown stronger to help with the sight you don't have, but . . ." He watched the man step forward and use the edge of the table to keep himself oriented. "You can't focus when you're upset." He gawked at the sage. "Who are you, really?"

The room waved, like heat escaping off a hot spring. The only door faded away becoming dust at the foot of an archway. The bookcases vanished. One by one, the burning candles darkened on the walls until the illumination fled. Several glim holders were broken, barley hanging upon the walls. Others were not there at all. As the light of the illusion faded, the table altered from wood to stone with carved out, pie-shaped, cavities slightly larger than the size of Ord's hand.

Lime mixed with ash and blood had been poured into the cavities. Handprints of others filled most of the spots around the table. Ord's had almost been next.

The dwarven staff in Visdor's hand became a gnarled stick. No lamp hung from the nonexistent, split curve at the top. The visage of the sage, although almost the same as with the magic cast illusion, showed a scar on the side of his left cheek.

The table was designed to magically bind the person who agreed to the sage's proposal. The word *contracts* hit Ord's mind when he looked at the table.

"How many others have you tricked into making the agreement?"

There was only one thing to do. Pulling the hammer from his back, Ord took aim, and struck the table center.

The hit echoed as the table cracked. Iridescent glows flickered up like the tips of flames. The mortar, holding each pie-shaped cavity together, crumbled from the vibration. The table shifted dangerously. The stones making up the cavities dropped one by one. They struck the floor as the magic that held it seeped away. With each strike, a ghostly form rose from the table to spiral up until it passed beyond the ceiling.

Thud. Crack. Snap.

Visdor screamed, "Stop, I command it." He pointed his hand in Ord's general direction, waving it as if uncertain of where Ord was.

Blue lightning leaped out. Ord dodged to the right and struck the table with the hammer a second time. More fractures rippled across the table surface. More ghostly apparitions rose up from the various handprints to pass into the ceiling above.

Visdor pointed his hand farther to the left trying to find Ord. A second burst of energy ripped across the room, but nowhere near the right direction, scoring on the far wall. The smell of ozone filled the air.

Hefting his hammer, Ord focused on the common spot to where the fissures in the table ran as the pie-shaped sections continued to fall.

Ord swung his war hammer down, bashing the top of the table a third time. The table supports sheered, snapped, and collapsed. What was left of the round tabletop slanted toward the right until it shattered against the stone floor becoming rubble and dust.

Ting.

Shamira kicked his chest armor.

Ord grinned at the ingenuity Shamira had used to get her foot uncovered and kick him, despite the maniacal actions of Visdor.

"I agree, Shamira" Ord said, feeling pride in his daughter's resourcefulness. "Let's get out of here."

Chapter 10

Visdor screamed. The blue lightning burst from his fingertips with no controlled direction or purpose. It struck stone walls, blew apart remaining glim holders, and scorched the floor black where the table laid in a ruined mess.

Ord silently skirted around the crazed Visdor toward the only doorway into the round room.

Contracts? Signatures? None of that makes sense, but at least I understand why I needed to keep Shamira with me.

Visdor shrieked. The shriek echoed within the chamber. The man continued to lash out with the blue lightning striking at every echo.

Ord ducked, guarding Shamira, feeling the heat as a burst rushed past his shoulder. The blue hot flame blistered the wall behind Ord.

By breaking those contracts, Ord thought, *what is happening to those who signed them?*

Stepping through the only exit from the room revealed a long hall, which ran left and right. He had no idea which direction was the correct way to go, and no immediate clue showed him how to get out of this building.

He glanced down at Shamira. She was wide awake now. He would have thought after all that excitement, she would at least be crying, but the delight in her wide eyes showed she was enjoying every moment.

What type of baby am I raising?

To his right, a slight breeze brought the smell of leaves.

Ord took off down the hallway toward the leaves trying to put distance between him and Visdor.

His left arm ached, the arm holding Shamira. The muscles needed to be stretched.

How long had it been before Visdor woke us up?

The stone walls stretched out into the distance with lit candles every twenty feet as he rushed down the hallway. What tapestries used to hang on the walls were either shredded or fallen.

Visdor's cries of fury became distant. The farther Ord went, the stronger the breeze became whipping at the candle flames and threatening to blow them out. The smells of the forest drove Ord to boost his speed until he came to a four-way intersection and stopped.

With a slight curve, the corridor to the right appeared to go deeper into the fortress, lit by periodic candles. The corridor directly ahead was the largest of the three new paths, descending a set of stairs with no light shining, daylight or candle. A burst of wind ruffled his hair from the left, lit, snake-like corridor.

Visdor's shriek echoed behind him much closer than before. The dwarf kicked into a trot down the left hallway, watching for a window or door that led to the outside.

Dust stirred in the crevices of the hall. Dirt swept along by the periodic bursts of air. A leaf floated down the hallway tumbling toward him. It stopped with a flip and remained fixed to the wall.

Several archways stood at the end of the passage as he approached. The farthest held the strongest draft with wisps of smoke tainting the air. Brief orange flickers of light reflected off the left side of the arch.

He slipped closer, listening for anything which might betray another creature's presence. When no noise came, Ord peered past the last archway into a room.

In one corner, broken furniture had been tossed. Chair legs had been snapped off. Table legs had been broken into three or more pieces.

He stuck his head farther in but kept close to the archway. Small bonfires burned in the room surrounded by straw sleeping mats. In the fires, pieces of broken furniture charred in the flames. Yet, most of the burning wood consisted of branches or cut logs. There were no windows, only additional doors at the far end of the room.

He listened closely but heard nothing except the crackling of the fire and the brief burst of wind as it entered the chamber. Disturbed leaves drifted amongst the fires. When a leaf tumbled too close, it smoldered until consumed. Sparks jump as the wood popped.

Where is the way out?

Ord's eyes darted to the various doors in the room, but nothing appeared to be the source.

It has to be coming from . . .

He looked slowly up.

Nature had indeed created an entrance. A hole in the roof was above his head and quite out of reach.

With a tinge of worry, he looked back to the contents of the room.

Everything indicated this room was used on a regular basis.

But where are the beings that live here?

He thought back to the contracts he had smashed when he had destroyed the phony round table and watched the spirits that had departed.

A shriek came from the hall behind him.

Visdor, the insane, is coming, he thought.

He swallowed as he silently counted the sleeping mats and slipped toward the far end of the room.

Shamira whimpered as her little stomach grumbled. She looked up at him with her big wide eyes.

Listening to the wind coming through the hole in the roof, he stayed close to the right wall.

So close, yet so far, he chided himself.

Toward the far left corner of the room, he spotted three smaller doors.

Visdor's next scream sounded farther away.

Adjusting his grip on his war hammer, Ord stepped past a bonfire. Burning wood popped. A piece of a branch higher than the others tumbled into the center, sending up flames. The sound of footsteps echoed from the area of the three smaller doors, but no one stepped from that direction.

Shamira's stomach grumbled so loud he cringed.

How often did a baby have to eat?

His own stomach grumbled.

Not me too.

He looked down at Shamira and whispered, "Working on the food thing, kid, but we need to get out of here in one piece, first."

She gurgled at him like the ravens, and he cringed as the sound echoed.

He continued in a whisper, "We're going to have to work on your stealth skills, too."

He dared not leave her hidden though it would be easier to scout the area. The water sprite's temple and the spiders had taught him a valuable lesson.

What in the dwarven kingdom am I doing with a baby here?

Ord frowned.

Am I sure this magical knowing, The Sight Jada had called it, really happened to me? Maybe I let my emotions make the wrong decision.

He slipped closer to the doors while keeping the wall to his right side.

Ting.

He stopped. A lump rose in his throat.

No other sound met his ears. He stepped past the next bonfire.

Pop. Ting.

This time, he felt where the sound came from and looked down at Shamira.

She had wiggled free her little foot, again, and kicked his armored chest.

"Young lady, you almost gave me a heart attack."

She giggled, talking in sounds he had no idea how to translate.

"At least you are not crying."

Visdor's next scream reverberated into the room, sounding closer.

"We've got to get a move on," he whispered. "How do I express to you we have to be quiet?"

From the hallway, footsteps echoed louder.

Ord slipped past the remaining bonfires and started toward the first door. From this location, he could see the entrance by which he had come and the exits he sought to explore.

He sniffed. The smell of burnt flesh grew in the air.

Shamira sneezed.

Ord wrinkled his nose.

He whispered to Shamira, "I agree. Something has been thoroughly burnt."

He placed an ear to the first door he reached and listened. The smell of fresh cedar wood help cut through the stink of the burnt flesh. Several of the boards on the door had been skillfully replaced.

Ord set his hammer down on its flat top beside the first door, lightly clutched the door ring, and pushed it in. It silently swung back, not the norm in a fortress with this much ruin.

A bowl with oil sat on the top of a three-foot-tall, wooden barrel. Alongside the bowl was a metallic mug that had a light mist of frost on the outside. Nails lay scattered on a crate next to the barrel. A small hammer leaned against the side of the crate.

Ord picked up the cold mug and sniffed it.

"Honey mead," he said out loud to himself though in a whisper, "and it's still cool. The carpenter cannot be far away." As if in agreement, Shamira gurgled.

He glanced down at Shamira and set the mug back on the barrel. "I wish it had been kefir."

His stomach grumbled at the same time hers did, and despite their circumstance, Ord chuckled.

He lifted the top of a crate that was no longer nailed down. As the firelight filtered in from the bonfire chamber, the sharp edges of iron daggers reflected the dull orange glow of the flames. He stepped back into the other room and closed the first door.

The second door, also, silently opened as he pushed it in. The orange firelight cast its flickering brightness, altering shadows on cut wood stacked against a wall. Oversized wooden wagon wheels leaned against the far right corner next to a worktable. Nuts and bolts filled the open wooden boxes next to the wheels. Long axles had been placed between four wooden posts. By the fresh wood he saw, they had been recently hammered into the ground.

Ord had seen these things drawn in a book at the dwarven library. And even if he had not, his experience on the battlefield would have been more than enough to put two and two together. These were parts to build siege engines, and the siege engines were used to storm fortresses.

The third door creaked as he pushed it to open. He stopped, went back for the war hammer, and then proceeded to use his foot to slowly open the door. A strong smell of urine hung in the air only disturbed by the door movement.

Troughs had been laid on both sides of the room. Water washed down the troughs. Benches with holes cut in the top could be positioned over the running water.

Ord coughed as he closed the door. They needed better air flow in the outhouse.

Stepping from the smaller doors, he sniffed the air. The smell of burnt meat hung there, slowly moving to fill the rest of the bonfire chamber.

Frowning, he searched the room and whispered, "So, unless the smell of burnt meat is coming from the outside . . ."

In the flickering of the firelight, the orange illumination played havoc with his eyes, constantly shifting from light to dark. He stepped closer to the corner, noting the way the stone pattern changed on the wall at a single, vertical location. Setting his hammer beside him, he traced the wall with his free hand another two feet. And then he saw it, the opening to a side hallway camouflaged by the pattern of the stones.

He reached back and picked up his hammer then stepped into the hallway. The smell of burnt meat grew stronger. And though he still wrinkled his nose, his stomach growled.

He looked down at Shamira and whispered, "What do you think? The aroma isn't too bad once you get used to it."

He sniffed again and then gagged.

Shamira attempted to cover her head with her blanket, wrinkling her tiny nose.

The more he thought about the area layout, the more he realized its similarity to dwarven barracks. That seemed odd in the middle of a territory not controlled by dwarves. Sleeping quarters, the latrine, supplies, and kitchen were all located in the same area. It made it more efficient so the soldiers could focus on learning to fight.

The burnt smell filled the air. The farther he walked down the hidden hallway, the more he realized that maybe it wasn't all burnt.

Voices grumbled. Someone hollered. Shouts went up from a large group outside of his view. Snippets of elven, orc, and human languages intertwined as the sounds echoed into the hallway.

"Shamira," he whispered, "it sounds like a dwarven wrestling match."

She looked up at him, her eyes filled with curiosity, listening to the clamor.

Two open doors led from the hallway, the first in the right wall. The second, five feet farther, was at the end of the hall.

A glance through the first showed a large mass of armor-clad warriors. They were gathered in the center of the room with their backs to him. From this distance, he could pick out dark elves in leather armor, orcs dressed in leather and metal combos, and humans in various mismatched armor pieces. They all stared at a spectacle in the center, packed in shoulder to shoulder, hollering at something Ord could not see.

A firepit had been set up in the far-left corner, its flames reaching up to lick the grease dripping into its coals. Meat, blackened on the bottom, smoked as those watching the spectacle ignored the food. Ord bypassed the first door and went to the end of the hall.

Stepping through the archway and past the open door, Ord reached a kitchen. A second doorway led from the kitchen into the main room where the spectacle took place.

Through the second doorway, he spotted the same large mass of armor-clad warriors. However, he was closer here and could see more details.

Against the wall, the roughly honed, dining tables and chairs had been shoved to make room for the fight. Human males and females, a sprinkling of hobgoblins, orcs, elves, dark elves and woodland elves at that, six to eight pixies, and a few dwarves helped to make a ring around the fight that took place in the middle of the room. There was more leather armor than metal. Some used heavy woven cloth. Several of the thinner ones were archers, but most had at minimum of a knife in their belt and at least one sword.

Ord's stature gave him an advantage on this side. Seeing over the throng, he spotted a dwarf standing in the middle of the ring. The border of the circular ring had been drawn on the floor using ashes from the firepit. Those shouting stayed outside the ash boundary.

Along with the dwarf in the center lay a human male, down for the count. The dwarf in the circle taunted another in the crowd with a come-forward wave, trying to provoke them to step past the ash border and into the ring. The unarmored dwarf bellowed, "Two rubies and an emerald say I'll put you down faster than the last."

The warriors, egging on the would-be challengers, hollered jeers. No one cared that the human on the ground wasn't moving.

There appeared to be only the two exits from the dining room, one to the hall and the other into the kitchen. Ord backed to the rear of the kitchen, as far as he could get from the horde. He headed to the corner where they appeared to store a variety of liquid refreshments from honey mead to hard ale, most contained in kegs. Even from a distance, he caught the labels of origin. The languages varied from elven to orc, even human.

Above the kegs, hung on the wall, were shiny, dust-covered, shields, similar in design to those of his homeland, but differing in the symbol worked into the center.

Definitely dwarven origin, he thought. *And probably here long before these marauders came.*

Ord eyed several jugs by a counter. Setting down his hammer, he picked up one, popped the large cork, and sniffed. His eyes brightened.

Kefir. Perfect. We're out of here.

A low squeaky voice said behind him, "Just put it on the counter. As soon as we're done, I'll let the cook know."

Ord froze. He turned toward the voice and said, "Put what on the counter?"

A pixie wearing dark brown pants, a darker brown shirt, and black belt raised an eyebrow at him. "The baby of course." A smile abruptly snapped across its face. "You didn't think I meant the kefir? Ha, ha, ha. No, no, take as much of the kefir as you want. It came on the wagon we hijacked. Had we realized what it was, we would have thrown it out before it got here."

The pixie gazed toward the fight. After a moment, it looked back at Ord. "Well?"

The dwarf glanced at Shamira. "Don't you think we better fatten her up a bit first? She does look a little thin."

The pixie peered down at the child. "I don't know. It might be better to eat her now. They poop too much."

"You're telling me." Ord nodded. "Just getting here I had to change her twice."

The pixie chuckled. "Oh, and the smell! I hate when I do an overnight pick up. It takes a ton of pixie dust to keep the air clean. And pixie dust has been hard to come by since I was expelled for my," he cleared his throat, "profession. Dorothy, queen of the pixies, doesn't approve of my activities, if you know what I mean."

The friendly face Ord portrayed almost dropped when he realized this pixie stole children, but he kept his expression steady. "You do that a lot? Pick up babies to eat?"

"Meh." The pixie shrugged. "My policy is if you see one alone, pick it up. Most parents have so many in Taika that they never know they're gone. Or, they are relieved when they realize a child is gone. The city has really turned into a place I wouldn't call home."

The very thought set Ord on edge. He fought to be civil. "Good to know." He nodded, struggling not to tighten his jaw further. "But I think with all the effort I put into this one, I want her to have a little more weight."

The pixie shrugged. "Suit yourself. But I'd keep a close eye. Some of these in here don't even bother to cook them," the pixie raised his voice, "right Agugh?"

An orc standing at the back of the ring of people grunted but did not turn to look at the pixie.

Ord nodded. "Thanks for the warning."

"Don't mention it, pal." The pixie turned to go but swung back. "Hey, by the way, what troop are you in? Next time I get a goblin child, I'll look you up."

The dwarf set the kefir jug down on the counter. "Troop?" He drifted his hand down until it toyed with the handle of his war hammer.

"Yeah, you know. The regiment number?"

The hammer will be too slow, Ord thought. *I will have to do something a little faster.* He threw a number out. "Regiment three."

The crowd in the dining area roared. Orcs beat upon their chests. Those with spears knocked the butt ends against the floor. The pixie looked confused, but his eyes darted toward the fight taking place. "I thought three was still over in . . ."

Smack.

Ord swatted him with his gauntlet.

The pixie tumbled, head over heels.

Crash.

It slammed against a line of skillets hanging next to the wall.

The skillets were loud, but not near as loud as the fight taking place in the dining area. Ord attached his hammer to his back as a few curious spectators glanced toward the kitchen archway but turned once more to view the fight.

Carrying both Shamira and the kefir, he strolled toward the exit that led to the hallway and caught sight of a smirk on his face in the bottom of a reflective shield hanging on the wall.

He felt much better after swatting the pixie. Had he been given more time, he would have made sure the pixie never stole a child again.

Less than a step past the archway, leading out into the narrow hall, Ord heard quick footsteps rushing in his direction. He no sooner pulled back into the kitchen and peeked around the corner, when a second orc stormed to the dining area, through the first open archway, and glared at the horde. "What in all of Taika are you doing?" the orc said, his voice booming against the dining room walls completely drowning out the sounds of the fight.

The roar of excitement produced by the gathered warriors dropped by degrees. Those near the outside of the group glanced back and abruptly turned. The motion continued until all the warriors, which had gathered around the fight circle, stopped shouting and stood at attention facing the orc standing in the hallway arch.

Grunt. Smack. Thud.

The warriors around the fight parted to show the dwarf in the center of the ring. Chest heaving and hands bloody from small cuts, he stood over three other opponents, which remained unmoving upon the floor.

The whole room went silent. The dwarf snapped to attention.

The orc stepped further into the dining area and growled. "You are soldiers, not hoodlums," he bellowed. "In formation now."

Warriors raced to change position, ignoring the fallen fighters. Metal clanged as they dodged by each other. The thunder of their feet echoed off the walls.

Ord took a last glance through the kitchen archway, which allowed him to view the dining area, before slipping into the hallway that led out. He skirted quietly behind the orc who glared at the soldiers. The orc turned about-face to eye him, a sneer on the Orc's face.

"Soldier, in line." The orc eyed the bundle in Ord's right arm. "And put that baby down, now."

Ord saluted, at least as best he could with the kefir. As the Orc stepped back to let him pass into the dining chamber, Ord belted the orc in the midsection with the jug of kefir.

The orc buckled forward, and Ord brought the jug down at the base of the orc's skull.

Crack.

The milky kefir poured out as the jug broke, oozing down the orc's head and neck. The orc dropped to the floor.

Shifting Shamira into his left arm, Ord ran.

The orc bellowed in rage and in an unsteady voice demanded, "Get that man."

Ord cringed as his face flushed. All the hostility he had taken from Aidan seemed to billow up inside him. He remembered Findor's cautioning words. He understood most races couldn't tell the difference between dwarves and men save for the height, but that was plain rude.

His nostrils flared. He wanted to turn around.

Ting.

He knew who it was without looking. The anger drained from his face while his stubborn pride tried to hold on a few seconds longer. The hallway was narrow enough that he could have knocked off the warriors two by two if it weren't for the baby in his arm.

Ting.

Shamira kicked his armor, again.

His lungs labored, sucking in air as logic fought through his irritation.

He wasn't about to let them put one finger on Shamira, and it certainly wasn't time for him to die.

Ord sprinted down the smaller hall. The smell of smoke from the bonfires wafted stronger the closer he came. At the corner, he dashed into the room with the sleeping mats, caught a flicker of movement near the far archway, and skidded to a stop.

Visdor stepped into the chamber.

The sage, or rather a human mage pretending to be a dwarven sage, appeared perfectly calm. In the mage's eyes, there was a sharp clarity of purpose that Ord had never seen.

As if in slow motion, the mage turned to face Ord and raised his hands. As Visdor locked his eyes onto the dwarf, lightning leaped from his fingertips.

Just as the dragon had appeared to Ord on the battlefield, so an image of himself zigzagging toward Visdor popped into Ord's thoughts. It made no sense. It was the last thing he wanted to do, but the feeling that it was the right thing grew as he dodged to the left.

The lightning from Visdor's fingers blackened the gray stone floor and sent wood, flame, and ash shooting into the air. Half-burned sticks struck the wall behind Ord, bounced back, and landed. Most burned harmless upon the gray stone, but some burning embers landed upon the straw mats and burst into flame.

The dwarf leaped over a small bonfire. Even through his armor, he felt a brief surge of heat. His feet touched down on the other side as the first of those who chased him erupted from the hallway, which led to the kitchen.

Visdor roared, somehow knowing of his failure to strike Ord despite his blind eyes. The lightning leaped again, ripping the air only a second behind the dwarf.

Stones burst from the wall as the lightning hit, revealing a second layer of stone behind the inside wall. The scorched rocks scattered as they hit the floor, breaking into even smaller pieces.

The warriors, which followed Ord from the kitchen hallway, scattered to avoid the lightning cast by Visdor. Blue energy crackled. Wood burst into flame. Black burn marks appeared on the stone. True to what Ord had seen in his vision, he zigzagged toward the mage.

Visdor was dead ahead. There was no ducking this time. Ord watched the buildup on the mage's fingertips crackle. A smug look crept across Visdor's face. And Ord knew there was no way this man could miss. Yet, the vision Ord saw said forward.

How can this be true?

With no other choice, rather than peeling to the right or left, Ord put on a burst of speed.

Behind the mage, the dark feathered shape of a raven darted from the corridor. A pixie shrieked. A human leaped back. The rest of the warriors, rushing from the hallway, tried to stop, but only slammed into those within the bonfire room who had already halted.

The raven soared in an arc, completed ninety percent of a circle, and looped directly toward Visdor. As the bird approached the mage, uncertainty danced across Visdor's features. The mage leaped sideways as if pushed by an invisible force. The raven lunged into a left turn and headed down the larger hallway.

Ord bolted past Visdor as the mage scrambled to rise. The dwarf's boots skidded on the stone as he tried to changed directions. Unable to avoid a collision with the right wall, Ord used his right arm to propel himself from it. Without a pause, he took off down the snake-like hallway toward the 4-way intersection from where he had originally come.

Still a short distance in front, the raven slowed, stretched its wings, and allowed Ord to catch up. Without the bird giving any other sign,

Ord knew what it wanted. The bird would guide him out.

But how did it find me?

As if it picked up that he understood, the raven flapped its wings and sped forward until it was ten feet ahead.

With the baby held tight, Ord followed the raven as it winged a path to the four-way intersection.

There had been no windows along this route and no additional doors for an exit.

How is Visdor's army getting out of this fortress?

Voices echoed behind him as those in command barked orders. After a momentary pause, running footsteps could be heard coming in his direction.

Around the next curve, the raven cut a tight circle in the air in the center of the 4-way intersection. While three of the lighted hallways were similar, the larger, darker one was not.

What is it doing?

The sounds of the warriors behind grew closer. He glanced toward the right hallway, which he knew would lead in the direction of Visdor's chamber.

Perhaps there is an entry farther down that hall?

He had no sooner decided to take it when the raven swept down the larger, darker hallway that descended deeper into the earth.

Ord hesitated. Of all the directions to go, this was the way he had chosen not to take, even at the beginning. Though it was the larger hallway, it had no light, which indicated to Ord it was not used by the bandits that called this fortress home.

With the siege engine parts in the workshop, there must be another way out.

The raven's gurgling cry echoed up to him from the darkness. The approach of those behind grew into a rumble as weapons clanged together and boots struck against the floor as they ran. At any moment, they would come around the snake-like curve of the hallway and be close enough to see him.

I hope you're right, raven, Ord thought as he took the left turn. He adjusted Shamira's hold. *For all our sakes, I hope you're right.*

As the candlelight faded behind him and his dwarven sight adapted to the dark, the steps he followed grew dim and changed from color to shades of gray. The left wall of the hall was made of natural cut rock. The right wall had been built of chiseled stone.

At one time, he thought, *before the fortress, this hall must have been part of a cave.*

Around a slight curve, still down more steps carved from the natural rock floor, a room with a pool in the center came into view. The pool had been squared off with carved steps all the way around it leading in from its sides. The floor of the room and pool steps had been covered in a type of mosaic tile. Each tile was approximately one foot by one foot. Glowing moss grew from the roman-like columns, which went from floor to ceiling. The moss cast a greenish light upon the room, and Ord's dwarven vision kicked out.

Drip. Drip. Drip.

The water glistened in the faint glow as drops from somewhere above created ripples in the pool surface.

The raven swept through the air, following the outer edges of the pool three times as it weaved around the columns. Cutting toward the center, it spiraled toward the ceiling.

Ord stepped out of the hallway to the edge of the pool steps and peered upward in an attempt to track the raven. He saw nothing but growing stalactites above the pool, the source of the drops which rippled the pool surface. Not even a hole in the rock let fresh air in from above.

Where is the bird going?

The raven rose to peak below a center stalactite and arced downward to dive toward the center of the pool.

He expected to see the bird curve, perhaps to head toward an unseen tunnel leading from the chamber, but it did not.

The raven plunged into the surface of the water. Ripples spread out from the raven's nosedive as water splashed upward.

Ord waited and watched. His fingers twitched on the arm holding Shamira as he heard the warriors behind. When the water drops fell back into the pool and ripples faded, the raven had vanished.

Ord stepped back from the edge of the water, his metal armor lightly hit together where the lining needed to be repaired. His lungs heaved as he listened to the warriors' approach behind him still waiting to see where the raven might emerge. It did not, and those that followed him had to be close.

He hurried to the right around the pool, looking to every corner of the room unable to understand where the raven could have gone.

The room appeared to have only one entry and that was behind him. The roman-like columns were decorated in olive branches with most of the columns standing against the walls.

Murals of bright colors depicted living things. These had been painted between each of the columns, upon the curved sections of the rock walls, giving the scenes depth and shadow. Blue skies, green trees, white-topped mountains, and forest creatures frolicked among the painted scenes. It was peaceful despite knowing that Visdor's warriors could storm into the chamber at any moment.

The raven had plunged into the pool and somehow escaped, for surely if it had died, it would have floated to the surface by now. Though he struggled to see the bottom of the pool, the greenish glow reflecting from the top of the water allowed him to see nothing below two feet.

Moved more by the ruckus behind him than belief that the raven had escaped, he stepped forward and placed his right foot in the water. The water flowed over his boot as he touched the first submerged step.

In the water sprite's pool, both he and Shamira had already had a bath today. He had no desire be wet again.

Although, he thought, *once the water nymph touched us, we had not stayed wet.*

From the other side of the pool where the entrance to the chamber was located, the thunder of the running warriors and the clang of their metal armor grew louder. If he was going to escape the way the raven had, it was now or never.

Shamira whimpered.

Ord knew she was hungry. Unfortunately, the kefir was gone, broken on the head of a commanding orc, and he had no way to get more even if he wanted to.

He gazed at the center of the pool where the raven had vanished. Despite the approach of the warriors behind him, he watched the ripples in the water as more drops fell from the stalactites above and looked for the truth of what to do next.

He gazed upward at the ceiling.

Surely, I am not supposed jump into the pool of water?

The words of the dragon echoed back from his memories, *Find the Branwen.*

He blinked and remembered when the ravens had guarded Shamira on the back of the wagon when he was first changing her. The same group of ravens had guided him to their nest to save them from the stone troll. They had also watched over him as he had fought the spiders.

And after my adventure with the water sprite, could a little more water truly hurt?

He bit his lip, mulling over his choices.

Who or what was this Branwen? Was it connected to the ravens or the dark elves or both?

Someone approached from the hallway that led to the pool. The step echoed to him as he stood silently on the first submerged step opposite the entrance to the pool chamber. They were searching now, uncertain where he had gone. In less than a minute, they would surely know.

He stepped into the pool. The water seeped between the joints of his armor soaking the pads beneath and filling his boots. Maybe it was the situation, but the water chilled him, sending a shiver up his spine, more than when he had stepped into the stream to help Frida.

He gazed from the pool to Shamira.

The water sprite helped the child. Would the sprite's magic still work without the nymph's presence?

Without effort, he counted three pairs of feet heading in his direction. At any moment, they would round the curve in the hallway. And while they may not know he was in the pool until they saw him, he didn't like the odds when they did.

Ord scrutinized the center of the pool while stepping closer to its depths. He did not like the murkiness that floated across the bottom, which hid the solid stone his feet walked upon.

He repeated to himself, *If the raven can do it, so can I.*

Though the ravens had never steered him wrong, he had not once encountered anything like this.

I have to believe. Perhaps . . .

An idea hit him.

A hole, he thought. *A center underground tunnel in the pool could have allowed the raven to dive down and emerge somewhere else. That makes sense.*

He stepped deeper. The chill of the water stung him as it reached his thigh. He inhaled, held his breath, and walked toward the center.

The water rose, reaching his waist. By instinct, he held Shamira higher.

Past the waist, the liquid brushed against his chest armor in waves, seeping through where the joints interlocked and the metal overlapped.

He shivered as his joints moved slower beneath the water, like pins stabbing against his skin. On instinct and using both hands, he brought Shamira up to his head. In a final step, he reached the center of the pool.

Nothing, he thought. *Nada.*

He stood there, a foot taller than the deepest spot and waited. The sting of the cold pierced through his resolve. The surface of the pool flattened as the ripples he generated by his movement faded away, replaced only by the waves caused by the stalactites' drips.

Ping.

A drop hit him on the top of his helmet.

Ping.

The sound grated against his nerves. He shifted to the right so the drops would hit the surface of the water.

His whole body shook, the coolness of the pool stealing the life from his limbs.

I cannot stay here any longer, he thought, his gaze going to the only entrance of the chamber.

The footsteps in the hallway were within seconds of arriving at the pool. He turned around in desperation, rotated right, and studied the murals to find a sign, a signal, anything to tell him how to make the pool work.

The hard pool bottom felt firm beneath his feet. The murky water in the greenish glow, stirred by his turning, swirled around him as he continued to complete his circle. The little clarity of the upper translucent part of the pool surface swept away as gritty mud rose from below.

Heart thudding, pulse pounding, he wondered if he could get to the pool edge in time to meet these warriors with his great war hammer in his hand.

This is no way for a dwarf to die, he thought, *trusting in a bird to show the way when I have a war hammer secured to my back.*

The footsteps coming down the stairs halted, and a warrior called out, "He has to be down here. Get the others."

Shamira remained quiet: no more murmurs or whines. The odd sense that she, too, waited permeated his being though he could not see her face.

He lowered Shamira to see her expression.

She gazed wide-eyed at the world until she spotted him looking at her, and then a wide smile brightened her countenance.

What does she know? he thought and then shook his head.

Nothing. She knows nothing. She is only a baby.

He could not fight without a weapon, and he could not hold Shamira over his head and draw the great war hammer from the sheath on his back.

He whispered to Shamira, "I'm right here, baby girl. I need to know if Cy's gift still works. I need you to trust me."

She gurgled unconcerned at his words and waved her hands without any particular direction.

Despite the cold, sweat dripped down the sides of his head inside his helmet as he touched Shamira to the surface of the pool. His heart beating like a drum, he dipped her down into the water.

The liquid encircled her wrapping, but the wrapping did not absorb the water. Inch by inch, he lowered her deeper until the cold pool water flowed over the wrappings and touched her face and hands.

Shamira played, delighted at the water around her. Her tiny voice babbled throwing in high-pitched sounds of joy.

"Shh." He shot a glance at the hallway entrance. Two warriors rounded the curve of the hallway, humans carrying torches. Unlike his kind, humans were not able to see in the dark. This gave Ord only a few more precious seconds.

He released his hold on Shamira and reached for his war hammer.

Shamira floated.

There is no way the wrapping could have done that by itself.

She giggled.

The warriors turned in Ord's direction as the giggle echoed in the chamber. They walked closer to the pool, swords ready, torches held up, trying to see across the water. The orange-red of the torches displaced the green glow to the edge of the torchlight. This worked against them but made them quite visible to Ord.

Ord let Shamira float though he reached out to keep her close with his right hand. At the same time, he drew his great war hammer with his left.

His armor's underpadding was soaked. Combined with the weight of the plate-mail armor, and sluggishness of his movements in the cold water, the odds did not look good.

But by all the dwarven gods, he thought, *I will not go down without a fight.*

He growled, the sound halting the two humans in their tracks, and then removed the war hammer from his sheath.

Where is that bloody raven?

Maintaining his hold on Shamira above the pool surface, he ducked his head into the water and scowered the murkiness for a sign before committing to the inevitable battle. The pool showed him the dusty swirl of ages, but there was no raven.

Lifting his head from the water, the liquid dripped from his helmet running down the helmet's sides to return to the pool. Calm settled over him. He focused on the two humans. Whether he liked it or not, he was trapped, the raven was gone, and he must meet his enemies.

From the entry hallway, additional torchlights brightened the stairs. The sound of rushing feet on stone sent vibrations across the pool.

The hairs on his arms stood up, and he knew a mixed hoard of armed warriors rushed toward him from the other end of the hallway. Once their combined torches lit the room, they would know exactly where he was.

Their war cries, the cry for the blood of the invader who had dared enter their own fortress, the invader who had challenged their master, was a familiar song, sung by his own race on the field of battle.

If I am going to die here, he thought, *I will go out swinging.*

Ord tightened his grip on his hammer, shifting it so that his right fist was closer to the hammer's head while keeping Shamira held to him against his left shoulder.

Bellows multiplied as additional torches, carried by more warriors, drove the green glow farther away.

Ready or not, he thought, *here we go.*

Ord tried to step toward the outer edge of the pool to meet the oncoming enemy. He leaned but his feet stayed in place. Waving the hammer held in his right hand to regain his balance, he fought to stay standing.

Snake-like tendrils encircled his legs, traveled past his knees, surrounded his thighs, and wrapped around his waist.

The warriors splashed toward the center of the pool. The shorter members dropped back.

The first archer drew his bowstring and let his arrow fly. With a jerk, the tendrils dragged Ord below the pool surface.

The arrow stabbed the water above him. Air bubbled from it as it slowed and floated upward. A second and third arrow struck the water, their angles steeper, their points stabbing down farther, but it was too late.

What little he could see went dark. The tendrils tugged him downward through the bottom of the pool that was no longer there.

"Sleep," said a female voice from everywhere around him but nowhere at all. "Sleep, you have been given permission to pass."

Chapter 11

Dreams filled Ord's thoughts, the distorted glimpses of people he had never met and places he had never been.

A room made of gray stone with the Mundgurun, the round table that had written upon it the Guardians' names, had appeared. However, the place it existed in was different than the illusion the deceptive Visdor had created.

And then, a huge lake where there should be none filled a valley. It faded away until a royal chamber with six thrones, each made of a different type of material, formed in his mind.

A grown up Shamira holding her staff gazed upon a huge lake. A man, unlike any he had ever met, flipped his fishtail up on land, and it transformed into two legs in a swirl of rainbow colors. A golden dragon gazed down at the man as its wings held up the falling partitions of realms in chaos.

Ord twisted and turned, struggling to open his eyes. He became conscious of his fingertips touching the inside of his gauntlets. The padding was dry and yet, his armor pushed through a thick medium of an unknown substance.

Where am I?

The thickness existed around him, and yet, it did not. Though he knew his eyelids were open, he saw nothing, and he realized the truth to his situation.

There is nothing to see.

Slowly, he parted his lips. Though he could feel the tip of his tongue touch them, he sensed no sensation beyond himself. The thickness that his appendages pressed through did not apply the same pressure to his face. When he opened his mouth, nothing entered, and nothing left.

What is happening to me?

Out of the absence of light and dark, pressure and no pressure, a boundary approached. He could feel a tug through every part of his being drawing him closer to whatever generated the pull.

The distance closed, although how he knew was not apparent. The tug grew stronger. As he accelerated toward it, a single image flashed in his mind.

It was a tiny hammer worn about the neck. The head of the hammer was shaped like his war hammer, but the handle held a dual twist creating the illusion of the points on a star. It matched the amulet he had thrown at the red dragon . . .

Ord sucked in air, not water-air like the nymph had provided. It was real, honest-to-goodness, air laced with the smell of forest, dirt, and water. He blinked up at a blue sky with sparse white clouds to his right. The sound of falling water caught his attention. It wasn't like the water sprite's thundering waterfall but more like the trickle of a small spring.

He felt . . . relaxed, like a great weight had been taken off his armored shoulders. Shoulders. Arms. Despite the stiff muscles, he lurched to a sitting position as he realized his left arm was empty. "Shamira."

"Shh." Jada smiled at him holding the little goblin baby as she rocked it in her arms. "You'll wake your daughter."

Beside her, a bottle of Kefir sat alongside a cloth with breadcrumbs lying on it. Some of the broken bread had been mixed in Shamira's elf-carved bowl. Half had been eaten.

His eyes felt as big as saucers. "How?" Confusion spread across his face. "Where? When?"

Other voices came from a distance. Ord could have sworn he heard Aidan talking with Frida.

Talking? he thought. *And no haughty remarks? I have to be dreaming.*

A large creature shifted in the trees grunting as it approached the clearing.

Jada looked up, a pleasant smile on her face. "He's awake, Vindr."

Ord watched the ravens settle around him. Their gurgling croaks varied in tone and frequency. And while some stretched their tail feathers as others rolled in the dirt, more of the ravens landed to cock their heads in his direction.

Jada's pleasant smile brightened. "They want to know if you are better."

Ord watched a raven jump on his armored leg and stare up at him. He slowly answered, "I . . . don't know what occurred to tell if I am better." He looked over his arms and legs. "Did something happen that I should know about? Last I knew, I was dragged beneath the surface of a pool inside some type of fortress." The dwarf paused, a frown forming on his face. "I didn't imagine that, did I?"

With a slight chuckle, Jada shook her head. "No, that was very real. The place you were at is called Halvardor."

"Whoa, whoa, whoa." Ord held up his hands.

Ravens fluffed their wings. A few stepped back. However, the one on his leg remained where it was staring up at him.

Ord continued. "Wait a minute. That was the place it would take us until morning to reach." His eyes caught the blue sky above him. "What day is it?"

Her face appeared sympathetic. "Between no sleep and no food, you collapsed when you stepped through the Halvardor's water portal."

Ord scrutinized her look to see if she was hiding anything or simply misinformed. He remembered being pulled down, not collapsing. He even recalled something saying *he was allowed to pass.* "And where did the portal go? To here?" He waved to the pool on his left. It was just beyond the border of the camp.

Jada nodded. "Should the fortress ever be taken, it was through this water portal the defenders could escape." She looked to the forest behind Ord. Her eyes narrowed as her face filled with worry. "We have yet to know if they did escape. If Halvardor has been taken, the City of Taika may be in worse condition than we thought."

Ord said, "The fortress was old and in disrepair. If it was taken, it happened long ago. I think these new bandits simply walked in and claimed it."

His words made her pause.

"Yes," she finally said. "How could I have forgotten?"

The raven on Ord's leg croaked at him. When Ord looked down at it, the bird turned an eye toward him and blinked. The dwarf glanced at Jada. "What is it saying?"

She snapped out of her thoughts and grinned at Ord. "*It* is a *she*. And she is thanking you for saving their children. A whole new generation will be born because of what you did."

The dwarf watched the bird eye him. In a quiet voice, he answered though he felt a little self-conscious, "You are welcome."

The raven fluttered her wings.

"Oh, wait," he said. Reaching for the echor on his belt, he opened the drawstring. Just as Jada had said, the single egg he had placed in it bobbed to the top. He picked it out carefully and placed the egg in his palm. The egg was still warm. Wrinkling his forehead, he set the egg on the ground beside him.

The raven hopped off his leg to stand alongside the egg. She moved her beak closer to eye the unborn bird.

Other ravens gathered around. Their gurgling croaks rose as if a huge discussion took place among them. When they stopped, the first raven rolled the egg toward Ord's hand. The female raven's head came up and looked him in the eye.

Jada said in a quiet voice, "It's yours, Ord. A gift from the ravens."

"But," he opened his eyes wide, "I don't know how to hatch an egg."

Aidan chuckled and for the first time Ord realized the male dark elf was listening to everything being said.

Jada gently rocked Shamira. "Place it back into the echor until you find a spot to keep it warm. It will keep."

Ord picked up the egg, remembering the aid these ravens had offered in protecting his daughter. "I am honored."

With careful fingers, he placed the warm egg back in the bag and pulled the drawstring closed. He darted a glance toward Jada. "You still haven't answered my question of where we are."

Aidan stepped within view and said, his voice sharp, "Past Halvardor. A day from Taika. If it weren't for you, we'd be much farther along."

"That's not true," Frida came in behind Aidan. "We've only just arrived."

Ord took in all three. "I don't understand."

Jada squinted at Aidan, throwing the elf a frown. "According to the ravens, you were found in the fortress of Halvardor. We were forced to slow our advance while searching for where you were taken."

"The ravens found you." Frida held an open palm toward the flock. "Vindr and I wanted to storm the fortress, but Jada directed us here saying we would meet you at the pool."

Jada nodded. "I knew of the water portal and told the ravens. If I were to guess, the old sage's magic affected your perception of time.

For you, it may have felt as if you traveled instantaneously to the fortress, yet, it was not so."

The ravens drifted over to the pool, past the edge of camp, and drank. Unlike the water nymph's basin, they had no problem frolicking at the edges and bathing in the waters. A few ravens splashed the others. Those farther back croaked in laughter.

"Maybe that would explain Shamira's reaction," Ord pondered out loud. "She was sleepy when we arrived . . ." He wrinkled his brow. ". . . and hungry. I was out of breath." The dwarf listened to the birds flapping as they bathed in the clear fresh water.

"Sleepy?" Jada looked down at the little girl and studied her features. "I don't think the sage realized he had taken two people at once."

Ord shook his head. "He didn't. He was a blind mage pretending to be a dwarven sage."

Jada's eyebrows rose. "A blind mage, you say?" She flicked her gaze toward Aidan. "That explains the rest of the story. If this is true, the situation is worse than we thought."

Aidan nodded. "Time is short. It may already be too late."

The dwarf squinted at the two elves as he rubbed his gauntleted thumb against his gauntleted pointing finger on his left hand. "Aren't you even curious as to what happened to me or is this one of those, *it's your test* scenarios?" Smoke wafted toward Ord as the wind shifted, and for the first time, he realized there was a crackling fire. He sniffed. The smell of roasting rabbit brightened his eyes.

Aidan huffed. "He has to ask."

Frida folded her arms and glared at Aidan. "Of course, he does."

"The ravens informed me of the situation," Jada said, with only a slight warning nod to Aidan. "The part they knew, that is. By the time we got to the fortress, there was no one at the ruins. Perhaps your appearance spooked them, and they changed campsites?"

Knowing you had already escaped and that time was of importance, we continued to follow the trail to where I knew you would be."

She adjusted Shamira in her arms. "And neither of you were worse from wear." She smiled down into the baby's face.

Shamira reached up trying to catch hold of Jada's long black hair as the wind whipped the strands to the front of her body.

Frida stepped closer to Ord, her club held against her right shoulder with her right hand. In her left hand, she held a small bundle tied at the top with a thin leather strip. She placed the bundle on the ground beside him.

He could smell the scent of garlic mixed with thyme used as a seasoning for some traditional dwarven dishes. His stomach growled much louder than he would have thought possible.

She giggled. "And just in time, too."

"Thank you." He had no sooner finished the words, than his hands undid the leather tie around the top of the bundle. He couldn't be certain, but it looked like lamb.

Placing the end of a sliced piece in his mouth, he let his tongue savor the seasoning used in just the right amounts. It enhanced the texture, merging with the natural meaty taste.

He bit in, forcing himself to chew slowly, tasting the juices. When he could not stand it anymore, he swallowed.

This is heaven, he thought.

The meat traveled down his throat and landed in his stomach. Ord closed his eyes and sighed. Taking a second bite, this one he chewed a little bit faster, his gurgling stomach demanding more.

"Ah," he took a third, "you're a life saver, lass. I mean, we dwarves are a hearty folk. We could go for days without food, but I'd rather not push it." He opened his eyes and grinned at her.

Frida blushed. "I'm glad you like it. It is a special treat that my third . . ." She tapped her lips. ". . . or was it my fourth husband enjoyed? Anyway, he loved it, that big ol' troll."

Ord opened his eyes wide. "Troll, you say? Third or fourth?" He glanced up at Vindr. "As big as your cousin?"

He looked down at the meat he was eating and squeezed it between two fingers. Juice oozed out.

In a quiet voice, he asked, "This isn't *human* is it?"

Frida chuckled followed by Vindr's odd grunts of humor.

"No," she laughed, "it is mutton." She patted his armored shoulder. "Vindr caught it for me on our way to the pool. I'd never do that to you, Ord."

"Huh," he sighed in relief, cut the sigh short, and sheepishly looked back at Frida. "I mean . . . ," he weakly chuckled, "ha . . . I knew that." Ord nodded though he did squeeze the meat a second time just to make sure of its texture.

"Ah, mutton," he finally said, relaxing. "Great food."

Would a bulder even care if the meal was human? he thought as he chewed. *Vindr certainly would prefer it.*

Ninety percent sure it was lamb, at least he was going to accept that it was, he ate faster than he probably should.

Frida placed a wooden mug beside him filled to the brim with sweet smelling ale.

Ord raised the mug, eyed the liquid as the sun glimmered in its translucent golden surface, and drank down a swallow.

He raised an eyebrow toward Frida. "Honey mead? Delicious." He stopped again and stared into the mug. "This is honey mead, right?"

She nodded her head, cracking a wide grin. "Yes, Ord. You know it is."

"Good, good." The dwarf sipped more, just to be sure of the taste. Satisfied, he continued to eat the mutton. When he picked up the mug again, he noticed the initials T.M. carved into the handle of the wooden mug. A gold base supported the bottom of the mug with a silver line running around its circumference in the middle. "A relative of yours?"

Frida glanced at the initials and nodded. "My last husband carried it when I met him, but I don't think it was his. I don't know where he got it." She gave him a whimsical smile. "You may keep it if you wish."

Tree limbs swayed above them as ravens took off from the upper branches. The smoke of the fire filtered up through the leaves.

"No, no." Ord shook his head, placing the mug beside him as he resumed working on the meat. "I would never want to keep a memory."

The female troll laughed. "I have plenty of mugs. It was just the first I took for my rucksack." With a raised eyebrow, she gauged his expression. "Tell you what? Just keep it for a while till you don't need it anymore. If you don't want it by then, I'll drop it back in, no questions asked."

Ord watched her for sincerity and thought, *I don't want to hurt her feelings.*

"Just for a while." He winked and turned back to the meal.

Frida blushed again.

Ord swallowed his last bite, watching her from the corner of his eye.

He looked down at his mutton. Only a piece or two and he would be done. He picked up one and chewed while thinking over what had happened to him and Shamira.

Most of the ravens had finished their bathing. The sound of the splashing of their bodies in the pool dwindled until it stopped. With a brief flap of their wings, the birds rose into the air and perched among the tree limbs above the pool. The wind and sun worked together to dry them.

"So, uh," Ord munched on his last piece of mutton, "who exactly pulled Shamira and me from the pool?"

No one answered.

He turned his head to catch the eye of those around him one at a time.

While Aidan added a small log to the fire, the dark elf turned away from the dwarf's gaze. "Don't look at me." He tilted his head as if listening to something and then walked toward the trees across the clearing to the south.

Three ravens darted above Ord and flew in the direction Aidan went.

"Come on," Ord peered at Jada. "You said the ravens told you what happened. If that's so, you have got to know how I ended up here."

She shook her head.

He continued. "Don't you see the conflict between the time it took Shamira and I to get here and the time it took the rest of you? And if not you, who pulled us from the water portal?"

Two ravens returned from the south and landed in the branches above the pool. Their gurgles caught Ord's attention, but he turned back to Jada and Frida.

Ord said, "Surely someone knows the answers my questions?"

Jada looked down at Shamira. "Ord, you were just here when we arrived. I knew where to find you. My vision did not give any details."

A raven fluttered down from a branch to land beside Jada. A series of gurgling croaks left its throat.

Jada nodded to the raven and then looked over to catch Ord's gaze. "Ord, please join Aidan. He will need your help."

"My help?" Ord chewed on the last of the meat. "Since when does Aidan need my help at all?" He drank some more of the honey mead and rolled his eyes at Jada. "He's got everything worked out already. Just ask him."

Jada said nothing, but her stern look spoke volumes.

Ord slowly chewed the last of the lamb watching her expression and thought, *She's serious.*

He downed the rest of the mead. "You mean it? Right? This is not some test-the-dwarf scenario?"

Jada did not blink.

Wiping off his mouth, he glanced to the right across the clearing.

Of course, he thought, *it will always take a dwarf to pull a dark elf out of trouble, especially Aidan.*

He set the mug down and turned to Frida. "Thank you."

She nodded. "You are welcome."

Ord slowly picked himself up, moved his stiff feet and ankles, and then, in gradual stages, worked out the kinks in his shoulders, arms, and back.

In the dwarven camp, armor was removed each night. And despite the superior dwarven padding inside his armor, he hadn't taken it off since the day of the battle.

How long was I out?

He took a few steps, the muscles becoming more flexible as he moved. Despite the strange dreams, he did feel rested.

He crossed to the south side of the clearing and passed into the forest, the last place he had seen Aidan go. A glance back showed Jada still holding Shamira as she talked to the baby in low soothing tones. With her eyes fixed on the trees, Shamira appeared to be listening, not to Jada, but to the ravens near the pool. Frida could not be seen.

A small path led through the undergrowth. From the periodic tracks, deer roamed through these forests. He looked closely for prints in the shape of the elven boots that Aidan wore. It was a good ten feet in before he spotted the first partial print.

He cringed as leaves crunched beneath his feet made worse by the heavy weight of his plate-mail. The armor was great for battle.

However, the weight made it near impossible to stay silent while he tracked through the forest.

The conifers of the upper hills were fewer here. Oak was more frequent than ash. Going south meant descending the mountainous areas of Eurig toward the great forests where the tribe known as the woodland elves lived.

It still made no sense to him about the loss of time and who had put him and Shamira beside the pool. It made even less sense that no one had even suggested a reasonable explanation.

Jada must know more than what she is saying.

Something grabbed Ord by his shoulder armor and attempted to pull him to the right.

Ord twisted around and stepped backward with fisted gauntlets raised and ready.

Aidan jumped to the side and growled in an elevated whisper, "What are you doing here? You make enough noise to wake the dead."

Ord narrowed his eyes at the elf. "Jada sent me."

Aidan pursed his lips. He finally grunted, "Fine. Just keep it down and stay out of my way."

Without looking to see if Ord followed, the dark elf started down the narrow trail.

To their right, a jutting rock face went up in sedimentary layers, reaching a height somewhere near the treetops. Vertical crevices had been cut into the rock face by water flow, creating recesses large enough for Ord to hide.

Despite both moving through the forest, they saw no one else. A few birds called in the distance. Wind rustled the leaves.

There is nothing wrong here except for the company, Ord grumbled in his mind. *Why in the dwarven kingdom did Jada send me to help?*

The trail reached a t-section, which branched to the left and right, along a winding creek some thirty feet below. The left traveled through the forest as the ground sloped to the winding creek. The right skirted a rock face with a two-foot ledge and a sharp drop. At this location, neither direction was climbable. They followed the trail to the left.

She has to be avoiding my questions, Ord thought.

The ground they walked on was a combination of black dirt, decaying leaves, and white shale rock. Green moss existed in patches on the south side of the trees and in shaded spots upon the ground. The trail wound away to the right, still following the creek, until the creek became hidden due to the multitude of trees.

Listening to something Ord could not hear, Aidan tilted his head, slipped off the path toward the creek, and kneeled before a fallen log. He peered at a view between the branches. However, before Ord could identify what the elf had spotted, Aidan stepped over the log and moved farther down the slope as if Ord wasn't there at all. Despite the elf's quickness, Ord stayed right behind.

A bluff, overlooking the creek, came into view. The land on the far side of the brook gently sloped down meeting what little water existed in the small depressions in the creek bed. Water flowed down the creek but only a trickle. The far side of the brook was the perfect place for a campsite, and someone had taken advantage of that fact.

Pointing, Aidan said in a quiet and grudging voice, "Do you recognize them?"

The dwarf eyed those around the cook fire. He said in a whisper, "I don't know them, exactly, but they are dressed like part of the same group I encountered at Halvardor." He pointed at those around the fire. "I know they have at least three companies out. Although, how many soldiers are in each company I did not have time to discover."

Aidan sneered, rolling his eyes at Ord. "Great scouting. No wonder the dwarves are losing the war."

Ord tightened his jaw.

"An elven scout would have noted not only the number, but the exact weapons, who was in command, and even the commander's preference for dinner." Aidan shook his head. "Tell you what, you go back to Jada, tell her you did your job, and let *me* figure this out." He eyed Ord's plate-mail with disgust. "I'll find out who they really are, and how many they run per company." Aidan turned in dismissal and started back up the slope.

Ord slowly stood. He watched the dark elf climb toward the trail. With purposeful steps, he worked his own way up. Before he reached the path, Aidan had already gone farther down and was almost out of sight.

Ord followed, moving faster than the elf's pace and keeping the dark elf in view. The trail curved to the right around a thick group of trees.

Aidan slowed.

Ord stopped within two feet of Aidan, hands at his sides and shoulders back. He said nothing.

Aidan turned to face Ord. "I said, go back. That was not a request. Perhaps the plate-mail helmet is stopping up your ears?" He reached forward to tap Ord on the helmet.

To Aidan's surprise, Ord caught his wrist. "Aidan, what in the dwarven kingdom do you have against me when you two brought me along?"

The dark elf sneered though when he tried to pull his arm back, he grimaced. He could not break Ord's grip. "You're a dwarf. Isn't that enough?" He glared at Ord's hold, daring him to keep holding on.

Ord growled. "And you're an elf, a dark elf at that. Your kind broke the truce, invaded our camp, and carried me off. For all I know your kind butchered the rest of my comrades-in-arms, although Jada claims that did not happen." He shook his head. "And the smell, by all the gods, you male dark elves should really bathe more often."

Well, maybe we all smell after no sleep and all this activity, he thought. *But the insult makes me feel better.*

Aidan opened his mouth to speak, but Ord pushed on. "But you don't see me attacking you at every step of the journey. Jada talks about how you two are different from the other dark elves. Maybe she is, but not you. And I'm done with it." He twisted Aidan's arm until the dark elf winced in pain, drawing the elf closer and glaring into Aidan's eyes.

The elf jeered. "So, dwarf, what's it to you? Just run along like a good puppy and go back to camp. I'm sure Jada will have other things to keep you entertained."

"Look," Ord prickled more, "I'm trying to work this out before it comes to blows." He thrust Aidan back, releasing his wrist. "Jada would not be happy if you got hurt."

Aidan rubbed his wrist and laughed. "You and what dwarven army? You wouldn't get two steps without me putting an arrow through the smallest crevice on the suit of tin you wear."

Ord took a deep breath. His eyes burned red. "And you wouldn't know constraint if it walked up and bashed you across the rear of the head."

The elf reached for his bow. "Maybe you're right. I'll make it a small wound so Frida can baby you a while."

Ord struck with his right gauntlet, knocking the bow from the elf's hand.

Aidan's face flooded crimson. His chest swelled. The dark elf roared in rage. He dove at Ord, disturbing two squirrels, which were quietly watching from higher in the nearest tree.

Aidan slammed into Ord at the waist. Ord jarred as he hit the ground on his back. Their bodies tumbled down the southern slope.

Even without gloves, Aidan used his elven fists to beat against Ord's armor. Flesh gave against metal. Cuts and scrapes decorated the elf's knuckles as they started to bleed.

Ord taunted, "The bugbear I encountered hit harder."

Though the elf could not harm Ord, the strikes came quick, making it difficult to fend them off.

They rolled down the sloping grade. Leaves crunched. Dirt flew. Branches broke. Birds shot into the air. A fox scurried away. Black arrows scattered from Aidan's quiver.

Ord spied a large rock before he rolled over and slammed into it with his armored back. At the same time, he knocked the breath out of Aidan with his left gauntleted hand to the dark elf's solar plexus.

Aidan tried to suck in air, but was unable to breath. He clung with one hand to the gorget protecting Ord's throat, desperately trying to catch his breath and refusing to stop in his attempt to choke Ord.

Ord grudgingly thought, *The elf certainly knows how to take punishment.*

The rock behind Ord gave, the ground shifted, and they fell through the air.

Aidan let go of Ord, pushing away and sending his own body to the left. Ord tumbled, forcing himself away from Aidan while noting the pooling water beneath them in the creek.

Splash.

They landed fifteen feet apart in a pool of water near the northern bank.

The liquid and mud shot in all directions. The mud rained down splattering them both.

Ord groaned, lying still as he sucked in air to fill his empty lungs. He looked at Aidan. The elf was on his left, wiping the water from his face.

To Ord's right, running feet splashed through the water and caught his attention, but his immediate problem was what Aidan would do next.

Aidan lifted himself up, having landed on his chest. Mud dripped from his leather armor, hairless face, and shoulder length hair. He glared at Ord as his lungs heaved. Without waiting, he used his hands to grab small exposed roots to crawl up the bank, slipping in the mud and dirt.

Ord slowed his heartbeat. He reached over and took hold of a tree root with his left hand. Slowly, he pulled himself up the bank until only his boots dangled in the creek pool.

An orc's familiar deep voice said, "I know you."

CHAPTER 12

Ord attempted to blink the water out of his eyes, which dripped down from his hair. As he focused on the orc, the blurry image came into sharper view. Generally, he couldn't tell one orc from another, but this one he had just met. "Agugh?"

Agugh growled, clenching his fists as he started around the pool toward the dwarf.

Ord struggled to get his feet under him, but his dwarven boots slipped in the mud, cutting grooves into the water soaked soil. He glanced at Aidan.

Water dripped off the dark elf's clothes, but at least the red flush was gone from Aidan's face.

Or was it? he thought. *The elf seems in no hurry to help.*

"So, Agugh," Ord grinned, "out with the rest of the troop?"

Ord reached back for his war hammer but found it gone.

That's right, he thought. *I had it in the pool before something jerked me down.*

With his peripheral vision, he looked for any object that he could use as a weapon while keeping focused on Agugh. "Out for a hike, maybe? Perhaps a stroll?"

Agugh snarled, stomping into the water directly in front of Ord.

Ord grabbed his boot knife, but the orc kicked it out of his hand.

Still keeping eye contact, Agugh reached slowly down, grabbed onto Ord's left foot with his right hand and dragged him toward the deeper water in the pool. The orc grunted out, "This is for Sebar, my pixie friend."

Ord clung to a tree root. It snapped. He scrambled to grasp a large rock but it pulled from the mud. He chunked it at Agugh.

The orc chuckled as the rock bounced off his chest armor.

Shaking his head, Ord sighed. "So, I guess we're not friends anymore?"

The orc evilly grinned and said in the common tongue, "You'll wish we were."

Ord rolled sideways toward Agugh's right hand, twisting his left foot out of Agugh's grasp and slamming his right foot into the orc's wrist.

Agugh snatched for the dwarf's right foot with his left hand but missed. The dwarf slammed a kick to Agugh's chest as the water seeped into his own chest armor.

Agugh staggered backward, caught his balance, and surged toward Ord.

Ord shifted onto his back, brought his foot up, and smashed it into the orc's groin.

Agugh roared.

Others ran toward them. They splashed down the creek from farther up the stream toward Agugh's campsite.

Aidan picked up a large branch, walked up behind Agugh, and slammed the branch into the base of the orc's skull.

Thud.

The branch broke. Agugh crumpled.

Aidan tossed the remaining piece of the branch into the pool and washed the blood from his knuckles. He glanced at Ord and then warily watched upstream. The running feet of others, probably Agugh's mates, came closer. He said with much less arrogance in his voice, "We don't have time for this nonsense anymore."

"No," Ord met his eyes, "we don't."

Rising from the pool Aidan walked over and extended his hand to Ord. "I don't like you. I'm not sure I can. But I'll not betray you. On that, you have my word."

Ord hesitated but reached up and grasped Aidan's extended hand. As Aidan pulled back to help the dwarf to his feet, Ord noticed the deeper cuts on Aidan's fists. "How are you going to explain this to Jada?"

Aidan sniffed. "I'm not saying a word."

Ord turned to spot his knife half-covered in mud, stuck about a foot above the water level. He cleaned it in the water, despite the sounds of others coming to investigate what had happened, and dried it as best he could before sticking it back in his boot sheath.

The metallic clang of weapons echoed from upstream as at least two warriors came from the direction of Agugh's campsite.

With a nod toward each other, Aidan and Ord raced downstream.

The north bank, though only about twenty feet up at their present point, was unyielding. No climbable trails gave way. Only sparse trees had attempted to grow out next to the water. More than likely when it rained, a deluge raged down this creek bed, exposing the additional roots of ancient trees farther up the sides.

Avoiding the water as much as possible, Aidan said between breaths, "It's the bow I'm worried about, not the cuts."

Around a bend, they spotted a bank with a forty-five-degree incline. Small four-foot trees had taken root into the north bank.

Using the small tree trunks as handholds, they climbed out of the creek and scrambled up the northern side of the stream, pushing through the underbrush in an unsteady line to the top.

The splashing sounds of Agugh's fellow warriors grew distant. Those who hunted them had moved farther downstream, had stopped, or had gone back to camp. In any case, if the enemy warriors had found Agugh's body, it would not be good. Ord and Aidan had to warn the others.

The trail, which followed the creek to the west and east, appeared through the trees. Ord's keen eye spotted only animal prints on the ground. It was their only good omen.

He dodged around a large oak tree and listened to the sounds of a quiet forest, caught in a wind, which blew from the west. Aidan and Ord slowed to a walk as both worked to catch their breath.

"And the arrows?" Ord questioned as they turned west toward the camp.

Without insults, he thought, *this is the longest continuous interaction I have ever had with Aidan.*

Aidan frowned throwing a glance at Ord. "More in the wagon."

They walked quietly for a moment before Aidan cleared his throat. "Look, as I said, I still don't like you, but . . ." He pursed his lips as if fighting a great battle inside. "I'll *try* to be more civil."

Ord nodded. "Mind telling me why you really don't like me?" He rolled his eyes toward Aidan. "Other than you're a dark elf?"

Aidan squinted at the forest in front of them. Nothing stirred as they headed back toward their campsite. He checked the ground but saw no footprints other than their own.

"Don't push it," he finally said. "This is only the beginning."

Clan Ravensmith: City of Taika
Preview

Ord, the six-foot dwarf, clad in plate-mail armor, hurried along beside the dark elf archer, Aidan. They rounded an outcropping of rock, following the westward trail as shouts of angry warriors echoed through the forest.

Aidan picked up the pace.

Ord leaped from a fast walk to a jog. The mud from their fall into the water had dried and begun to flake off as he hurried through the forest. After their tumble down the side of the hill into the creek and their encounter with Visdor's patrol, he really wanted a bath. At least one good thing had come out of the fight between him and Aidan, a grudging respect from both sides.

Responding to the dark elf's last statement, he caught Aidan's eye and said, "And a beginning that needs to wait." He turned his head, trying to get a better feel for where the warrior shouts came from.

The direction is wrong, he thought, and then said out loud, "The warriors are not behind us."

As the leaves swirled around them, a burst of wind ruffled Aidan's shoulder length hair. The elf shook his head while keeping in step. He placed a hand before him. As the wind blew through his fingers, he squinted toward the right. "That's coming from our camp."

Both spurred themselves into a run. Leaves crunched along the track. A raven darted past, only to change course and zip up behind them. A shrill call gurgled from its throat.

"What's it telling you?" Ord asked between exhales with a single nod at the raven. Despite his and Aidan's truce, he'd be horsewhipped before he let the dark elf reach the camp first. And he was sure Aidan felt the same.

The elf raised an eyebrow never easing up on the pace, but no insult left his lips. "It's not telling me anything. It's letting Jada know where we are."

Continued in Clan Ravensmith: City of Taika

Pronunciation Guide to Clan Ravensmith, Abridged

Bob the Pixie's comments for each name, place, or thing will be between the square brackets. They may or may not make sense for he is a pixie after all. The comments within standard parentheses are my author notes and will be denoted AU.

Not all words may be in this book, Clan Ravensmith, as Bob the pixie does tend to ramble on without realizing it. Hopefully, I have verified them all. However, if I missed one, please let me know.

Who is Bob the Pixie? Pick up a copy of The Wall Outside, the first book in the Xun Ove series, and find out for yourself, if you don't already know.

~ James William Peercy

Agugh ('Ag-you-guh / ag-' yü-gə) – [Burr up the . . . (AU: See Clan Ravensmith.)]

Aidan ('A-done / ā-'dən) – [Burr up the . . . (AU: See Clan Ravensmith.)]

Anryulong ('ahn-roo-long / 'än- rü- lȯŋ) – [Could be a dragon, could be something else...Teasing not advised. (AU: See *Twisted Fates*.)]

Bugbear ('bug-bear / ' bəg-ber) – [Poor thing! (AU: See Clan Ravensmith.)]

Bob (bob / bäb) – [Pixie extraordinaire; Winger through the skies; Recorder of all things Xun Ove. (AU: The pixie kept circling around me until I added his name, too. However, he still refuses to give his real name. I will keep trying. See *The Wall Outside*, *Partition Majik*, *Twisted Fates*, and *Tainted Soul*. Is there ever a book Bob isn't in?)]

Branwen ('bran-ween / 'bran-wēn) – [Such dark beauty . . . (AU: See *Clan Ravensmith*.)]

Daarkob (dar-'cob / dār-'käb) – [Color is no excuse for bad manners! (AU: See *Clan Ravensmith*.)]

Dimur ('dimmer / 'di-mər) – [Yes sir! Ready sir! (AU: See *Clan Ravensmith*.)]

Dubhruya ('dub-roo-'yuh / 'dəb-rü-'yə) – [(AU: See Clan Ravensmith.)]

Enaid (in-'a-id / in-'a-id) – [Three become one . . . (AU: See *Clan Ravensmith.*)]

Eurig ('you-rig / ' yü-rig) – [territory of; shining glitters of _____ . . . you fill in the blank. (AU: See *Clan Ravensmith.*)]

Findor ('fin-door / 'fin-dȯr) – [Everyone needs one . . . (AU: See *Clan Ravensmith.*)]

Frida (fri-duh / fri-də) – [Carries a mean club . . . (AU: See *Clan Ravensmith.*)]

Havilah ('have-uh-lah / 'hav-ə-lȯ) – [sand, sand, sand . . . (AU: See *Clan Ravensmith.*)]

Hekta ('hek-tuh / 'hek-tə) – [Too tall for a pixie; too short for a dwarf. (AU: See *Clan Ravensmith.*)]

Jada ('jay-duh / 'jā-də) – [Hair as black as night . . . (AU: See *Clan Ravensmith.*)]

Lucasta (lu-'cast-uh / lü-'kast-ə) – [pure light shining in the night. Oh the delight of . . . (AU: See *Clan Ravensmith.*)]

Learned-One ('lure-ned-one / ' lər-nəd wən) – [Wow, they really exist . . . (AU: See *Clan Ravensmith.*)]

Mundgurun (mund-gu-run / mənd-gyü-rən) – [Shh, not so loud! (AU: See *Clan Ravensmith.*)]

Rin (rin / rin) – [Long, twisty, and cold . . . (AU: See *Clan Ravensmith.*)]

Shamira ('shuh-'mear-uh / 'shə-'mir-ə) – [Soooo cute, uh, for a . . .you'll find out! (AU: See *Clan Ravensmith.*)]

Taika ('tay-kuh / 'tā-kə) – [Mysterious gems glowing in the dark . . . (AU: See *Clan Ravensmith.*)]

Platoon Fimi (' pla-toon Fem-y / plə-'tün fem-ē) – [Turnabout, halt! (AU: See *Clan Ravensmith.*)]

Väinämö ('vah - nah-'moe / 'vä-nä-'mö) – [I like him! (AU: See *The Wall Outside*, *Partition Majik*, *Twisted Fates*, *Tainted Soul*—you get the picture.)]

Vindr (ven-'der / ven-'dər) – [Talk about a thick skin . . . (AU: See *Clan Ravensmith.*)]

Visdor Odenash ('vis-door 'o-den-'ash / 'viz-də 'ō-dən-'ash) – [All is not as it seems . . . (AU: See *Clan Ravensmith.*)]

Vulkodlak ('vull-kahd-lack, 'vəl-käd-lak) – [No dark alleys . . . bad, bad, bad. For that matter, just keep your distance if you can . . . (AU: They are not all that way. See *Twisted Fates* and *Tainted Soul.*)]

Vytiwa ('vi-ti-way / 'vi-ti-wā) – [Ha, ha, ha. Did you expect to see it in this book, too? (AU: I am clueless as to what he means. See *Tainted Soul.*)]

Xun Ove (zon ove / zən ȯv) – [The anointed one. Oh, come on. Surely you've heard of this by now! (AU: Bob rolled his eyes. See *The Wall Outside*, *Partition Majik*, *Twisted Fates*, and *Tainted Soul.*)]

ABOUT THE AUTHOR

James William Peercy fell through a portal into the publishing biosphere in 2012. Previously, he had observed and recorded his own worlds since the age of 10. James continued to write while attaining a degree in Computer Science, getting married, raising dogs, and starting a business.

Since all worlds simultaneously exist, he has written four book series: the *Cliff Fulton* mystery series, the *Xun Ove* fantasy series, *Ivan, Universal Space Tech* series, and the newest, *Clan Ravensmith*, a fantasy. With a constantly moving mind, he devotes his downtime to writing, traveling, and adoring his wife, Claudette.

If you like poetry, fantasy, sci-fi, and mystery check out his website:

http://www.JamesWilliamPeercy.com
http://www.StoriesToTell.com
https://www.facebook.com/jameswilliampeercy
https://www.instagram.com/jameswilliampeercy
https://twitter.com/JamesWPeercy

If you enjoyed Clan Ravensmith: The Beginning, drop him a line. He will appreciate the feedback. As in the words of J.R.R. Tolkien, 'May the hair on your toes never fall out!'

Made in the USA
Coppell, TX
11 November 2023

24108105R00132